T0246296

MORNING PAGES

Advance Praise for
Morning Pages

"Feiffer's novel is a seductive meditation on the shifting roles women play as daughters, mothers, wives, and artists. Full of wise observations and a scathing wit, this smart, engrossing read will stay with you long after you've finished. Original and enthralling."

    —FIONA DAVIS, *New York Times* bestselling author of
    The Spectacular

"*Morning Pages* plies a withering wit in the service of an open-hearted exploration of love, career, and family. As the play-wright-narrator tackles her block through the writers-class exercise of early morning free association, we feel the squeeze of her sandwich-generation predicament, caring for a declining mother and an inscrutable and increasingly distant adolescent son. Not since Andrew Sean Greer's *Less* have I laughed so much and, at the same time, been so moved."

    —GERALDINE BROOKS, author of the Pulitzer
    Prize-winning book *March*

"I laughed out loud at Kate Feiffer's comic characters and clever way with words. Her protagonist Elise is caught in the all-too-common middle-aged pickle of being sandwiched between a disengaged teenage son and an overly engaged parent, while at the same time, trying to revive her flatlining career and moribund love life. Feiffer's inventive framework of a play within a novel deftly reveals the challenging issues beneath the humor. The reader roots for Elise to find a path forward and show us the way."

    —ALISYN CAMEROTA, CNN

"A compulsively readable tale of a woman writer in a full-fledged 'sandwich-generation' crisis. Her interior monologue is a hilarious, poignant blend of existentialism and stand-up comedy. Feiffer's playfully eviscerating-yet-compassionate observational humor is so incisive, I could barely refrain from calling friends to read snippets of it aloud. And her prose is simply addictive: each new paragraph brings some delicious wordplay; I want a Phrase-a-Day calendar stolen from Elise's morning pages."

—NICOLE GALLAND, author of *Stepdog*

"Kate Feiffer has done with words what she is best known for with her illustrations, making us laugh out loud but also feeling the profound power of heartwarming love."

—NANCY SLONIM ARONIE, founder of
Chilmark Writing Workshop

MORNING PAGES

A Novel

KATE FEIFFER

A REGALO PRESS BOOK
ISBN: 979-8-88845-131-1
ISBN (eBook): 979-8-88845-132-8

Regalo Press
New York • Nashville
regalopress.com

Published in the United States of America
1 2 3 4 5 6 7 8 9 10

For my writers' groups

"In order to retrieve your creativity, you need to find it. I ask you to do this by an apparently pointless process I call *the morning pages*. You will do the pages daily through all the weeks of the course and, I hope, much longer. I have been doing them for a decade now. I have students who have worked with them nearly that long and who would no more abandon them than breathing.... What are morning pages? Put simply, the morning pages are three pages of longhand writing, strictly stream-of-consciousness."

—JULIA CAMERON, *The Artist's Way*

"Being a grownup means assuming responsibility for yourself, for your children, and—here's the big curve—for your parents."

—WENDY WASSERSTEIN

"Madame Bovary, *c'est moi*."

—GUSTAVE FLAUBERT

"People write in diaries, but diaries never write back. It's the same with these Morning Pages. Unrequited confessions."

—ELISE HELLMAN

PLAYS BY ELISE HELLMAN

Simple Syrup

Too Tall for the Short Girls

I Love Your Dad

But, Maybe

Little Dalton

The Groom of the Stool and the Royal Fool

Middle-Aged Mermaids with Bad Backs

Stealing Obituaries

Ibid, Again

Matzo & Mistletoe

The Golden Age of Insomniacs

January 5, 2013

Dear Elise:

The Players Playhouse will soon be celebrating its 25th anniversary! When we started this theater company to nurture the talents of emerging playwrights, we could only dream that we would be instrumental in launching voices that would shake up and redefine American theater. Yet, by producing the work of playwrights like you, this is precisely what we have done.

For our 25th anniversary, we have decided to offer commissions to the five playwrights whose work premiered during our first season. Elise, you are one of our selected playwrights. Your first play, *Simple Syrup*, offered a visionary approach to a woman facing mid-life: her pursuit of having the perfect mid-life crisis captured the angst of a generation. Many of us at The Players Playhouse still remember your brilliant line: "My career hasn't met my expectations. My marriage hasn't met my expectations. My children haven't met my expectations. I am now at the age at which I am expected to have a mid-life crisis. I'm not going to screw that up too."

Thanks to an anonymous benefactor, we can offer you $50,000 to write an original play which would premiere during our 2014 season. We are unfortunately working with an unusually tight timeframe, and if you will honor us by accepting this commission, we will need your finished play by December 1, 2013.

Elise, my enthusiasm to work with you again is unmatched! I eagerly await your reply.

Sincerely yours,

Samuel Ronstein
Executive and Artistic Director
The Players Playhouse

DAY 1

Morning Pages. Day 1.

I will do these. Every morning.

First thing.

Before coffee. Before my brain kicks in and kicks out again.

Morning pages. Day 1.

I already wrote that. Shit.

How should I begin?

I used to love beginnings. The sloppy adrenaline rush of starting something new. Thinking faster than I could type. Not anymore. These days, beginnings feel ravenous and needy. "Give us a middle!" they shout. Middles are hungry for conflict though, and that's a problem for someone as conflict-averse as I am.

I don't like what I've written so far.

It doesn't matter. Keep writing, Elise. Just keep writing.

I'll write about yesterday.

Mom got stuck in her bathtub. Alan called. It was around 2:00 in the afternoon. Before Marsden got home from school. Alan has never called me before. I've known him since I was five, and yesterday was the first time I'd ever spoken to him on the phone. When I picked up and heard, "Hi Elise, it's Alan, the doorman from 212," I got so excited I shrieked into the receiver, "Alan! Oh my God, I can't believe you're calling me!"

I don't know why I did that.

Alan's voice sounded serious, not quite somber, but weighed down with discomfort. He said, "I'm sorry to bother you, Elise, but there's an issue with your mother; she seems to be stuck in the bathtub." Neither the absurdity of his words nor the soberness of his tone resonated. I was delighted that my favorite doorman had called me, and I responded by asking him, "How are you? How's the building? How are things in New York?"

"Elise, your mother is stuck in the bathtub, in her apartment, she can't get out of the bathtub."

"Oh no. That's terrible," I replied this time.

It's possible, I suppose, that we may have never known that Mom was stuck in the tub until it was too late. We only found out because Aunt Rosemary had a premonition that something was wrong. At least that's what she said. Mom wasn't answering her phone and Aunt Rosemary got worried. Instead of calling me, she called Mom's building and told Alan that there's an emergency, that someone needed to check in on her sister right away. Alan alerted the super—there's a new one but I can't remember his name—maybe it's Elon. I still can't believe Mr. Fuchs died. This super is baby-faced and handsome and polite and no match for Mom, and when he found her in her bathtub she was agitated and swearing like a woman who has an expansive enough vocabulary to comfortably perform triage and discard the respectable words.

I wonder what he said when he found her there. "May I please help you out of the bathtub, Mrs. Hellman?"

And her reply? "Who let you into my apartment? Get the hell out of here, you perverted motherfucker!"

After that, Alan called me. He didn't want to chitchat. "Elise, what would you like us to do?"

I wanted to say, "Keep her in the tub." The idea of sentencing my mother to the bathtub for the rest of her life is, I'll admit, somewhat appealing.

Instead, I said, "Alan, thank you so much for letting me know. I'll figure something out and get back to you."

I called Aunt Rosemary and filled her in and asked if she would go uptown to Mom's to help her.

She said, "Wild horses couldn't keep me away. I sensed something was wrong. I always know when something is wrong with Trudy."

I don't know if Aunt Rosemary actually had a premonition. All I know is that she has a nose for drama. Even the way she looks is dramatic. At 77, her hair is still a passionate shade of singed auburn. It doesn't so much frame her face as form a separate entity around it. It's a dome under which her face resides—that mountainous forehead, over-chlorinated pools for eyes shielded by a pair of wire-rimmed bifocals, a perfectly fixed nose, and cheeks that seem shaped differently every time you see her. And when she speaks, her lips not only form words. They mold each and every letter within those words. I suspect Uncle Bill found a lot of pleasure in those all-encompassing lips.

Aunt Rosemary took a cab uptown. I know this because she likes to complain about the high cost of taking taxis yet says she'd rather be waterboarded than ride the subway and compares taking the bus to a slow dance with eternity. I called the super and stayed on the phone with him while we waited for Aunt Rosemary to arrive, which seemed to take forever, so while we were waiting, I asked him if he'd try again. "Tell her, 'I'm talking to your daughter, and she has asked me to help you out of the bathtub.'"

But Mom didn't believe him. "You're not talking to my daughter. She's working on her play. She refuses to talk to anyone when she's working. I know what you're really after."

When Aunt Rosemary arrived, the super told her that he'd wait in the front foyer, but when he heard screaming, he ran into the bathroom and found Mom draped in a towel and standing over Aunt Rosemary who was lying on the floor hollering, "My back is broken!"

This is what was reported back to me by Alan. The super called for an ambulance and the EMTs raced in and brought Aunt Rosemary downstairs on a gurney.

I couldn't get Mom on the phone until late last night, and when I did, she said, "She's fine. Of course she's fine. You know how your Aunt Rosemary is. It's always something and then it's nothing."

She also said she decided not to go to the hospital with Aunt Rosemary because she was famished and exhausted, so she scrambled some eggs and crawled into bed—which was also her excuse for not picking up the phone even though I must have called 30 times.

Aunt Rosemary called me from the hospital just before midnight.

"Elise, they drove like my life was slipping away. I almost had a heart attack, and then I spent four hours in the blood-stained bowels of the emergency room listening to a concert of falsetto screams before being seen by a magnificently incompetent doctor."

"Oh, Aunt Rosemary, I'm so sorry this happened. How's your back?"

"They claim it's spasming," she said.

I should drive down to the city to make sure they're both okay. If I leave Dedham at noon, I'll miss rush-hour traffic and will get to New York by 3:30. But Marsden is with me this week—and I was going to force myself to sit at my computer and write. No excuses. No procrastinations. But maybe this isn't an excuse. This is an emergency.

It's not really an emergency.

Mom is okay. Aunt Rosemary is probably fine. What would I do if I went? I'd get in a fight with Mom. I'd lose a day of writing. I have deadline creep. I can't lose a day right now. I need my days. I'll stay.

I need to be here for Marsden also. To make sure he focuses on his college essay—and not his bong.

I've written three pages. Three pages-ish. I have finished something. Accomplished something. Morning Pages Day 1 is completed. I have two months and four days—which I have calculated is 65 days—to finish *Deja New*. Sixty-five is a robust number. It's more than nine weeks. But barely. God creating the world in one measly week has set up unhealthy expectations for the rest of us, but nevertheless, I can surely finish writing a play in 65 days.

DAY 2

SUNRISE IS FAST approaching. After lying in bed, repositioning my pillow, and mentally composing today's Morning Pages for over two hours, which was a huge waste of insomnia, I have forced myself out of bed to write these. I think I work too much in bed. When I work in bed, I don't sleep. Now I'm in the kitchen. Maybe if I work in the kitchen, I won't eat.

The floor feels like an ice pack. It's not even cold out yet. Why is it so cold in the house? It's still September.

I should put on socks. No. I don't want to punish my feet and make them walk back to the bedroom. It's dark and quiet and I'm going to sit here at the kitchen table under a bare light bulb—an expensive designer light made to look like a bare lightbulb—so stupid. I'll whip out these Morning Pages so I can go back to bed and hopefully get an hour of sleep before the alarm rings, and I reemerge as the cheery, crepe-making lady.

For what? Marsden will sleep through his alarm. I'll wake him up and he'll grunt while tossing his long, gorgeous limbs over the side of his bed.

"I made crepes," I'll say.

"Cool," he'll respond.

Four crepes stuffed with fresh berries, bananas slices, and a schmear of Nutella will then slip down his throat. A plate of food disappears within seconds. The only thing he does with any speed is eat. The rest of his life moves at a *stop rushing me I'll get there when I get there* speed—only he doesn't get anywhere. He's in a perpetual state of slowly going and never getting. Except when he eats. He eats without chewing. I tried talking to him about the health benefits of chewing and the usefulness of teeth. He nodded mechanically and said, "Y'I know." I tried engaging him with stories about teeth that might interest him. I told him about the serial killer who extracted his victims' teeth and kept them as keepsakes, and he said, "Cool." I told him about the pilot from Connecticut who killed his wife and put her through a woodchipper to dispose of her body and that the investigators only broke the case because they found one of her teeth in a woodpile. "Teeth can withstand a woodchipper, Mars. They are great assets, and you should make better use of yours." And I proposed the idea of a mother-son movie night where we watch *Marathon Man* together. I'm still waiting for that to happen.

When did I lose him? I somehow missed the moment he started to disappear. Was there a moment? There are so many moments I can remember. All the firsts. First word. First step. First night without wearing a diaper. First bike ride. First day of kindergarten. First day of high school. But I can't remember the first long uninterrupted silence.

I try talking to him about his day, about school, about applying to colleges, about taking a gap year. I try talking at him, with him, near him, behind him, in the car sitting next to him. He nods and his eyelids droop. Is he stoned? Is he always stoned? When was the first time he smoked pot? Surely the first time wasn't when he got caught with Tommy Kane on Ralph Riverton's deer cam.

Tommy said, "It wasn't us." Marsden said, "It looks like us." Ralph Riverton said, "Don't fucking come on my property again you stupid-ass delinquents." Elliot said, "Ralph, they're just kids experimenting." I said, "Marsden, do you promise to stay off Mr. Riverton's property?" Marsden said, "Sure." June said, "Can we please not turn this into a trespassing issue? Our children are being accused of doing drugs." Tommy stood his ground, "Mom, I told you it wasn't us." "Marsden?" I asked. "Was it you?" He repeated, "It looks like us." "What the fuck, Marsden," Tommy said. "That's not us." "Tommy, watch your language," June said. Elliot told Riverton, "The kids will stay off your property. Marsden, Tommy, please." "Yeah, of course," both boys replied.

He doesn't even try to hide his smoking. Sure, his drug paraphernalia is in his shirt drawer, but he doesn't bother to cover it. I used to take his pot when I found it and pepper him with stories about fried brains and ruined lives. I was on him all the time. Then he said, "Yup. Got it. You know, Mom, every time you take my weed, I buy more, and it costs me a lot of money." He had a point. Maybe it's laziness on my part. Maybe I'm a lousy mother. Or maybe the best course of action is inaction, and I should let Marsden find himself. But nobody really finds themselves. They just find new places to get lost.

It is a wonder, though, how Marsden had more words as a toddler than he does as a 17-year-old. He was speaking in full sentences before he was two. At 17, sentences barely exist.

I can't feel my fingertips. I should go back to bed. I'm too hungry to go back to bed. I think I'll make myself a crepe and chew and chew and chew and chew.

DAY 3

JULIE DROVE DOWN to the city from Syracuse yesterday because Aunt Rosemary was having muscle spasms, or as she described it, "Poseidon's furious waves of pain." Julie is a great daughter. I wonder if I'd travel that far if Mom was having a tidal event. I'd probably sit at home and hope that one of the waves would wash her away.

I cannot believe I just wrote that.

What the hell is wrong with me?

I should be a better daughter.

No. It's okay. I can be a bad daughter here.

Mom kept calling and calling yesterday. She seemed a little out of it and even forgot who she was calling a few times.

MOM: Who's this?

ME: It's me, Elise.

MOM: Who?

ME: Elise, your daughter. You called me.

MOM: Oh darling, it's so nice to hear your voice. I know you're busy writing, so I'm trying not to call too often, but I wanted to tell you that I miss you.

ME: I miss you too.

Twenty minutes later she called again.

MOM: Elise, this is your mother.

ME: Hi Mom.

MOM: I've been up all night. I couldn't sleep at all.

ME: You should try to take a nap.

MOM: I'm too exhausted to nap.

ME: I can't talk right now. I'm writing.

MOM: I'm out of Ambien. I can't sleep without Ambien. Can you send me some?

ME: Why don't you call your doctor and ask him to refill your prescription?

MOM: I already called and spoke to his cunt receptionist. She said he won't give me a refill until I come in for an appointment.

ME: Can you not call her that? She's just doing her job.

MOM: I won't call her that again.

ME: Why don't you go in for an appointment?

MOM: Why would I do that?

ME: To get your prescription refilled.

Something happens to my upper body when I talk to Mom on the phone. It involuntarily pitches forward, then swings back like I'm one of those glass toys—the drinking bird with the long neck and the bright colored liquid inside. I walk around holding the phone to my ear, tipping, swinging, and bobbing while she's bitching and cursing.

Then the third call.

MOM: I'm changing doctors.

ME: Why would you do that?

MOM: My doctor should have his license revoked.

ME: For not refilling your prescription?

MOM: For being a prick.

ME: Your doctor is a good doctor if he wants to see you before refilling your prescription. That's pretty much the definition of being a good doctor.

MOM: All he has to do is pick up the phone and call in a refill, but instead he wants me to schlep across town. It's criminal.

ME: I've got to get back to work. I'm on a deadline.

MOM: Please talk to me. Elise, you never talk to me. You still haven't told me what your new play is about.

ME: I've told you.

MOM: I must not remember then. But I'm sure I'd remember if you told me.

Is it possible I never told her what my play is about? I withhold so much from her I think I may not have told her. I think all I've said to her about the play is, "I'm working now. I'll tell you later." God, that's awful of me. I don't think I've told her. And I did it again yesterday.

ME: I'm working now. I'll tell you later.

Fourth call—an hour or so later.

ME: Hi Mom.

MOM: Who's this?

ME: It's me, Elise, your daughter. You called me.

MOM: Elise, I need to talk to you about something. I couldn't sleep at all last night and my doctor refuses to refill my prescription for Ambien. Can you help me?

ME: We've already talked about this. There's nothing I can do.

MOM: My doctor wants me to schlep across town to see him, but I don't have time to do that. It will take all day.

ME: We discussed this before. What else are you doing today? Go to the doctor.

MOM: I've made a decision. I'm going to find a new doctor.

ME: I'm on a deadline.

MOM: Just talk to me for a minute more. Elise, tell me what's new with you. Have you talked to your father recently?

ME: I talked to him a few weeks ago. He's fine.

MOM: Is he still married to that slut?

ME: Lucy's not a slut.

MOM: She's a social climber.

ME: Well, she's not a very good one if she's using Dad for her ladder. I've got to go, Mom.

MOM: You never want to talk to me.

After that I tried turning off the ringer, but I couldn't focus because I was wondering if she was calling, so I turned it back on and spent the day fighting with her about her doctor. My work life is being conducted in short intervals between calls from my mother.

I'm going to write down all the times she called. I want to keep a record of this. If I never finish *Deja New*, I'll at least know why.

8:46

9:02

9:56

10:25

11:02

11:30

1:15

1:50

2:00

2:11

2:17

2:48

3:47

4:01

4:03

4:51

5:33

5:38

6:06

6:36

6:46

7:04

8:21

DAY 4

I NEED TO pee but I'm going to hold it in until I finish writing today's Morning Pages. Even if all I do is write about the sensation of needing to pee for the next three pages. What does needing to pee feel like? What are some good need-to-pee adjectives? Needing to pee is making me feel blocked. I can't think of the right words to describe what it feels like to need to pee. It doesn't matter that I'm only stream of consciousnessing. Stream of consciousnessing—is that a thing? If it's not, it should be. Like procrastinating. If only someone would hire me to procrastinate. Maya assures me that procrastination is part of the creative process. And Maya, being Maya, will cite a study to prove it. I can then feel good about doing anything but what I'm supposed to be doing, until I start to freak out because the days keep falling off an eroding cliff and I still haven't figured out how to end my play.

"I think I'm going to miss my deadline," I told her last week. "I'm stuck."

"Start doing Morning Pages," she said.

I'm four days in.

"Start drinking blueberry and kale smoothies," she said.

I've had two.

"Have sex. Lose your divorce virginity."

It's been so long. I don't remember how.

How did I become a celibate middle-aged woman with writer's block who is about to pee herself?

I'm going to hold it in. This is the new me. The hold-it-in-to-let-it-out me.

I called Mom yesterday to tell her about *Deja New*. Detail by detail, with this disclaimer: "Just so you know, I didn't write this in hopes that this becomes a life-imitates-art situation. But the play is about a single woman whose divorced parents move in with her. For the record, I definitely don't want that to happen."

"It might be nice."

"Are you kidding me?"

"Of course I'm kidding, Elise," she said. Like this is a thing she does, kids around. Never. Not once in my life.

I started telling her about the play. Act 1, Scene 1—

"Laurie and Granny are at a restaurant—"

She cut in before I got my next sentence out.

"You're writing a play about a grandmother. How wonderful and how very dull."

"I'm not writing a play about a grandmother. Granny is a guy. He's 40. His actual name is Granville. Granny is his nickname."

"A man named Granny. Elise, that's brilliant!"

"Thanks, Mom," I said. We were having a nice moment.

"That must have a terrible burden. Is he impotent?"

She ruined the moment. I didn't answer her question. Just kept explaining what my play was about. Like I didn't hear what she had said.

It's Laurie's 40th birthday and she and Granny haven't seen each other in over ten years. They are talking and kind of laughing about a pact that they made in college. If they were both single when they turned 40, they'd get married. And here they are—both single at 40. They seem to be avoiding talking seriously about the one thing they'd both like to talk seriously about.

She cut in again. But this time her feedback was useful. More than useful. Brilliant. "There needs to be tension between them, tension that might be confused with sexual tension. And don't forget the cultural tension of being a successful single woman. What they say to each other is as important as what they aren't saying."

Mom was right. I need more layers of unspoken tension between their words. Laurie and Granny haven't seen each other for ten years. What does that body language look like? They're both single. Do they lean in toward each other when they talk? A never-married professionally successful woman at 40 will have gone through her 30s dodging questions. *Are you married? How come you're not married? Aren't you worried about your biological clock? Did you know children born to women over the age of 35 have a greater chance of having learning disabilities?* She will be used to fielding these types of questions in the same way one is used to fielding questions about the weather. *Is it cold out? Why haven't you been married?* She will be used to questions people ask and the suppositions they make. People view married women differently from how they view single women and women with children, whether they're married or not, differently from women who don't have children. I think I have too many one-liners but not enough substance. But maybe my characters are hiding their nervousness behind the one-liners. How can I play off of that?

Mom loved Grace. That was a relief. I was worried she'd be upset. She was delighted though. "She's not really based on you," I tried to tell her.

But she knew. Of course she knew. "Don't bullshit me, Elise. Of course she's me. I am honored to have inspired a character in your play. Just please don't make her a prude. You tend to sanitize the characters you create who are based on me."

I told her that I will make Grace sexually inappropriate if that's what she wants.

"I've never been inappropriate," she said. "Just because I'm not repressed like you, Elise, doesn't mean I'm inappropriate."

"I know that. But you are inappropriate."

"You never have anything nice to say about me, do you?"

We were getting into it. It always happens this way. Thankfully she wanted to talk more about Grace.

"Don't let the father get away with being charming. After he moves in with them, you mustn't allow the character based on me to become a satire of herself. You don't want to let your anger toward me and your fond feelings for your father ruin your play."

She's right. I have to make sure I figure out who Grace really is. I can't let my anger at Mom create, then destroy this character.

It was strange talking to her about it. It was almost as if Mom could see the play I should be writing instead of the play I am writing. Her emotional intelligence for fictional characters is incredibly high. And yet, she seems to have little emotional intelligence for interacting with actual people.

Early on I used to talk my plays out with her, but then I stopped. Why did I stop? When we talk about books and movies and theater, we don't fight. That's not true. We had a fight a few weeks back about *The Big Sleep*. She was telling me that the character played by Martha Vickers was based on her.

"The underage manipulating seductress murderer younger sister to Lauren Bacall's character? You think she was based on you? I don't think so."

"There's a lot you don't know about me, Elise. You never wanted to know about me."

"Well maybe that's the reason why," I told her. Then of course I said, "I've got to go. I have a deadline." I'm a lousy daughter.

(LAURIE, dressed in a cautiously sexy outfit, is out for her 40th birthday dinner with her best friend from college, GRANVILLE (GRANNY). They are at a trendy restaurant. The walls are covered with what looks like street art. The restaurant's decor with the paintings should be projected on a large screen behind them. Along with the place settings at the table, there is a candle that resembles a phallus. The scene starts with Laurie and Granville looking at their menus. Granville is wearing a pair of readers. Laurie is squinting and holding her menu out in front of her with both arms. She moves it to the left and to the right and stretches her arms out so far that they are in danger of popping out of their sockets.)

                    GRANVILLE
Do you want me to hold it for you?

                         (Laurie lifts the menu up
                         over her head and tries to
                         read it like that, then
                         brings it down in front
                         of her. She picks up the
                         candle and holds it close
                         to the menu.)

LAURIE
Oh my! Does this candle look like a…?

GRANVILLE
Wow. It kind of does.

LAURIE
Do you think they did that on purpose?

GRANVILLE
They must have.

(Laurie examines the candle.)

LAURIE
Granny, I'm going to make a confession. This
is the closest my face has been to a penis in
three years. I can't believe I just said that.

GRANVILLE
Three years isn't that long. Ten years is
though. What I can't believe is that we hav-
en't seen each other in ten years.

LAURIE
I know it. That's crazy. And now we're old.

GRANVILLE
You look the same as always. You look fabulous.

LAURIE
Maybe on the outside. My insides are looking
pretty ragged. They've been ravaged by the
pressure to get married, to have kids, to
make money, to have friends, to keep up with
politics and movies and books and celebrity
scandals, to have arcane interests but not
too arcane, and to sleep through the night.

GRANVILLE
I'm feeling it too. I thought it would feel
different. But it just looks different.

LAURIE
(Still holding the phallus candle) I don't
think they really want us to order. The print
on this menu is tiny. Have you noticed that
everything is getting bigger and bigger these
days except for fonts? People are driving
around in cars that are the size of houses.
I bet there's a car out there somewhere that
has a bowling alley or a pool in it. And the
houses. What's up with all the McMansions?
But then you go to a restaurant and the print
is so small you can't read the menu.

GRANVILLE
I once read about a limo with a jacuzzi in it.

LAURIE
You're kidding.... I can't believe we're
forty. Forty!

GRANVILLE
This is the decade where menus become impossible to read.

LAURIE
That sucks. I love reading menus.

GRANVILLE
Really? I didn't know that about you.

LAURIE
I feel unwanted here. Let's find another
place to eat. One that respects font sizes.

GRANVILLE
I think we should hold our ground and stay.
The food is supposed to be phenomenal.

                    (A hip looking WAITRESS
                    walks over to their table.)

WAITRESS
Are you ready to order?

LAURIE
(Cheery) Hi, how are you today? Do you by any chance have a large print menu? I'm having a hard time seeing this one.

WAITRESS
We don't. But we do have the menu on audio if you prefer that. It comes with information about the art on our walls, which was done by a twenty-two-year-old Cuban street artist. You can rent a headset for two dollars.

LAURIE
Excuse me?

WAITRESS
Here.

(She pulls a headset out of her apron and holds it up.)

LAURIE
You're really nice to offer that. You're like a waitress and a docent all in one. But I'm okay. Thanks.

WAITRESS
My job description, if you can believe it, is customer advocate and culinary consultant.

GRANVILLE
That's impressive.

WAITRESS
Can I get you a drink to start?

GRANVILLE
Two glasses of champagne. It's her birthday.

WAITRESS
Please take this. It's my birthday gift to you.

(The waitress hands Laurie
the headset and Laurie puts
it on. The waitress walks away
humming "Happy Birthday.")

LAURIE
What do you think an invigorated eggplant
involtini is? I think it sounds like it could
be good. Mmmm. Listen to this. Skuna Bay
salmon crudo with blood orange gastrique. I
wish I spoke foodie. I don't understand what
anything on this menu is.

GRANVILLE
So, what's new? Are you seeing anyone?

*too abrupt?
what's his
agenda*

(Laurie takes off the
headset.)

LAURIE
Not for a while. When I was dating, it was like
I kept going out with a carbon copy of the
same guy. Unavailable. Smart. Self-involved.
Kind. Conflicted. Detached and tormented.
But they came in different body types. I
thought that changing out body types might
help. It appears men can have the same demons
whether they're tall and lanky or stocky and
barrel-chested. Granny, the truth is I've
never had a relationship that's lasted longer than a year and a half. The times between
my relationships always last longer than my
relationships. Is there a word for that? The
time in-between relationships?

GRANVILLE
Celibacy...at least for some folks.

LAURIE

I went into my last two relationships waiting for them to end and when they did, I
felt an incredible wave of relief that the
waiting was over. I've been checked out of
the dating scene for a while now. I think
the expectations are too high and I've buckled under the pressure…. What about you? I
can't believe we're so out of touch with each
other. We don't even live that far away from
each other. How did we let this happen? I
should know about your dating life.

GRANVILLE

I've had girlfriends. Some serious. But I
don't know, nothing really felt like it
clicked. You know that sound people make
when they click?

LAURIE

Like when they finish each other's sentences
but they're not talking over each other.

GRANVILLE

Exactly. Do you remember Marta?

LAURIE

Of course. Marta was great.

GRANVILLE

I really loved Marta. I could have married
her but when she decided to go to medi-
cal school in California we broke up and
that was that.

LAURIE

I guess it wasn't meant to be.

GRANVILLE

I don't buy that. Is anything meant to be?
It works out and we assume it was meant to
be. When someone you love gets into medi-

cal school in California and you've got a job in Boston, you convince yourself that maintaining a long-distance relationship is impractical. Does that mean it wasn't meant to be? Marta and I figured we'd both find someone else closer by. And she did. Were they meant to be?

                    LAURIE
I believe that some things are meant to be. I think I was meant to be alone. I've come to terms with it, really. Well, as much as I can.

                         (Granville puts both his
                         hands on the table and leans
                         toward Laurie.)

                    GRANVILLE
Do you remember our pact?

                    LAURIE
Oh my God—we were going to get married at forty if we were still single! And here we are. Why did we choose forty anyway?

                         (Granville leans back and
                         puts his hands in his lap.)

                    GRANVILLE
It seems kind of random. Fifty would have been better. Or thirty, so it would be easier to have kids.

                    LAURIE
Do you think we thought we'd have it all fig-ured out by now or that we knew we wouldn't?

                    GRANVILLE
It's strange how far away forty seems when you're twenty. Do you think sixty seems that far away now that we're forty?

(The waitress returns
holding two flutes of
champagne.)

WAITRESS
These are on the house. Have you decided what
you'd like for your birthday dinner?

LAURIE
What about this or this?

(Laurie starts tentatively
stabbing at the menu.)

Granny, can you read these?

GRANVILLE
Brussel sprouts kulambu. Beef carpaccio.
Skuna bay salmon.

LAURIE
Oh, and let's get that eggplant thing. Do you
think that's enough food?

WAITRESS
You can always get more if you're still hungry.

(The waitress walks away
humming "Happy Birthday"
again. There's an almost,
but not quite, uncomfort-
ably long silence before
Laurie talks.)

LAURIE
Granny, I can't believe you went into tech.
You were the consummate English major. You
always had a novel in your hand and never
understood why I was a math major. By the
way, I love my MatchIT App, Granny. It was
genius to think that people would want to

have appliances that match their personality profile. You're kind of a visionary.

GRANVILLE

I'm not a visionary. I had a good idea, and I caught the moment. We're expanding into other household items and beyond. It's extraordinary how eager people are to have their possessions match their personality.

LAURIE

Well, I'm proud of you. It's great to see you. I've missed you.

Why didn't they stay in touch?

GRANVILLE

I've missed you too. I think about you a lot. Probably more than I should. Is it okay to say that?

(Laurie leans back and crosses her arms.)

LAURIE

Did I tell you that my mom has moved in with me?

GRANVILLE

Oh no. Is she okay?

LAURIE

It's temporary. She totaled her car. She was banged up but is fine. But I don't want her driving anymore. She's a terrible driver. Way too nervous. The bigger problem is her place is almost impossible to get to without a car, so, she's staying with me for a while.

GRANVILLE

And how's it going?

LAURIE

Honestly, it's hell.

GRANVILLE

I'm not surprised. I remember your mom well.

LAURIE

Did she try to seduce you when we were in college?

GRANVILLE

Not really. I think she just wanted me to be appreciative of her sex appeal.

LAURIE

No wonder I'm so fucked up.

GRANVILLE

You're not that fucked up. I've been think-ing a lot about our pact. Not as a joke. Like thinking about what if we did.

LAURIE

How *Sleepless in Seattle* of you.

GRANVILLE

It's more *When Harry Met Sally*. But not really.

LAURIE

It doesn't matter, as long as I get to be Meg Ryan.

GRANVILLE

I see you more as Tilda Swinton.

LAURIE

That's even better! She's kind of hot-nerdy. Have you heard of Euler's Identity?

GRANVILLE

I can't say I have.

LAURIE

Euler's Identity is the perfect equation. E to the $i\ Pi$, plus one, equals zero. I know this sounds geeky, but in this one equation there are all of the most important mathematical elements, and the beauty of Pi and an imaginary number. I'm not exaggerating when I tell you that people have compared this equation to a Shakespearean sonnet. I used to use Euler's Identity as a metaphor for life. *E* stood for Enrichment—a fulfilling career and friendships. *I* was Good Health.

> GRANVILLE

Shouldn't *I* be for Illness?

> LAURIE

Or Immortality.

> GRANVILLE

Is that what you want?

> LAURIE

Not with my mom living with me. *Pi* is for Plentiful and Delicious Food, naturally. And then there's the Plus One, and that plus one is true love…. Like the perfect equation, together those elements equal a happy and fulfilled life. For a long time, I'd wake up every morning and it would be the first thing I said—*E* to the *i Pi*, plus one, equals zero. It was my mantra. But it didn't matter.

> GRANVILLE

You had a Plus One problem.

> LAURIE

Yeah. I had more than just a Plus One problem. But the Plus One was an issue. Then it dawned on me that there's too much pressure to love. We're supposed to love our parents. Love our friends. Love our jobs. Love sunny days. Love what we're wearing. And then find a soulmate to love on top of that.

GRANVILLE
What if it's all bullshit? What if the pressure and the pursuit are real but that's all
that's real?

LAURIE
We were so drunk that night. Do you remember?
You peed on a tree, and I yelled at you.

GRANVILLE
And then we made the pact.

LAURIE
And now we're forty and I'm living with my mom.

                    (The waitress arrives with
                    their food and puts it on the
                    table. While she is placing
                    it down, Laurie is squinting
                    and trying to decipher
                    what's on the plates.)

GRANVILLE
I think we should honor it.

LAURIE
Look at this food. It looks like an art project and the portions, the portions here are
as tiny as the fonts. (Singing softly almost
as if to herself) Happy fortieth birthday
tooooooo me.

BLACKOUT

DAY 5

I REWORKED THE first scene of the play yesterday, then walked around Kendrick Pond twice with Maya. First loop—we discussed whether it's more important to visit the mother who drives you nuts or stay home in case the son whom you drive nuts needs you.

Second loop was focused on what Maya should do for Stu's upcoming 50th. It was late afternoon but the sun was lingering in the sky like a teenager defying curfew, which was good because Maya seemed to know everyone there with a dog and we had to stop and chat every 20 steps. Amazingly, she knew not only the names of all the dogs we passed, but also of the owners who stopped to talk. "Do you know them?"

"We met them last week here, remember?"

No. I never remember. Maya remembers everything. Birthdays. Lines from movies. Titles of books. Names. Even the names of plants and animals. She collects information, stockpiles fun facts about everyone she meets and creates a storied world filled with fascinating details and tidbits of trivia. She makes the banal interesting.

Maya wants to throw Stu a surprise party. I told her I thought he would prefer to let the day pass without notice. Stu had the misfortune of being born into this world minutes after Walter Cronkite informed the country that JFK had been assassinated. The news had spread throughout the hospital and everyone in the birthing room, including Stu's mother, was crying while he was crowning. After the delivery, the doctor disappeared. Stu's mother figured he stepped out to tell her husband that he had a healthy baby son. But that wasn't the case. Stu's father didn't learn the news of his son's birth for another two hours and the doctor wasn't seen again until the following day.

Being born on a day of tragedy makes for a lousy birthday and Stu's mother used to break down in tears every year during his birthday party, and for Stu, no matter how many times he'd blow out the candles wishing his birthday was on a different day, it came again and again on November 22. So now, understandably, he reviles his birthday and never celebrates. He's made such a big deal of not acknowledging his birthday that it's one of the few birthdays I actually remember, and every year I slip up and wish him a happy birthday by mistake and every year he tells me to mind my own business. "Elise, what is it with you?"

Maya is convinced he needs to get over his birthday issues. "It's been 50 years. It's time to celebrate. I want to go big," she said.

"Why?" I asked her. "Why not just let him hate his birthday? Can't some issues just remain issues? So what if Stu hates his birthday. Isn't that his prerogative? I think he'd be happier ignoring his birthday or having a nice quiet dinner with just you and the kids."

"He's turning fifty. Fifty!" she said. "I'm not going to let this birthday pass like it doesn't matter."

"It doesn't matter if Stu doesn't want it to matter," I told her. I wanted her to see that maybe she wasn't thinking about what was best for Stu. Maybe she feels the need to throw him a party because it's best for her.

And to that, she said, "I want to do this because I believe with my heart and soul that he'll be really happy once he sees everyone he cares about in the same room together. It's going to be a love fest. It'll make him happy."

I want to believe her. Maya has an almost magical ability to heal people who don't know they need healing and to help the people who do. Sure, she can be annoyingly heavy-handed about it, but she usually—not usually, she always seems to know how to help someone out of their rut. She knows what to do to get you to think a bit differently, to get you to shift your perspective, however determined and dedicated you may be to seeing things the way you want to see them. But this party for Stu. It feels all wrong. Why is she throwing this at him?

She tried to explain—although I think her story was more distraction than explanation (the magician's trick)—by telling me about a girl in her kindergarten class named Candy Carmella. I don't know if that's her real name or if Maya invented a sticky toffee name so I'd remember it. Apparently, a boy in her class named little Jared Shithead—or something—saw Candy Carmella extract a booger from her nose and eat it. This was an event he decided was exceedingly newsworthy. As the conveyor of good gossip, little Jared Shithead ascended a few notches in class rank to most popular boy and Candy Carmella landed the role of class pariah. When the birthday calendar posted on the classroom wall showed Candy Carmella's birthday was a few weeks away, word got out that the booger-eater's birthday party was an event to be boycotted. Of course, none of them at that age knew about actual boycotts or organizing political movements, but essentially that's what they were doing.

And then the invitations came. Maya was one of the three girls in the class who got invited to the class pariah's birthday party. Maya and the other two invitees decided to counter-attack and whispered in voices that were meant to be overheard about how Candy Carmella's party was going to be the best party ever and that only three kids in the class were lucky enough to get an invitation. One of the girls brought her invitation to school and secretly revealed it to one, then two, then most of their classmates—telling them, "I'll show it to you, but you can only look at it for a second." The kids got a sneak peek at a picture of a prancing pony wearing a tiara with little flickering lights. The birthday party fast became viewed as an exclusive event that only a lucky few were invited to. And, in fact, the three girls had a great time at the party—intimate gathering that it was. After the party, Candy Carmella was no longer the class pariah and while little Jared Shithead remained popular, his reputation took a bit of a bruising. But what really came out of this tale was that Maya, at the age of five, started to understand the power of reshaping a narrative and this is exactly what she wants to do for Stu.

I told her I still didn't think the surprise party was a good idea.

"Noted," she said.

I asked her what became of Candy Carmella.

She said she's lost track of her, but little Jared Shithead is now the CEO of a Fortune 500 company. Figures.

DAY 6

LAST NIGHT, SLEEP came in cycles. I fell asleep at 11:00. At midnight, I was jolted awake by the fire alarm. I jumped out of bed and ran into the hallway to get Marsden. Then I realized the fire alarm wasn't actually going off. I'm still not sure if I dreamt it or if my brain actually set off an alarm. *Don't sleep now, Elise, there's too much to stress out about. What are you doing? It's midnight. Time to set the foundation for your 2 a.m. ruminations. After you do that, you can settle in for another round of sleep.* All night I cycled. Sleep. Stress. Sleep. Stress.

Why must we have so many cycles? There's the cycle of life and the seasonal cycle. The planets cycle, the economy cycles, moods cycle, musical intervals cycle, politics cycle, and then there's my favorite cycler of all—the washing machine. Everything comes in cycles. My career as an exciting new voice in the theater cycled into a career as a substitute teacher who can no longer get plays produced and is now cycling back, at least it will be if I can finish this play.

It's been seven years. Seven years of rejections. Seven years of tears. Of bouncing back for more rejection. Of rewrites that lead to another round of rejections. Of new projects that go nowhere. Of half-finished plays. Of ideas that soar then stagnate. Of feeling lost. Of giving up but not really. Of convincing myself to quit. Of convincing myself not to quit. Of starting over. Of stopping. Of not being able to get to write a decent play or get any play produced. And then Sammy Ronstein unexpectedly cycled back in.

I sent him congratulatory emails when Players Playhouse plays got rave reviews and moved to Broadway. He never once replied. I haven't heard a word from him since *Simple Syrup* closed and that was in 1989. I was 24 years old in 1989. He didn't even reach out to me after I won a Drama Desk award for *Stealing Obituaries* or got an Obie nomination for *Matzo & Mistletoe*. And then out of the blue last winter, he cycles back in with a letter offering me a commission to write a play.

I thought about turning him down. Or ignoring him. How great it would have felt to reject Sammy Ronstein.

Instead—I called him and said it would be an honor to write a new play for the Players Playhouse. It was the truth and a lie.

I was tortured by Sammy's silence. I still don't know why he shut me out, but I suspect it was a reaction to two things that happened. I stupidly blamed him—how could I be so damn stupid—for losing Uma Thurman in *Simple Syrup*. We had her. We celebrated. I told everyone. I bought a $500 pair of ballet flats because my feet deserved a little Audrey Hepburn while my ego was inhabiting Wendy Wasserstein. Then Uma left. Didn't even make it to the first day of rehearsal. I asked Sammy what happened. He thought I was accusing him. We recovered, but not really. I knew he was holding the Uma accusation against me. I could feel Uma's presence every time I wanted to challenge something he said. I would start to speak, and then, there would be Uma—her tall lanky limbs holding my tall lanky limbs at bay. Her long fingers covering my mouth. So I stopped challenging Sammy and became agreeable. Well,

I'm already agreeable, but I became even more agreeable. The agreeable woman's agreeable. Which means I disappeared. The real Uma would have been disappointed in me, but my Uma understood that this was what I needed to do.

The reviews for *Simple Syrup* were generally raves. The run was extended. It was my first play and I was getting called a "playwright to watch." I was ecstatic. But then at the closing night party, Sammy came in for a congratulatory hug and he rubbed my back. Under my shirt. I jumped back and stepped away. First, I accuse him of losing Uma and then I don't let him hug me the way Sammy likes to hug.

The thing is, Sammy has two settings. That's it. His default— a charisma-oozing hyperbolic enthusiasm. "Beyond brilliant! BEYOND!" This one is easy to stomach but can be tricky to digest. But who cares about digestion when the food tastes magnificent? He makes you feel seen and heard, even if he doesn't believe what he's saying, even if you suspect he doesn't believe what he's saying, he wants you to believe it and you want to believe it and he's so charming it's hard not to believe him.

When Sammy Ronstein is happy with you, his eyes don't look past you, or through you, nor do they jettison from table to chair avoiding you, as so many eyes do. They hug you. Sammy is a giver of eye-hugs, so when his eyes go cold, it's bad. He lets it out slowly—he's not one of those blow-his-top types. His rage is constipated, and so you wait, knowing it's coming. He sucks his lips into his mouth and bites down on them. His philtrum flattens and his eyes harden.

And when it arrives, it cuts through you like a targeted drone. You are discarded. Eliminated. Guillotined. Maybe not guillotined, that's insensitive to people who legitimately got their heads cut off. I shouldn't have written that. Maybe defenestrated? I did kind of feel like I was unceremoniously tossed out a window. I suppose that's insensitive too. Screw it. Morning Pages are a safe space for insensitivity. My stream of consciousness shouldn't have to be considerate to others. If I can't even say what I want to here, I'll never finish my play. I'm scared that I've self-censored myself numb and dumb. I want to nurture my stream of consciousness's ugly side—I want to be able to let it out in these pages. I want to let it out.

DAY 7

HAPPY BIRTHDAY MARSDEN! 18. My baby is 18. 18!!!

Marsden doesn't hate his birthday the way Stu hates his, but I'm starting to wonder if what happened when he was born might be having an impact. Like he somehow knew that my mind was on something other than him and now he has low self-esteem because of it. He was almost two weeks late. He's always running late. I was desperate to not be pregnant any longer. We had gone to the hospital a week before he was born and I told my obstetrician I was having contractions that were coming a few minutes apart. "Ooooohhhhhh! Ahhhhhhhhh! Owwwwww!" I moaned as we rushed in. Elliot whispered to me, "What are you doing? Are you faking your contractions? You sound like you're having an orgasm." "Ouch! Ewwww!" I yelled trying to sound less orgasmy and more contractiony. She sent us home. Then, unbelievably, the morning the verdict was going to be announced, my contractions kicked in. I spent my entire pregnancy watching the O. J. Simpson trial and writing *Middle-Aged Mermaids with Bad Backs*. I was so addicted to the trial I named three characters in the play Ito, Darden, and Marcia. There was no way in hell I wasn't going to be home to watch the verdict. But my contractions were coming faster than the verdict and Elliot forced me to go to the hospital.

At 1:11 in the afternoon of October 3, 1995, Marsden Hellman Walthers was born—just minutes after the verdict was announced. Elliot, bless him, said, "O. J. was acquitted."

My doctor said, "You have a son." The first words out of my mouth after the birth of my only son were, "I can't believe he was acquitted." Why didn't I say, "I can't believe I have a son"?

It's hard to imagine that Marsden is now 18. Eighteen is considered the end of childhood, only Marsden must be well aware that 18 is little more than an entrée into a pimple-prone, porn-curious, infantilized-yet-over-inflated adulthood.

Yesterday Mom called every hour on the hour with updates about Aunt Rosemary. "Mom," I finally told her, "Thanks for letting me know, but I don't need real-time updates."

And her response: "Sorry for bothering you. All I am is a bother to you."

"You're not a bother. I was simply trying to get some writing done," I told her. "I love you, but I'm on a deadline."

And her reply: "I'm eighty-one years old and will probably be dead soon, so you won't have to worry about being interrupted by my calls much longer."

My mother is an octogenarian adolescent.

Marsden is 18—the inverse of 81. She is moody. He is sullen. She wants attention from me. He wants me to go away. She screams. He sulks.

Last week I tried to tickle Marsden. He looked confused and rebuked me.

"What are you doing?"

"Tickling you," I said. "You love to be tickled."

"No, I don't," he replied.

I didn't tell him that he was wrong, that I never knew of a child that liked to be tickled as much as he did. Doesn't he remember?

"More Tickle Monster Mommy!"
"Mommy, where's the Tickle Monster?"
"Mommy, I can't see the Tickle Monster."
"Mommy, did the Tickle Monster get lost?"
Yes. The Tickle Monster is lost.

I want to tickle him for his birthday. Just once more. With every inch of height he adds on to his ever-growing body, Marsden moves inward. I think there must be a connection between physical growth and parental disdain. It's more than hormonal, I'm convinced the contempt teenagers feel for their parents is in their growing bones and stretching muscles. But then where is the contempt a middle-aged woman feels for her mother? If only I could loofah it off like dead skin and treat Mom like she deserves to be treated and love her like she deserves to be loved. I want to forgive her. To start again. From birth. Let's get it right this time.

This push and pull between Mom, Marsden, and me is starting to feel very Sandwich Generationy. That might not be a bad thing. I've long felt lost in the shadowy existence of a cusp Gen X/Baby Boomer, unsure if I'm first year Gen X or Baby Boomer backwash. Cusps have no real identity, and I wouldn't be surprised if some of my insecurities developed because I was born into a generational mash-up. But now I feel the intense squeeze of two slices of bread, one stale and crusty and one baked on pot. I am going to claim the Sandwich Generation as mine.

I wonder what kind of sandwich I'll be—a tuna melt, PB & J, or maybe I'm a burrata with marinated cherry tomatoes on ciabatta? When did sandwiches become so complicated anyway? Did the wrap ruin the sandwich? It's not that I don't like wraps, it's just that anything you roll up isn't a real sandwich. Neither is anything that uses roasted red peppers or aioli mayonnaise. Aioli should be used in Scrabble when you have too many vowels, not in sandwiches. Sandwiches are for Hellmann's. I think I'm a bologna sandwich with mayo on white bread.

DAY 8

MIDGE CALLED YESTERDAY asking me if I'd join them at Marsden's birthday dinner. Actually she said, "Elise, join weee for Marsden's birthday din din tonight palease." Midge speaks a sort of Eastern European Suburban Illinois baby talk. The only part of this verbal affectation that makes sense is the suburban Illinois. I wanted to answer, "Me no want to join we for this last-minute invitation to my own son's eighteenth birthday. Me pushed this baby out without epidural and it is me who he should be with—not babyspeak youeee." But I bit my tongue, swallowed a hefty intake of air, and said, "Midge, that's a most lovely offer. I would love to join you." And she replied, "Fantastic shmantastic!"

They had made a reservation at The Daily Catch in the North End. The three of them drove up from Wellesley and I drove into Boston from Dedham. I was the one-woman show, they were the ensemble, their bodies moving together as they walked through the restaurant to the table where I was already sitting.

Elliot apologized for them being 15 minutes late. "Midge wanted to skirt up the back roads, I insisted on the Pike, and it was crawling. I should always listen to Midge."

"Don't be silly. Elliot. We'd be latey-late if we took my way too." Midge always agrees with Elliot, even when she doesn't.

I hugged Marsden—squeezed him tightly enough for him to understand that I wouldn't let go until he draped his limby arms around me. I reminded him that it was his 18th birthday.

"Eighteen. Can you believe it?" I asked him.

"Yup," he replied.

Midge and Elliot sat down at the table while I was holding onto Marsden. They sat across from each other, which left me seated across from Marsden, sandwiched between my ex-husband and his girlfriend. Fucking sandwich generation.

Since I assumed Elliot was picking up the tab, I ordered the lobster fra diavolo. Midge asked me and Elliot if we remembered our 18th birthdays. It was the type of leading question that somebody asks because they have a story they want to tell. Elliot went first and told his tale of turning 18 that we've all heard many times before. His parents gave him a car that wouldn't start. They wanted him to understand that now that he was legally an adult, he needed to figure out how to navigate a broken world. If he wanted a car of his own, he'd have to find a way to fix this one. And Elliot being Elliot got an afterschool job at a garage and learned how to repair cars. While he was telling this story and putting on a dazzling display of paternal engagement by emphasizing the lesson in it for Marsden, Midge smiled and nodded. I nodded too but probably didn't break a smile until I noticed all the lines on Midge's face. She's five years younger than me and her face is already sectioned off into rows of cheek. She's aging in double time. Keep smiling Midge. Keep smiling. My turning 18 story was about going out to famed literary hangout Elaine's for dinner with Dad and Lucy and seeing what looked like a casting call for famous writers and actors. Everyone from the wimpy and horny—Woody Allen—to the burly and horny—Norman Mailer—to the sexy and horny—Warren Beatty—was there. And I drank Tom Collins after Tom Collins because the drinking age was 18 back then and Dad didn't seem to notice that I kept ordering drinks for myself. After dinner, Elaine herself brought out a cupcake with a candle on it and informed me that there would be no singing tonight, but she assured me to wish carefully because my wish would come true.

"And so what did you wish for?" Midge asked.

I looked over at Marsden to try to gauge how tuned out he was.

"I wished that I would find a way to help make the world a better place," I said.

"That's beautiful," Midge said.

Elliot gave me the eye. He knew I was lying. The truth was I had just seen *Star 80* and *Flashdance* and I wished that one of the famous men eating at Elaine's that night would discover me. For my 18th birthday I had one wish, and I wished to be discovered by a famous man. I wouldn't tell that to my son, I wouldn't tell that to anyone. I will burn these Morning Pages when I'm done because I'd prefer to go out with the mythology of my life, because whatever that mythology is it'll be more posthumously palatable than the warty truth.

But I haven't yet gotten to Midge's inappropriate and probably apocryphal story about "popping her cherry"—her words—on her 18th birthday with a singer in a "super-duper" famous band that she refused to name.

So we guessed.

"R.E.M.?"

"Not going to say."

"Rolling Stones?"

"I said I'm not going to say."

"U2?"

"I'm not going to tell you."

"Talking Heads?"

"I wish."

And so it went on until Elliot put a stop to it.

Then she told us that this famous rock star who most certainly wasn't Bruce Springsteen or Jon Bon Jovi gave her herpes.

And I yelled out, "Yay!" At least I yelled it out to myself.

Midge wanted to use this story to lecture Marsden about the importance of using a condom. And she blathered on and on about STDs, and when she looked over at me for some parental reinforcement, I said, "I agree, it's important to use a condom if you're having sex with a rock star."

And Elliot laughed.

My baby is 18 and now he has his own story.

DAY 9

SMALL RONSTEIN WANTS to know how the play is coming. "When can I read something, Elise?" he asked. "I'm tingling with excitement."

I'll send him the first act today and keep trying to figure out the ending.

I'm still stuck. This is my ninth day of Morning Pages and I've had no epiphanies and no new ideas. I still don't know how to shape the ending. Or what the ending should be. How did this play get away from me? The play I intended to write when I started disappeared, and now I don't have an ending.

I feel the kind of stuck you get in dreams when you're being chased but your legs won't move. I'm not breathing right. I'm eating too much. I'm slouching. I have less than two months to finish and I spent two hours yesterday cyber-sleuthing online trying to find out what became of Candy Carmella. Why did I do that?

Today I will sit up straight, focus, focus, focus, and write a brilliant play.

Then I can have my career back.

Or whatever it was that I had. It's hard to remember.

It's been eight years—no, seven—since *The Golden Age for Insomniacs* opened and a nasty-assed reviewer wrote: "While clearly not her intent, Hellman's plodding play should help even the insomniacs in the audience fall asleep." Not even Maya—who is truly a talented publicist—could corral an audience into the theater after that review. We had fewer than 30 people a night in a 200-seat house. I wonder if they were insomniacs hoping for a respite or season ticket holders?

Marsden was 11 when *Insomniacs* opened. He hadn't yet had his growth spurt and he'd lie on the floor and curl himself around Sinatra and I'd curl myself around him and Elliot would curl himself around me and we were like a big beautiful nautilus. Marsden called me Mommalommydoodle back then. I guess words still had syllables when he was 11. I wish I could remember when they started dropping off. Elliot and I were happy. He took me to Belize after the play closed to try to get me to stop moping. We had good sex and got bad sunburns. I thought everything would be okay. We came home and I got back to work, but no one wanted to produce anything I wrote. I focused on my failings. And on Sinatra. I walked him five times a day. Walking. Walking. Walking. Trying to flesh out scenes. Characters.

I should have focused more on Elliot and less on Sinatra. I shouldn't have blurted out, "You are soooo handsome!" every time I walked into the room and saw them together.

Elliot would be on the couch reading. He'd smile. Sinatra, snuggled up next to him, would wake up and look at me. "Sinatra, you are the handsomest guy I've ever met."

Elliot's smile would collapse. "Are you talking to the dog?"

I bruised his ego. Time and time again. Sinatra was handsome though. I miss his bright blue eyes, his shiny golden ginger coat, his sweet licks, and gentle bark. When Sinatra died Elliot asked me if I would be crying as much if it were him who had been hit by a car.

"I don't know," I said. I don't know why I said that.

(*LAURIE and her father, LARRY, 70s, nice looking but not particularly dashing, are seated at a table in a retro style diner—the diner decor can be projected on a large screen behind them. Larry chews loudly while he eats a hamburger. Laurie is picking at a salad, which was served in an almost comically large bowl. Between bites, she stretches her arm across the table and eats fries off Larry's plate. Laurie points to her chin, to signal that Larry has ketchup on his.*)

LARRY
What? Do I have something on my chin?

LAURIE
Ketchup.

LARRY
(Wiping his chin) Gone?

LAURIE
Yup, but now you have hamburger on your cheek.

LARRY
I put it there on purpose. I want it there. Tell me, how have you been?

LAURIE
Good. Busy at work. It's great actually, but it can be challenging keeping up with changing regulations and market volatility. I think they put an entire head of lettuce in my bowl. Do you want some salad? There's too much for me. Can I have another fry? I love the fries here. I don't know why no one puts fries in salad. Don't you think French fries could be a delicious addition to a salad?

Laurie is so happy to be at lunch w/ her father. Almost giddy? Does that come across?

63

> (Larry reaches across the
> table for a bite of salad.
> He stabs some lettuce,
> picks up a fry and stuffs
> the salad and French fry in
> his mouth.)

LARRY

That is good. You're on to something, Kiddo.

LAURIE

You have salad dressing on your nose.

LARRY

Leave me alone. You haven't seen or talked
to your old man in months.

LAURIE

I'm sorry. I've missed you Pops. I've got
some news to tell you. It's about Mom.

LARRY

Must you ruin my appetite?

LAURIE

Something happened that I think you should
know about. Mom was in a car accident—

LARRY

Your mom's always been a lousy driver. How's
the car? I hope she wasn't driving your car.

LAURIE

Mom is fine, if you care to know. Everyone
was fine. Where's your compassion?

LARRY

I'm not sure. Let me summon it. Compassion,
where are you? Compassion, are you in here?

(Yells out) Waitress. Waitress. Can you bring
me some compassion? Mine seems to be missing.

                    LAURIE
Shhhhh!

                    LARRY
Am I embarrassing you? Tell me what happened
to your mother.

                    LAURIE
Her car is a mess.

                    LARRY
I hope she has good insurance.

                    LAURIE
She's blaming the car's accelerator for being
too far from the brakes. She insists that
male engineers design cars for men's shoes,
and that's why she rammed the car in front
of her. She wants to sue the auto industry.
We're lucky no one was hurt.

                    LARRY
I'm glad she wasn't hurt. Honest I am.

                    LAURIE
I know you are. Mom shouldn't be driving
anymore. But that's not what I wanted to
tell you. She's miles away from everything
and can't live there without a car. I don't
know why she ever moved out to the middle of
nowhere. She was in a survivalist phase. She
wanted to move far away from the terrorists
and her back-stabbing friends.

                    LARRY
I thought she moved out there to escape me.

(A WAITRESS walks over to
the table.)

                    WAITRESS
How is everything? Can I get you anything else?

                    LAURIE
I'm stuffed. Thank you. What about you, Pops?

                    LARRY
This is a good burger.

                    LAURIE
Are you still working on it?

                    LARRY
Of course I'm still working on it.

                         (He   looks   over   at
                         Laurie's bowl.)

You've barely touched your salad. Do you
remember when we used to play the one-more-
bite game?

                         (Larry picks up a fry
                         and holds it in front of
                         Laurie's mouth.)

One more bite. Just one mooooore biiiiiite.
One more bite or the bite monster will get
you. ROAR! You loved that game.

                    LAURIE
(To the waitress) I'm sorry about my father.
(To Larry) I hated that game. Pops, there's
something else.

                    WAITRESS
(Walks off as she's speaking.) I'll come
back in a bit.

LARRY

You've finally met someone! It's about time. Nicolette and I have been wondering what's taken you so long.

LAURIE

That's nice. But what I was going to say has to do with Mom. She's moved—

> (Laurie pauses and leans forward to make sure her father is really listening.)

Mom has moved in with me. Well, it's temporary. But she's going to be living with me for a while.

LARRY

(Howling with laughter) You're kidding? Your mother has moved in with you? Have you lost your mind? As you may well remember, your mother is not easy to live with. I do recall the temptation though. When I met your mom, every head would turn when she walked in a room.

LAURIE

I can't believe you just said that. That line is the biggest and grossest cliché in the book.

LARRY

But it's true. Your mom had magnetism. She was drop-dead gorgeous, and she had a seductive brilliance to her. She radiated charm and intelligence with movie star sex appeal. Everyone wanted to date her, but she picked me. I was the one she chose.

LAURIE

And then you tossed her back.

LARRY
I didn't realize what a killer seductive
brilliance could be. If I had stayed with
your mother, I would have died young.

LAURIE
So you left and you're still going strong.

LARRY
I'm happier than I've ever been. Nicolette
is the best thing that's ever happened to me.

(The waitress returns.)

WAITRESS
Are you done?

LARRY
Done? What's done? Is one ever done?

LAURIE
I'm sorry about my father. Yes, we're done.

WAITRESS
Can I get you anything else? Coffee? Tea?

LARRY
Peppermint tea for me. I'm off sugar.
Nicolette has me on a strict diet. No meat,
no wheat, and no sugar.

LAURIE
But you just ate a huge hamburger.

LARRY
(Lifting finger to mouth) Shhhhh, that's
between you and me. A father and daughter
should have some secrets. By the way, I
have news too.

LAURIE
Please, do tell.

                    WAITRESS
Anything else for you, ma'am?

                     LAURIE
Oh, I'm sorry. Yes, I'll have peppermint
tea as well.

               (The waitress walks off.)

                 LAURIE (CONT.)
So what's your news Pops?

                     LARRY
I sold my place. Nicolette and I bought a terrific house just a few miles down the road.

                     LAURIE
What? You what? You moved? Why didn't you
tell me you were moving?

                     LARRY
I'm telling you now.

                     LAURIE
Why didn't you tell me before you moved?

                     LARRY
You were busy at work. I didn't want to
bother you. You'll love the house. It was
just built. Nicolette decided she wants to
go into the interior design business, so I
bought her a house to get her started. You
should see what she can do with a room. I
never noticed rooms before. They were all
the same to me. Some had couches, some had
beds, some had tables, but mostly, they were
all the same. Nicolette sees things that
should be in a room that I never thought
about. She has a vision, which is good, since
I've almost lost mine.

LAURIE

I'm a little confused. You bought a house so
Nicolette can become an interior designer?

LARRY

Nicolette is serious about finding something
she loves to do and since I'm in a position
to support her, I want to do that. She's
envious of you, Laurie, because you found
and followed your passion.

LAURIE

I'm sorry. What? She thinks I am passionate
about being a financial advisor? No. Wow.
Well...just so you know, I didn't find my
passion. I didn't follow my passion. I got an
MBA to become financially self-sufficient.
It was important to me but had nothing to do
with passion.

LARRY

You always loved numbers.

LAURIE

What's that have to do with anything?

LARRY

Let's just say, you had a calling.... Nicolette
is an artist. It's different.

LAURIE

Nicolette isn't an artist!

I didn't have a calling. Why didn't you tell
me you moved? What's the new place like? ←

I'm sorry. I shouldn't have said
that. Maybe Nicolette is an artist

LARRY

It's spectacular, the most beautiful house
I've ever seen. And it's got a pool. You'll
have to come for a swim.

LAURIE

You have a pool? I begged you for a pool when
I was a kid. My entire childhood was spent

lobbying you for a pool. You said you hated pools. You told me it was against your religion to have a pool. You actually invoked religion so I would stop asking you for a pool. And now you're suddenly a born-again pool lover? I'm not comfortable with you having a pool.

                    LARRY
I've softened my stance on pools. Plus, Nicolette insisted.

of course she did
                    LAURIE
Is it a big pool?

                    LARRY
It's a pool-sized pool.

                    LAURIE
I can't believe you got a pool.

                    LARRY
I don't know why this is bothering you so much. Can't you just be happy for me? I'm madly in love. You should try it sometime. But if it makes you feel better, I won't swim in the pool.

                    LAURIE
Please swim in your pool. I insist that you swim in your pool.

                         (The waitress walks over
                         with two cups and puts them
                         down on the table. Laurie
                         looks up at her.)

Thank you. Thank you so, so, so much.

                    BLACKOUT

DAY 10

LAST NIGHT, MAYA and Stu had a dinner party.

There were four couples, including Maya and Stu, and there was me, the single. The table was set for nine, an awkward number. There's no symmetry. Rectangular tables weren't designed to accommodate divorced friends and there's no way to mask it. Four chairs on one side of the table, a little too close together, three on the other. Because dinner party rules dictate you shouldn't sit next to your spouse, Fiona, Bobby, and Sarah were seated on the three-chair side and I was seated on the four-chair side, with Jack and Mike to my left and Erick to my right. But then Fiona and Erick said they were left-handed and wanted to swap seats. We stood up and started to shuffle about, and that's when Bobby started tapping us on the back of our heads. Duck. Duck. Duck. When he got to Erick, he said Goose and started running around behind us and taunting Erick to chase him, which of course he couldn't resist. We were all laughing, but I could tell Maya's laughter was forced. It's not like her to forget that Fiona and Erick are lefties.

When we got down to eating, they all wanted to discuss my dating life. No one asked about the play. No one wanted to talk about the government shutdown or the Affordable Care Act. Or talk about the movies they had recently seen. I was the hot-topic, the feature presentation, the centerpiece of the table.

I even looked the part of a cornucopia in an autumnal earth tone shirt that I wear too often because someone once told me it brings out my inner beauty.

SARAH: Elise, are you dating anyone?

ME: I've had a few uninspired dates.

MAYA: Elise needs to get laid.

BOBBY: Don't we all.

ERICK: At your service, hon.

ME: I'm fine.

MAYA: I am convinced that Elise needs have sex to get her creative juices flowing.

BOBBY: We'll get your juices flowing. This should be easy. You're still hot and I can think of a million men to introduce you to.

ERICK: Darling, she needs to meet straight men.

ME: How come only gay men tell me I'm hot?

MIKE: Because I'd get in trouble if I said that. You do have a great smile though. I think I can safely say that—

FIONA: Yes, dear. That's fine. I know someone you have to meet, Elise. He's a journalist. He's inquisitive and fascinating and doesn't have an ego. He's one of those guys who knows everything but doesn't weaponize it. He travels a lot on assignment, so you'll never feel suffocated.

MIKE: Honey, if you'd like to be married to someone who travels more, I'd be delighted to oblige. Tomorrow morning I'll book a surfing trip to Costa Rica. Stu, would you care to join me?

I jumped in to try to squelch any brewing marital eruptions.

ME: Where does this journalist live when he's not off traveling the world? I don't want a long-distance relationship.

FIONA: Actually, he lives not far from here, with his mother. He's never been married.

ME: He lives with his mother? How old is he?

FIONA: Fifty-ish. He never got his own place because he travels so much. It was a financial decision, it's not like some weird mommy thing.

ME: I don't want to date anyone who still lives with his mother whether they have a mommy thing or not. I don't want Marsden to get the idea that living with your mother when you're 50 is an option. The next man in my life has to have his own place. I'm pretty sure that's a basic requirement.

ERICK: I've got someone who would be perfect for you. You absolutely need to meet him. His name is Roger, and he lives in his own apartment. He's a scientist and brilliant, a bit of an introvert, prefers reading to talking, but may be the nicest person I know. I love men on the spectrum.

BOBBY: Sorry to disappoint, dear.

ME: I like talkers.

SARAH: I've got the guy for Elise. Five kids. An attorney. Loves the theater. Sees everything he can and takes all five kids to New York every year for a Broadway musical. They sing show tunes around the dinner table. His wife died of cancer a few years ago. It was heartbreaking and he's just coming out from under. He could probably use some good adult conversation and, Elise, who better than you to sing show tunes with.

ME: Five kids? I've been overwhelmed with one. Just the thought of five kids gives me anxiety. And I'm really not that good with show tunes.

It didn't stop. They were coming at me from all sides of the table.

BOBBY: I have the perfect man. His name is Dashiell Hammett, but I call him Dashing Dashiell.

ME: Dashiell Hammett is dead. He died before we were born. I've gone out with unavailable men before, but never that unavailable.

BOBBY: My Dashiell is very much alive. He writes mystery novels just like his namesake, and has two kids named Nick and Nora, and a dog named Sam Spade. It's a meta touch.

ME: It's actually kind of creepy that he named his kids and dog after real Dashiell Hammett characters. I don't see anything meta.

BOBBY: Trust me when I say Dashiell is all meta-man.

ME: Bobby, I have no idea what you're talking about, so I'm going to make this easy and break up with him before I even meet him. This way we can skip the heartbreak and hard feelings, and little Nick and Nora won't have to wonder why I'm no longer in their lives.

MAYA: Elise, don't be so closed down. You could be his Lillian Hellman. Lillian Hellman said she wrote her best plays when she was with Dashiell Hammett. I think this is meant to be. You're a playwright named Hellman and he's a mystery novelist named Hammett. It's kismet. Imagine the work the two of you will produce when you're together. Elise, you're always droning on about not being able to finish your play. Maybe you need your very own Hammett. Just one date. How about it? Test the waters to see if he is the Hammett to your Hellman.

BOBBY: Come on Elise, one date, just to see. If it works out, the world gets Hellman and Hammett: The Sequel.

ME: I don't think most of the world knows about Hellman and Hammett: The Originals. And I highly doubt anyone is waiting for the sequel.

BOBBY: It's a done deal. You're perfect together.

ERICK: Bobby, love, lay off her. She doesn't want to go out with your Dashing Dashiell and I don't blame her. But Elise, do I have another guy for you....

And so it went, an entire dinner party conversation devoted to finding Elise a date. But all Elise wants is to finish her play. When Elise decides she wants to be everybody's go-to for their single male friends, she will say so. But it will be on her terms and on her own time clock. And if that time is in two weeks or 20 years, it shouldn't matter to the people at Maya's dinner party. Elise feels used. She didn't sign up to be the party entertainment. And now, because her singleness, singletude, and singledom was the focus of conversation for an entire evening, Elise has started writing about herself in the third person.

DAY 11

SAMMY RONSTEIN CALLED at 8:00 yesterday morning to say that reading the first act of *Deja New* reminded him of the feeling he gets when he walks by a street musician who should be playing Carnegie Hall. At first his call inspired me, but after an hour of typing and deleting, I realized his enthusiasm was more inhibiting than inspiring. I mulled over every word. Was that word worthy of Carnegie Hall? None of them were so I gave up and decided to pick an item from my to-do list in an attempt to finish something. Finish anything. The act of finishing seemed important. I chose a low-priority task: sort through old handbags.

I hate getting rid of things. It feels like a betrayal. Or like I'm being the mean girl. I tried being the mean girl, I was more accomplished at being the bullied girl, but honestly my strength was staying under the fray. Now I aim to be all-inclusive. It doesn't matter how old or stained or ugly you are. You matter. Plus, as a writer I want to hold onto my memories. A bag is not just a bag and the bags I have kept tell the story of my entire adult life. There's the hipper-than-thou bag that I slung over my shoulder when I lived in the East Village and worked at PS 122, the I've-got-a-real-job-now bag that I used when I moved to Boston and worked in the development office at the American Repertory Theater, the scuffed-up backpack from weekend getaways to the White Mountains with Elliot, the many bold-colored look-at-me-I'm-a-playwright bags, and the you'd-never-guess-how-much-this-bag-cost bag during my life as the wife of a successful entrepreneur living in a suburb with six sushi restaurants. And now the canvas tote bag of the divorced-single-mother-with-writer's-block-living-in-a-suburb-with-far-fewer-sushi-places bags. These bags moved with me over the years, from a studio apartment with heroin addicts living in the hallway, to a tiny apartment with no heroin addicts in the hallway, but a junkie roommate, to a larger apartment in a different city with three fabulous roommates, to a small apartment with a future husband, to a big boastful house with a husband and son, to the house with no husband. I gathered these bags and arranged them in a large chronological circle and sat in the middle of them. Surrounded by my life in bags, I tried to decide what the criteria was for probable future use.

I exhumed playbills and stubs for plays that should have gone to the accountant, notebooks filled with ideas and character studies, business cards for people I don't remember meeting, used tissues that I saved for some reason—for what? DNA samples? Or because I can get nostalgic about snot? A pack of unopened chewing gum from a trip to France, a small stone with a single white band around it, crumpled up receipts for cups of coffee, a half-eaten cookie, lipsticks in many shades, concealers, and hair clips. But most importantly, in an old, embroidered backpack from my Boston days, I found a marked-up copy of *The Artist's Way*. Julia Cameron would call it "synchronicity." How else do you account for the magnificent coincidence that less than two weeks after I start doing Morning Pages, I find my long-neglected copy of *The Artist's Way*?

The part of the book about disengaging from your inner censor jumped out at me. My inner-censor reminds me of a theater critic for a local paper. She's opinionated, but doesn't feel like she should offend, so her criticisms are couched in nice-speak. Her name is Franny, but she wishes it were Françoise. She would probably be more successful if she were less benignly diplomatic. I think an eviscerating inner-critic would be easier to contend with. I could counter her lacerating barbs, but my Franny would never be so bold as to suggest that what I'm working on is worthless drivel. She's too much the ambassador and is more interested in unifying the left lobe and the right lobe than nuking the entire region. Sometimes Franny is even kind and supportive—a cheerleader. *It's passable*, she'll say. What kind of self-respecting inner critic acts like that? It occurs to me that Franny is afraid of being too critical. My inner critic doesn't want to go out on a limb. She fears rejection. I have an inner critic who is afraid of being criticized.

I didn't finish sorting through my bags. I told myself it was okay, that non-finishing was part of the process. Figuring out the process is a bigger part of the process than I ever thought it would be. Should I take another day away from the play? Will the ending reveal itself to me? I can distract myself and await a revelation. I can go back to my to-do list. I don't even know if I can even call it a to-do list anymore. My to-do list has exploded and found its way onto napkins and receipts that are now scattered around the house, posted to the fridge, and stuck in memos on my phone, only to be lost, neglected, and forgotten about. My to-do list is spawning indiscriminately.

I'll write a half a to-do list. I wonder if it's better to have a tome with several volumes across multiple platforms or make sub-lists? Maybe I can trick myself into believing my to-do list is manageable.

To-do list deception sounds a little bit like cheating at solitaire. Well, what's so bad about cheating at solitaire anyway? Is there any evidence that people who cheat at solitaire also cheat on their taxes or their spouses? Actually, I wouldn't be surprised if there is a correlation. I'd bet a million dollars and a Porsche that Elliot cheats at solitaire. Not that he needs to. Elliot wins when he plays solitaire. The cards know it's him playing and behave accordingly.

I'm going to do away with my to-do list. To-do lists are oppressive. They render us failures through guilt. I'm going to throw mine out and start an Eschew List instead. From now on every morning after writing my Morning Pages, I will make a list of all the things I will not do.

Today I will eschew:

> Paying bills
> Calling the phone company to get a better phone plan
> Taking the moldy food out of the fridge
> Getting annoyed with Mom

DAY 12

MARSDEN WAS AT Elliot's, and I worked in the house in near silence until noon yesterday. The only sounds interrupting my flow all morning were old house sounds. The creaks and occasional random thumps that this house emits makes it feel like the authentic fake it is. When Elliot left, he bought a new farmhouse designed to look like an old farmhouse for me and Marsden to move into.

"You always said you loved old farmhouses," he told me.

"But this isn't an old farmhouse," I had to point out.

Elliot likes new things that look old. He left me for a woman who is five years younger than me but looks ten years older. I like new things to look new and old things to look old, but I am still surrounded by new things that look old. A deep-hued red underlayer of paint peeks through the steel blue overlayer in spots on the kitchen cabinets that have been sanded down to look like wear-and-tear. The exposed wooden beams that frame the house aren't just made from reclaimed wood, they are reclaimed wood that was further battered and beaten.

Everything in this house is distressed, even its inhabitants.

In our old house everything looked perfect, because if we looked perfect, we'd be perfect. Only we weren't. I didn't believe it when Maya told me she heard that Elliot might be having an affair. "With who?" I asked.

It didn't strike me as possible that he was sleeping with somebody else, but I was curious as to who he would have a rumored affair with. Who did people think he was sleeping with? "Midge Montgomery," Maya said.

"Who's Midge Montgomery?" I asked before reassuring her, "Elliot's not having an affair."

When I tried to picture what someone named Midge Montgomery would look like, I could only conjure an image of Elizabeth Montgomery from *Bewitched*. Could Elliot be secretly cavorting with a woman with a magical button of a nose? No. Of course not.

Maya didn't bring it up again. Not directly. But the idea had infiltrated my thoughts. I reassured myself with the knowledge that Elliot was too nerdy and too honest to have an affair. But I watched him more carefully. At that point, he was spending almost all his free time in the backyard working on his fruit trees. He was experimenting to see how many different types of fruit he could successfully graft onto a single tree. His most successful had nine different types of fruit growing on it. But he wanted more.

That was the part of his personality I hadn't considered. Elliot always wants more.

And then one night after he got home late from a squash game with Mike, I asked him, not because I believed it was true, but because I wanted his reassurance that it wasn't.

I honestly felt guilty about asking.

ME: Elliot, I have a crazy question for you. Maya mentioned something and I keep thinking about it, so I'm just going to ask you. I'm actually asking more for Maya than for me.

ELLIOT: What's your question Elise?

ME: Never mind.

ELLIOT: Okay. I'll never mind.

ME: Okay, I'll ask. I'm sorry to ask this, but are you having an affair? Maya heard something.

ELLIOT: Do you want me to call Maya with the answer, or would you prefer that I tell you and then you can relay my answer to Maya?

ME: I shouldn't have asked.

ELLIOT: I'm seeing someone.

A year and a half after that conversation, the house with the fruit tree that grows apples, pears, nectarines, plums, and peaches had been sold and Elliot had moved out on me and in with Midge Montgomery, who thankfully looks nothing like Elizabeth Montgomery.

And a year after that, Maya tells me I need to stop obsessing over Elliot.

I told her, "If time was money, I only spend a dime a day on Elliot." I probably sounded defensive, too *thou dost protest too much*-ish. But I don't believe, like Maya implied, that I am self-delusional. She didn't just imply it. She said it straight out: "Elise, stop creating characters for a moment and look at yourself. You are self-delusional."

After Elliot emptied out his side of the closet, after his toothbrush and shaving supplies were gone from the bathroom and space opened up for new signs of sickness in the medicine cabinet, after he left his wedding ring on his bedside table, where he used to keep a pyramid of three books—the books would change but the pyramid always stayed the same—the one thing he couldn't take, the thing he inadvertently left behind was his scent. He had moved out, but our bedroom still smelled like Elliot and for three months I didn't wash the sheets, sweep, vacuum, or even clean the toilet, for fear of losing his scent. When Elliot announced that he planned to sell the house and would buy a smaller place for me and Marsden, I was forced to clean. Maya came over and helped me. We sniffed everything that had touched Elliot before scrubbing and sanitizing, and then to commemorate the end of *eau de Elliot*, we opened a bottle of Veuve Clicquot and curled up on the bed and planned my future.

I don't want to be thinking about him, but he lurks and he lingers.

DAY 13

I WONDER WHAT it would be like to be a writer who bangs out a first draft. Who can see a story in its entirety before beginning. I jump in at a sprint, but then I stop and circle back to make sure I haven't gotten too far without forgetting something. It's like racing out of the house because you're in a rush to get somewhere, then running back inside to make sure the stove is off, which it always is but it's still good you checked, and while you're back inside you quickly pee, glance at the stove, which is still off, get back to your car, and realize that you've misplaced the keys. That's how I write. It's nearly impossible to get to your destination with this kind of writing style.

I might not be getting traction on my ending, but at least Laurie is finding her voice. The problem with having an introvert as a main character is that she doesn't want to have all the attention focused on her. My secondary characters were leading an insurrection and moving into the primary roles. They were getting all the good lines and the only thing left for Laurie to do was react. Yesterday I figured out how to get her back, but now I have other issues. I have too much extraneous dialogue, a boring monologue that's way too long, and a near pathological lack of stage directions—it's as if I'm worried about seeming too pushy or demanding. I need actors. I need to listen to the rhythm and flow and figure out what's making sense and what's not.

If only I could blink my eyes and *Deja New* would be finished. I'm scared I'm blowing this, my first commission. Blowing it. I wish I could blink this play into existence. Blink. Sammy Ronstein's email is in my inbox telling me that *Deja New* has Wendy Wasserstein's insights, Sarah Ruel's poetic voice, Neil Simon's humor, no not Neil Simon, but who? I want her to say I am the female who? Oscar Wilde? John Guare? Yasmina Reza? Yasmina Reza is a woman. But she's French. I want to blink and turn myself into the American Yasmina Reza. I'll blink past Sammy's notes. Sammy calls himself a hands-off producer, but while the words, "I don't want to insert myself," are coming out of his mouth, he's handing you a tome of notes. I'll blink past casting, and past opening night and the pain of reviews, and I'll blink this play onto Broadway and, why not, the Tony Awards. I'll write an acceptance speech. I'll thank the talented cast, the amazing director, and of course, I'll thank Sammy Ronstein. "Sammy, you believed in me when no one else noticed I was still writing!" My voice will be strong but full of emotion. I'll thank my incredible son, Marsden, and I'll thank my mother and father for the gift of great material. I'll thank Maya for her friendship, and I need to make sure I remember to thank Aunt Rosemary. She'll feel rejected if I don't thank her.

Deja New won't be commercial enough for Broadway, but someday I want to write something that smashes people to smithereens and then elevates them into a near orgasmic euphoria. I want to write something that people refer to as "an emotional tour de force." Imagine what it's like having someone say that about something you've written. "Elise Hellman has given us another emotional tour de force." Applause. Invitations to speak. More commissions. I'm ready.

For now, though, I'll trade tour de force for a good final act. Not contrived. I don't want to write another play that opens the door for reviewers to grouse about how it fell apart at the end. Yes, we know. We didn't need you to tell us. Why do things need endings anyway? Are they even necessary? Resolution is overrated. Everyone is always talking about closure these days. Fuck closure. Let's stop suturing the wounds and leave them open to fester.

That's what real life is. When did we all get so obsessed with closure? Was it after the Revolutionary War? I somehow doubt John Hancock signed the Declaration of Independence and said, "Now we finally have closure."

Seeking closure has consumed us. It's become our North Star, our American identity. We are closure-obsessed. I cannot count the number of times people have asked me if I feel like I've found closure with Elliot. What if my play doesn't have an ending? What if there is no closure?

DAY 14

No.

No. No. No, Bobby. No is a short word, a favorite amongst two-year-olds, two letters that go together naturally. What other consecutive two letters in the alphabet actually form a word? I can't think of another one. Wait. Hi. Hi is another one. It doesn't matter. No is an honest, organic, and impactful word, and yet I avoid it because I find it aggressive, authoritative, and mean and I don't use it enough.

It is fascinating to see who gets offered up as date material. Being single is an excellent way to find out what your friends really think of you. Who are the men they deem fit for a match? Are they attractive? Intelligent? Are they kind? Are they decent? A bit boring? New-agey? Cynical? Professionals or artists? Are they murderers? What does that say about me if a friend sets me up with a murderer?

Bobby called yesterday morning, early.

"Hi love, give Dashiell a call. He's waiting to hear from you."

"Who?"

"Dashiell Hammett. You can't possibly have forgotten. Call him before you get too saggy or soft. Dashiell is spectacularly handsome and deeply mysterious. I told him all about you and I bet he can't wait to get in your pants."

No.

No. No. No.

I wrote down the number and called.

"It's Dash, if you're up for it, leave a message, and if you're not in a message-leaving mood, I don't blame you." His outgoing message was sweet and goofy, so I left a short a message and he called back within minutes.

Two tickets had just dropped in his lap for a performance of a show that was getting a lot of buzz as a need-to-see experimental theatrical experience. Was I free to join him?

No.

Yes.

At six o'clock a silver Porsche, a car specifically designed for a man interested in advertising his midlife crisis, pulled up in front of the house and a slightly weathered golden man with silver hair emerged from it. He was trim and fit, had a firm handshake, and was overly scented. He reminded me of Sonny Crockett in *Miami Vice*. Big smile. Bright white teeth. Too white for tooth whitener. Probably caps.

Bobby is setting me up with a handsome writer with super white teeth who drives a Porsche and smells like a cedarwood forest. That's who Bobby thinks I should be dating.

He started driving and I asked, "How'd you get into crime writing? Don't most crime writers start off as lawyers?"

"That's the cliché. I'm not interested in clichés, so I chose not to go to law school."

"You're a middle-aged man driving a Porsche, how can you say you're not interested in clichés? I'm sorry, that was rude." I apologized to him and silently chastised myself.

"Appearances are deceptive. You learn that in Crime Writing 101."

"Okay, so you weren't an attorney. Did you start out as a reporter? Isn't that the other route people take to get into your line of work?"

"I never worked for a newspaper, although I've been written about quite a bit."

I should have looked up this Dashiell Hammett online, but I had found my focus and was making progress on the play. I barely had enough time to figure out what to wear—a periwinkle blue V-neck sweater that reveals just a hint of cleavage and black jeans that make me look like I might have an ass—how much makeup to put on—politely pink cheeks and low-beam lips—and what to do with my hair—I straightened it to get out the frizz then curled it for bounce.

"If you weren't an attorney or a reporter, how did you come to write crime novels?"

"I'm not sure you really want the answer to that question," he said. I looked over at him, expecting an enigmatic and slightly flirtatious smile, but his expression was solid.

"I want to know."

"You know the advice we're all given, write what you know. I did exactly that. I killed someone and decided to write about it."

He was speeding down Washington Street toward Jamaica Plain.

"Excuse me?"

"I didn't mean to shock you. I've discovered over the years that the best to way to let people know about my dark past is to be straightforward. Bobby didn't tell you I gather."

"No, Bobby didn't mention this. And I don't actually believe you. But you had me for a moment."

"Glad to hear it."

"So how did you get into crime writing?"

"Unfortunately, I was telling you the truth."

I still didn't believe him, and tried engaging him in a conversation about being a murderer, as a lark. I thought we were kidding around.

"Okay, so have you killed a lot of people or just one person?"

"Just one."

"That's good. But why'd you stop with one?"

"You still don't believe me. Do you?"

"Of course not!"

"Why don't you call Bobby and ask him. You know how Bobby is. I'm sure he'll say he didn't tell you because he wanted you to be surprised. He likes to stir the pot. He's a child."

"He is a child. I agree with you." An uncomfortable and suffocating silence filled up the car. Was I sitting next to a murderer? He was speeding and I wanted to tell him to slow down, but what if?

"To be clear, the guy I killed was a monster. He deserved to die. Maybe you believe nobody deserves to die, but if that's the case, I suspect it's only because you haven't met a true sociopath." I think he started telling me his story to break through the tension. "And it was justifiable homicide, at least I believe it was. You can read about it in my first book. The title is *Slip Cover* and it's still in print. 'Slip cover' has a double meaning. The murderer is clever and slips cover, but he also disposes of the dead body in a couch's slipcover."

"Did you do that?"

"After I killed him, I was on the lam for three years. Then I got caught."

"And what happened after you got caught?"

"There was a trial. I got lucky. Evidence in my case was tampered with and there was a mistrial."

"That's good." I think I was trying to sound supportive. What do you say to a person you just met who you are starting to believe is a murderer? I told him I would read his book, and we changed the topic to the weather and our children. I couldn't focus on the play. Experimental theater is hard enough when your mind isn't racing.

I was set up on a date with a man who smelled like cedarwood and has murdered someone. I sat next to him wondering if the reason he was wearing so much cologne to mask the smell of being a murderer? Could it be that murderers smell better than the rest of us?

DAY 15

I CALLED MAYA to tell her about my date with the murderer.

"Missed opportunity," was her response. "Sleeping with him would have helped you get over your writer's block and given you something to write about. A double win!"

She kept at me with her infuriatingly forceful yet captivatingly caring relentlessness. Her Maya-ness.

"Elise, having sex with someone else will help you purge Elliot from your amygdala, where he's been starring in scene studies from Elise and Elliot's Marriage for the past two years. Don't let him hold you hostage. You need to lose your divorce virginity."

Divorce virginity. I hate the term. I tell her so. She doesn't care.

"It's a great term. You should take it and run with it."

She even came up with the idea for a sitcom called *The Divorce Virgins* that she thinks I should write after I finish *Deja New*—a kind of *Sex and the City* meets *Golden Girls* about best friends who get divorced around the same time and join a dating world that looks a lot different from the one they had left behind to get married.

I know she's trying to help me. I know she doesn't understand writer's block—or any block. Maya is a get-it-done type. I am a think-about-getting-it-done type. She is trying to help me squeeze the final act out. She's bossy about it

94

though. Demanding. Pushy. She calls it supportive. "Get laid, Elise. Fall in lust. It'll help you write your final act sex scene."

"What if I don't want to have a final act sex scene?"

"You will."

"I don't think so. Not in life and not in theater."

I have been on exactly three dates since my divorce.

There was Mikel, who was once named Michael but changed it to Mikel while studying landscape design in France. It was during a visit to Giverny. He claims Monet spoke to him, like God. "Mikel, revere the land like a literary master-piece," said Monet. "And change your name." After the visit to Giverny, he went from Michael to Mikel and shifted the focus of his studies to the narrative landscape. Maya met Mikel while she was doing publicity for the American Society of Landscape Architects or some organization like that. He told her he loved to read and talked more about books than landscaping, and he had the arms of an Adonis and deep-set brooding eyes which Maya described as "sexy, yet serious."

She sent him an email and bcc-ed me:

Dearest Mikel,

Please excuse the unexpected email. You've been on my mind recently as my daughter is reading *A Midsummer Night's Dream*, and the other night she blurted out: *I know a bank where the wild thyme blows, where oxlips and the nodding violet grows.* I was reminded of the Shakespearean garden you designed, and it occurred to me that you might like to meet one of my dearest friends, who is a brilliant play-wright and happens to be single. Come what may of this, her name is Elise Hellman and I'd love to connect you.

Yours,
Maya (Your Voice PR)

Mikel and I went out for coffee and three sips in, he said
he'd like to cut to the chase and talk about "rumpscuttle and
clapperdepouch."

"Excuse me?" I said.

"I'm interested in your favorite coital contortions," he
replied.

"Are you asking me what positions I like to have sex in?"

"You're distressingly prosaic for a playwright," was his
response.

"And you're a licentious pretentious weed!"

I didn't say that. I wish I had. I did respond with some
query along the lines of, "Do all landscape architects tend to
use such floral language?"

To make up for Mikel, Maya introduced me to Richard,
who she promised was more mature. By more mature, she
meant he was 75-years-old.

"He's in great shape. You'd never know he was over fifty,"
she insisted.

"But I'm not even fifty," I reminded her.

I look like the kind of 48-year-old who could date someone in their 70s or someone in their 30s. I don't particularly
want to look like that kind of 48-year-old, but my face has
aged into a face that people can't seem to figure out. The lines
around my eyes come and go, like the folds of theater curtains,
and I keep my skin so well moisturized I sometimes look dewy
to the point of damp or even greasy, and while my smile is big
and toothy and has been called contagious—although mostly by
hypochondriacs—my thinking face has inspired random people
passing me on the street to say things like, "Don't worry, it's
not so bad."

"Forty-eight is the new seventy-five," Maya assured me.

"I thought seventy-five was the new fifty," I told her.

"It goes in both directions," she said.

"So does that make me seventy-five and him fifty?"

We went to an Italian restaurant that had recently opened. He ordered a bottle of red wine, an antipasto, and an entree. And he chewed loudly and slowly, which was proof that 75 is not the new 50 and 48 is not the new 75. Forty-eight is the new 50 at best. Richard's stories reminded me of the ones Uncle Bill used to tell, and after he finished his tiramisu, I asked if he wanted to meet my Aunt Rosemary. "I think you two could have a lot in common," I told him.

"I hope you won't judge me too harshly for sounding like a cliché, but women of my generation are no longer of interest to me," he said. Straight face. Tiramisu on his chin.

DAY 16

MOM CALLED AT noon yesterday to ask me what time it was.

"It's twelve o'clock," I told her.

"In the daytime or night?" she asked.

"It's noon. Look out your window. It's light out."

"I had terrible insomnia last night and didn't fall asleep until five in the morning. I just woke up and was worried that maybe I had slept through the day."

Two hours later she called to tell me she was furious at Dad.

"He's stealing from me."

"Dad's not stealing from you," I assured her.

"He is. He's sneaking in here and taking things."

"He isn't sneaking in. The doormen wouldn't let him up."

"He's paid them off. They'll do whatever he wants."

"Trust me. Dad has not paid the doormen off. He's too cheap. Besides, do you really think Alan would take a bribe?"

"Maybe not Alan, but the others. They're all on his side."

"No, they're not. No one is allowing Dad to sneak in and he's not stealing from you."

After I said that, she accused me of taking his side too. Everyone is always on Dad's side. She called an hour later to say she had proof that Dad was stealing from her.

"My first edition *Madame Bovary* is missing. I've looked everywhere and I can't find it. I'm calling the police. Your father stole it from me."

I tried reasoning with her. I suggested she look for the book again. Maybe it got pushed behind another book on the bookshelf. Maybe it's under the couch.

"I'm sure it's somewhere. Trust me, Dad didn't steal it."

"It's not here," she said.

"I'm sure it is," I told her.

"Are you accusing me of lying?"

"No, I think you misplaced the book. It's somewhere in the apartment."

"You always blame me for everything, Elise. I'm calling the police and telling them to search your father's house."

"Mom, please don't call the police. I promise you Dad didn't steal your book."

After we hung up, I called Dad to make sure he didn't happen to have Mom's first edition of *Madame Bovary*.

"Why would I have anything of your mother's?" he asked me. "I've been divorced from her for forty years. Best forty years of my life."

"Yes, I know," I said. Dad loves to remind me how happy he is now that he's not married to Mom.

"Lucy saved me," he said. "I was drowning, and she pulled me out of the water." And he loves water metaphors. If he's not drowning, he's diving into something new, or treading water until the next wave comes. I tried to explain that Mom noticed that her copy of *Madame Bovary* was missing, and she thought he might have had it all these years. I didn't mention to him that she accused him of bribing the doormen, breaking into her apartment, and stealing a book that was probably worth far less than she believed it was. He doesn't need more ammunition to hate her.

DAY 17

THE FIRST TIME Mom called me yesterday she told me that her loneliness was like a deep hole that she's trying to eat her way out of, but she's scared of getting fat, so she threw out all the food in the house. She said it happened when she got up in the middle of the night and ate a cheese sandwich, then she made two hard-boiled eggs and ate those, then she finished the peanut butter, then she ate a leftover lambchop, then an apple to be healthy, then more cheese. Then she went back to bed but couldn't sleep so she got up and emptied the fridge into a garbage bag and threw it out.

"I'd rather die of loneliness than get fat," she said.

I encouraged her to eat whatever she wanted. I told her she was beautiful.

"All my friends have abandoned me," she said.

"Of course they haven't abandoned you," I told her.

She then told me that her life is empty, and she's filled with resentments and covered in age spots.

I suggested she invite Aunt Rosemary over for dinner.

She said she was done with Aunt Rosemary.

The second time she called she told me she missed me and that she loved me and that she was going to the grocery store to buy some food.

The third time she called she said she wanted to hear about Marsden, so I told her that he was supposed to be figuring out what colleges he wanted to apply to and that I was trying to convince Elliot to take him on some college tours but Elliot didn't want to pressure him, and I was worried that I'd get stuck taking him when I have a deadline—not just any deadline—the deadline that could change everything for me.

"I can take him to see colleges," Mom said.

"Thank you. That's so sweet. But he should go with one of his parents."

"I'd take him if you let me. You don't let me see him. He's my only grandson and you're punishing me by keeping him away."

"That's not true," I told her.

And then the kicker. "You still hate me because your father left. You never stopped blaming me."

Could she be right? Do I still blame her?

Dad smelled funny. I remember that. He said, "Elise, pumpkin, we need to talk to you about something."

And I said, "I need to talk to you about something. You smell funny."

And he said, "You're right. That's because I smell like someplace else."

And I think Mom said, "Someone else," but maybe she didn't.

I do distinctly remember Dad saying, "Your mother and I no longer love each other, but we still love you, and will always love you, Elise."

Dad moved out that day. The following day he came over to get me for the first of many outings into the world as a child of a broken home. We were going to his new apartment then heading to Macy's to shop for furniture for my bedroom. "You can get anything you want," he said.

"Can I get a pony?" I asked him.

"If there are ponies at Macy's, we'll get you one," he replied because that's the kind of father he is.

I suspect it wouldn't have taken much to set Mom off, but the pony is what triggered it. "Don't lie to her you piece of shit! You're not getting a pony, Elise. Your father is trying to turn you against me. Don't you understand? He's trying to kill me. He wants me dead. That's what he wants."

"Mommy! Stop saying that!"

She walked to the open window and leaned out of it.

"If I jump, will that make you happy? Will that make you feel better?" she yelled to the world, to Dad, to me.

"Mommy! Mommy! Noooooo! Please Mommy! Please Mommy! Please Mommy!"

Dad grabbed onto me. "Have you lost your mind, Trudy?" he shouted.

"Please Mommy, No! Please Mommmmmmmy!" I sobbed.

Do I still feel the anger of an eight-year-old child? Do I blame her for him leaving?

Kind of. And she knows it.

But what I told her was: "Of course I don't blame you. I know it was difficult when he left. You were in a lot of pain, and I understand why, but I am trying to write and I need to go."

I hung up—read and reread the beginning of the second act. It had meandered off track, so I deleted it and called Mom back.

"Hi Mom."

"Who's this?" she asked.

"It's Elise. Your daughter. The only person in this world who calls you Mom."

"Elise, darling, I'm watching *Jaws* on Turner Classic Movies. Do you remember that it was filmed on Martha's Vineyard the summer we were there? That was the summer your father left me for that cunt."

"Lucy's not a cunt. It's been forty years. Can't you get over it."

"It's a good movie."

"It is a good movie."

She hung up and I didn't speak to her again. I was so relieved that she didn't call back that I couldn't sleep. My relief kept me awake all night and now it's seven in the morning and I feel like I need a nap.

(Laurie's house. There is an open layout
living room/dining area, with the kitchen
behind an island. There is a couch with a
coffee table in front of it, a comfortable
lounge chair, and a dining table with four
chairs around it. It is simple and clean and
looks much like a Pottery Barn showroom. Off
to the side is the front door of the house.
LAURIE, dressed professionally, walks in
and looks around with a somewhat quizzical
expression on her face. GRACE, who we can't
fully see but is wearing an elegant long
dress, is in the kitchen preparing dinner.
Laurie walks into the kitchen.)

                    LAURIE
What are you doing?

                    GRACE
Is that how you say hello to your mother?

                    LAURIE
I'm sorry. Hi Mom. How was your day? Wow, you
look stunning! Are you cooking something?

GRACE

I'm making dinner. Why should you always
have to make me dinner?

LAURIE

I make you dinner because this is my house
and you are my guest.

GRACE

I'm your mother. A mother isn't a houseguest.

LAURIE

Of course you're not a houseguest. But I like
making you dinner anyway.

GRACE

Should Grace complain more here? List her woes?

I'm wasting away here while my car
gets repaired.

LAURIE

You don't look like somebody who is wasting
away. Why are you so dressed up?

GRACE

I wanted to look nice for my daughter. I'm
going to start making us dinners.

> (Laurie lifts up the lid on
> a pot on the stove.)

LAURIE

What's this?

GRACE

Broccoli.

LAURIE

That's broccoli?

GRACE

I steamed it.

LAURIE

For how long?

GRACE

I thought you'd be home earlier. It's almost
nine o'clock. Laurie, you work too hard.
Nobody knows better than me how hard a single woman has to work to pay the bills, but
darling, you can't work all the time.

LAURIE

We have a big audit coming up. Things are
crazy right now and I'm under a lot of pressure. It's not always like this. Thank you
for making dinner. I really appreciate it.
What else did you make?

GRACE

Meatloaf.

LAURIE

Wow, you got this dressed up for meatloaf.
It smells fantastic. I'm starving. I'll set
the table.

(Laurie reaches up and pulls
open a cabinet door.)

Where are my plates?

GRACE

They're over there.

(Grace points to the other
side of the kitchen.)

I moved them.

LAURIE

Why?

GRACE

They were on too high a shelf. You reach for
one and they're all about to come crash-
ing down. It makes more sense to keep them
over there.

LAURIE

I liked my plates where they were. I'm moving
them back.

GRACE

Darling, give them a chance.

> (Laurie opens another
> cabinet.)

LAURIE

Where'd the glasses go?

GRACE

(Pointing) Over there. It's more convenient.

LAURIE

(Both annoyed and amused) It's not more convenient for me. I had things where I wanted
them. If I wanted my plates there (points)
and my glasses there (points) I'd have put
them there.

GRACE

Please don't start in. Can't we have a nice
dinner together? Let's not fight tonight.

LAURIE

I wasn't fighting with you.

> (Laurie sets the table and
> Grace brings over the food.
> They sit down and start
> eating in silence. Laurie

is scarfing her food down.
Grace is savoring her meal.)

GRACE

You were fighting w/ me. You can't even tell when you're fighting w/ me anymore. It's up to me to tell you.

∧I called the garage about my car today.

LAURIE

Oh, what did they say?

GRACE

They said they haven't looked at it yet. It's absolutely outrageous. I told them I needed it back. How long does it take to look at a smashed-up car? First, they make you wait and then they charge you for waiting.

LAURIE

Mom, I don't think you should be driving anymore. I wouldn't worry about the car. It's not going to be worth repairing anyway.

GRACE

Add ~ well you would if you ever came to visit!

I can't manage without a car. You know where I live, Laurie. It's not possible.

LAURIE

or too much?

You'll stay here until we figure things out.

GRACE

I don't need to figure things out. I need my car. You shouldn't eat so fast, Laurie. It's not good for your health.

LAURIE

I like to eat fast. It's efficient.

GRACE

How do you like the meatloaf?

LAURIE

(Sincere and enthusiastic) It's fantastic! It's absolutely delicious. Best meatloaf

ever! Something seems different in here. Did
you do something?

GRACE

You might not know this, but I understand
what you're going through.

LAURIE

What am I going through? What do you mean?

GRACE

I was single when I was forty too. Dad
decided to blow up our beautiful family two
months shy of my fortieth. We already had the
party planned.

LAURIE

I wouldn't say he blew up our family.

GRACE

There you go again. Defending your father.

LAURIE

I'm not defending him. My point is that saying he blew up our beautiful family is a
bit hyperbolic. He fell in love with someone else. I know it was awful for you. This
meatloaf really is delicious. Can you give
me the recipe?

GRACE

He never loved me.

LAURIE

What? Of course he loved you.

GRACE

I was a conquest.

LAURIE

You don't usually marry your conquests. I'm
sure he loved you. Come on, it's Dad. He

falls in love with everyone. Look at how many
times he's been married.

> (Laurie pauses for a moment,
> thinking.)

I'm sorry he left.

GRACE
I'm sorry for the way I treated you.

LAURIE
You were in a lot of pain.

GRACE
You were only a child…but you were dreadful.

LAURIE
What?

GRACE
All you did was yell at me.

LAURIE
All you did was yell at me.

GRACE
Because you were so angry with me. He left
and I had to deal with your rage.

LAURIE
You were the parent!

GRACE
I was a victim of fraud. I'm telling you
that your father never loved me. He manip-
ulated me. Then you fell under his spell.
"Daddy didn't do anything wrong. Mommy, you
did." Do you know how that felt when you used
to say that?

                    LAURIE
I can't believe this. I can't believe this
is happening. (Laurie stabs at the broccoli and is clearly frustrated. She picks
up a few limp dangling stems of broccoli
and angrily holds them up.) This is not how
you cook broccoli...this is disgusting! I've
lost my appetite.

                    (Laurie gets up from the
                    table and storms out. Grace
                    slowly stands up and runs
                    her hands down the front of
                    her evening gown.)

                    BLACKOUT

DAY 18

I SPENT MOST of yesterday doing switchbacks on the phone with Mom and Aunt Rosemary—trying to repair a rift that mostly I felt needed settling. It began with a call from Aunt Rosemary to say that Mom is shutting her out of her life. She wanted me to know that she doesn't care, that she's done with Mom too. "Of course you're not done with her," I said and started making excuses for Mom. She'd never shut you out of her life. Nobody knows her better than you. I called Mom as soon as we got off the phone.

ME: Aunt Rosemary thinks you're mad at her.

MOM: I'm not mad at her, I'm done with her, and I told her so.

ME: Why would you say that?

MOM: She bothers me. She's always bothered me, but I put up with her because she's my sister. The other day I was thinking about it and I decided I didn't want talk to her anymore. Why should I?

ME: Because you love her. Did something happen? Did you fight?

MOM: I've stopped loving her. I don't have the energy to love her. Loving your Aunt Rosemary is a full-time job. I've retired.

ME: I think you're exaggerating.

MOM: Do you know how often she calls me? She's always calling. It's very disruptive.

ME: What exactly is she disrupting you from?

MOM: I don't know. I'm busy.

ME: She calls because she cares about you. She's checking in. It's kind of her.

MOM: She calls because she's needy. She makes a big show of everything in order to get attention. She keeps talking about how she was in that dreadful hospital, and then she says, "Darling, I don't blame you." Of course she blames me. So I told her to go fuck herself.

I got off the phone with Mom and called Aunt Rosemary to apologize for Mom's behavior.

AUNT ROSEMARY: I'm constantly fighting with her. It's nearly impossible to have a conversation with your tempestuous mother without getting into an argument.

I agreed with her and called Mom back.

MOM: Did you know that your Aunt Rosemary once pretended she was kidnapped? She wanted to have everyone looking for her. I found the ransom note. I knew the moment I saw it that she had written it herself, so I tore it up.

ME: I can't believe you did that. What if it had been real?

MOM: The kidnappers would have gotten back in touch.

ME: So what happened?

MOM: I can't remember. You'll have to ask her yourself. I'm not talking to her anymore. I feel nothing for her.

I called Aunt Rosemary.

ME: Mom told me that you once tried to fake your own kidnapping.

AUNT ROSEMARY: I wanted to see if anyone would notice if I went missing. I wrote a ransom note and my mother found it, ripped it up, and threw it out.

ME: Really? You think your mother would do that?

AUNT ROSEMARY: She claimed she never saw it, but I knew the truth.

ME: I see.

AUNT ROSEMARY: Our parents were so overwhelmed by your mother's behavior that they usually forgot I was alive. Your mother consumed everyone and everything. She got in trouble for stealing from the penny store. She cut school. She plagiarized Emily Dickinson. Once when I was about six, she told me she wanted to play hair salon with me. I couldn't have been more excited. She positioned me in a chair. "Sit up straight Rosie, shoulders square," she said. She draped a smock over me, brushed my hair, and looped my long curly locks into a sensational French twist, securing it for the centuries with her chewing gum.

ME: She's a lot.

AUNT ROSEMARY: All I wanted was for her to play nicely with me.

ME: That must have been hard.

AUNT ROSEMARY: I endured it because I worshiped her, in spite of everything she did. Your mother might be a terror, but she can be very engaging. I don't know how she does it.

ME: It is a wonder.

When I got off the phone with Aunt Rosemary, I tried to work.

I feel like I've forgotten why I wanted to be a playwright. I want to be able to capture that spark and drive I used to have. But I'm just going through the motions. I think my characters simply want to hear themselves talking. Maybe that's it. Maybe that's what we do these days. Talk not because we want other people to hear us, but because we want to hear ourselves talking. And we write to believe we are writers. I picked up *The Clean House* and read it for inspiration. So brilliant. Every word. Maya is wrong. I don't need to lose my divorce virginity to get over this block, I need Sarah Ruhl.

I called Mom back.

ME: I spoke to Aunt Rosemary.

MOM: What did she have to say?

ME: She told me you once stuck gum in her hair while you were playing hair salon.

MOM: I never did that.

ME: Maybe you forgot.

MOM: Your aunt makes things up. But she's not a talented playwright like you are. Her stories are limp, like a—

ME: Mom, don't go there. Will you please call her?

MOM: You want me to apologize?

ME: That would be nice.

MOM: I'll apologize, but I'm doing it for you. But she needs to call me. If she calls me, I'll apologize.

And so I called Aunt Rosemary and asked her if she'd call Mom so Mom could apologize.

ME: She's too stubborn to make the call, you know how she gets.

AUNT ROSEMARY: I've decided to stop kowtowing to her. She can call me if she wants to apologize.

And so I called Mom back.

ME: Please call Aunt Rosemary to settle this.

MOM: To settle what?

ME: To apologize.

MOM: I didn't do anything wrong. I don't need to apologize to her. She should apologize to me.

ME: Please just call her!

MOM: Fine Elise, I'll do it for you. I'll do anything for you. I hope you know that.

ME: I do. Thank you.

Not able to leave well enough alone, as they say, I called Aunt Rosemary an hour after getting off the phone with Mom to find out if Mom had called her yet.

AUNT ROSEMARY: I haven't heard from her.

And so I called Mom back, again.

ME: How come you didn't call Aunt Rosemary?

MOM: I tried.

ME: So what happened?

MOM: I couldn't.

ME: Why couldn't you?

MOM: I don't know her phone number.

ME: What do you mean you don't know her phone number?

MOM: I can't remember her phone number. I'll call her when I remember it.

Now that I am done with today's Morning Pages, I am going to pack up some things and drive to the city.

DAY 19

GOOD MORNING FROM my childhood bedroom, Morning Pages. Today is Day 19 of writing these. Some mornings I don't write enough, but for the most part, I think doing these has been helpful. This early morning journaling has helped me purge the excess ruminations that I tend to hold onto like a hoarder.

Yesterday I planned to drive to the city in the morning, but then I had an idea and started writing. Why is it that I always have my best ideas when I'm heading out? It's when I have nowhere to be that the siren call of web-nymphs, the urgency of my laundry, and the pangs of sudden hunger make it almost impossible to write more than a few lines of dialogue.

I worked on *Deja New* until about 2:00, then texted Marsden to tell him I needed to go to New York to check on Grandma Trudy and that he should stay at his dad's until I got back and that he should work on his college essay while I was away.

He texted back.

Sure.

I gassed up and drove into a traffic jam that added a good 45 minutes to the drive. Finding a parking spot in the city is a mix of luck and skill. The skill, of course, is knowing not to drive down a block behind someone else obviously looking for a spot, driving slow enough to let a spot open up but not so slow that someone passes you and gets a spot further down the street that you hadn't yet seen, or if you're on a one-way street, driving slowly down the middle of the street so no one can pass you, but not so slowly that people start honking and cursing at you. The trick is to identify anyone who looks like they may be heading to their car, and to analyze which blocks have the highest come and go ratios and focus on circling those blocks.

I found a spot and celebrated by pumping my arms in the air and looking up at the sky victoriously while stepping sideways off the curb and falling onto my knees. No one saw. The humiliation was mine alone, but when I walked into Mom's building I was discombobulated and bedraggled with Medusa hair and dirt-dusted knees.

"Elise, are you alright?" Alan asked.

"I'm fine. Thank you. It's nice to see you, Alan."

I wasn't in the mood for talking. I wanted to get upstairs.

"Welcome home," he said, even though I have now lived away from the building longer than I lived in it. Alan has always been kind to me. I tend to be in moods when I'm coming and going. I arrive ambivalent and conflicted and leave frustrated and angry. I'm rarely simply coming or going. "Thanks Alan." I picked up my stride and hustled to the elevator.

A hand reached out from inside the elevator and stopped the door from closing.

"Well, hello. Welcome back."

It was the gorgeous man who lives on the 16th floor who I've kind of been elevator flirting with for the past two years. Honestly, I don't know if he realizes we're having an elevator flirtation. Maybe he's this solicitous and sweet and sexy with everyone he rides the elevator with. Maybe he's a serial elevator flirt. This man in Mom's elevator is the only person I've felt any sort of attraction to since Elliot checked out. I don't know his name. I don't know anything about him other than he lives on the 16th floor and has luscious lips. I love Mom for living on the 15th floor of a pre-war building with a slow elevator. I knew I looked like shit but the way he was looking at me made me believe that, somehow, he didn't notice.

HANDSOME ELEVATOR MAN: It's nice to see you. (Eyes twinkling.)

ME: I just arrived. How's the elevator been while I was away? (Eyes twinkling.)

HANDSOME ELEVATOR MAN: Quiet and dull. We're glad you're back. How long will you be in town?

ME: (Heart pounding.) I'm not sure. I came down to check on my mother.

HANDSOME ELEVATOR MAN: Is she okay?

ME: She's been acting a little odd lately. Well, she's always acted odd, but something seems to be going on and I wanted to check in on her.

HANDSOME ELEVATOR MAN: Kiss me!

I fell into his muscular arms which he wrapped around me as my lips pressed into his and the space between our bodies disappeared.
Oh God, can I do this?
If I write it, will it happen?
"Kiss me." I fell into his muscular arms which he wrapped around me as my lips pressed into his and the space between our bodies disappeared.

If I write it, it will happen!

"Kiss me." I fell into his muscular arms which he wrapped around me as my lips pressed into his and the space between our bodies disappeared.

Well, if I write it, it will be written.

The elevator door opened, I said good-bye to the handsome elevator man, stepped out into the hallway, and realized I urgently had to pee. I unlocked the door. The TV in Mom's room was blaring. There's no way she could have heard me come in, so I raced to the toilet. Full confession, Morning Pages, no, I didn't quite make it in time. I sat on the toilet and decompressed for I don't know how long. I think I may have even dozed off. There's something about the toilet of your childhood that is unlike all other toilets.

Mom was lying on top of her bed, dressed in a shapeless shirt and baggy pants and folded in three parts, with her legs bent at the knees. Mom was once known for her fabulous legs. She'd flaunt them by wearing hot pants all summer and high heels and short skirts in the winter. She'd manage to have her legs available for onlookers even in the worst of weather. It was a kind of public service.

"Hi Mom," I said.

She turned to me and shrieked, "Elise, what are you doing here?"

I told her I drove down to see her. That I missed her. She sounded pleased and invited me to join her on the bed to watch Clark Gable and Claudette Colbert in *It Happened One Night*. I pulled a chair up next to the bed instead. Her hair was longer than she usually wore it. She wasn't wearing makeup, but even without makeup, even at 81, she is stunningly beautiful. When Mom was in her 20s and living in California, she competed in beauty contests. I have a photo of her and the other contestants in bathing suits lined up in a row, all of them standing on their toes, smiling. I bet she smelled floral. If someone were to walk past my mother and the bathing beauties by her side, they'd probably think they were walking by a flower garden filled with roses, honeysuckle, jasmine, and lavender.

"Every housewife and closeted husband in America wanted to fuck Clark Gable after this film came out," she said.

She's fine. Mom is fine. When she stops trying to rattle me is when I should start worrying about her.

Even though I went to bed feeling relieved, falling asleep was a nightmare. Ha! If only I had gotten enough sleep to have a nightmare. My thoughts were pinging around from Mom to Clark Gable to the handsome man in the elevator. My arms were impossible to place, my legs were cramping, and my stomach felt too stomachy.

DAY 20

I'M WAKING UP for the second morning in my childhood bedroom, which doesn't feel at all like the bedroom of my childhood. Mom didn't waste any time repainting and refurnishing once I left for college. She gave away my big-girl wooden desk with a drawer that locked without telling me. My journal and a love letter from Pete Freelander were locked in that. I took the key with me. I still have that key somewhere.

I was 18. A baby. I remember my first call home.

ME: Hi Mom, I'm calling from the payphone in the hallway and there's a long line of kids waiting for it so I can only talk for a minute.

MOM: They can wait. How are your classes?

ME: Pretty good. The kids here all seem to know what they want to do with their lives. It's a little intimidating.

MOM: Intimidation can be motivating. Use it to your advantage. Elise, I'm fixing up the apartment. I started in your room and gave your desk to one of the doormen who needed a desk for his daughter.

ME: But it's my desk.

MOM: You don't need it. You left.

ME: Going to college is not leaving.

MOM: To me it is.

By the time I got home for Thanksgiving, all that was left of my childhood bedroom were the books on my bookshelf, which all these years later are still here and still smell like high school crushes and bubblegum lip-gloss. *A Separate Peace, To Kill a Mockingbird, The Catcher in the Rye, A Portrait of an Artist as a Young Man, The Sun Also Rises, The Scarlet Letter, Great Expectations, The Great Gatsby, For Whom the Bell Tolls, Sons and Lovers, Pride and Prejudice, To the Lighthouse, Demian, The Odyssey, Slaughterhouse Five.* It is the bookshelf time stopped for. I underlined practically everything. I didn't want to miss something important, pass over some symbolism that I was surely not understanding, and I put a little star next to every mention of a setting sun or rising moon.

Yesterday Mom and I had breakfast together and I asked her why she gave away my desk.

"You said you didn't want it anymore," Mom said. Instead of getting into it with her about the desk, I asked her if she wanted another piece of toast.

She had an appointment scheduled for a haircut, and put on makeup and a velvet shirt, unbuttoned unnecessarily low. I went with her to a tiny salon, barely noticeable when you walk by, just off of Broadway.

Mom introduced me to her haircutter as "a brilliant playwright." Her haircutter said, "Your mother is a fascinating woman." Mom returned the compliment, I think, by calling her "the Georgia O'Keeffe of haircutters" and announced to us both that I could use a haircut. So after Mom's cut, the Georgia O'Keeffe of haircutters snipped, styled, and blew out my hair.

I was elevator ready and had errands to run. Mom needed food. Mom needed toilet paper. Mom needed lightbulbs. Mom needed laundry detergent. In running these errands I managed to get two elevator rides with my handsome elevator friend. We traversed 30 floors together. I've ridden elevators with other men but have never felt this kind of intimacy. When I'm with him, I feel us counting the floors together. It feels like foreplay, no, *floorplay*. We're standing in the same enclosed space—a step away from spooning. Breathing the same air, practically kissing. I could ride the elevator with this man forever.

I know I should have been writing, not making up excuses to ride the elevator, not hanging out with Alan the doorman for over an hour, but it was nice catching up with him and hearing the latest building gossip. Alan is both incredibly discreet, and a first-rate gossip, which sounds like a contradiction, but for New York doormen it's not. Gossip is big currency in the city, and New Yorkers pride themselves on the high caliber of their inside information. The city's doormen are privy to more good gossip than anyone else. But they're like priests, or shrinks, or bartenders. It's almost impossible to get anything out of them. The amount of scandalous information they are in possession of is so secure and solid that it's probably providing additional structural support for the city's buildings. To break through the sacred covenant between a doorman and his tenants, you have to pretend you're not gossiping, so conversations go something along the lines of: "Do you know if it's supposed to rain again tonight?"

"I believe there are supposed to be intermittent downpours, as in the past three nights, but they've been stopping by 2:30, around the time Madonna leaves Mr. Handler's apartment."

"Okay, good to know, thanks."

I don't know why I've waited this long to get the low-down on my elevator crush, and I certainly couldn't tell Alan why I was interested. I managed to get quite a bit of information without being too revealing, and he seemed happy to gossip, without being too revealing. What I surmise from Alan's roundabout way of revealing information is that my elevator crush sometimes has boldface name visitors. Mostly musicians. Most notably a Beatle—"There aren't cockroaches in the building, but there have been beetle sightings." I wonder if it was Paul or Ringo? I think he works in the music industry, but that was harder to ascertain. I am certain that he's got three kids, all adults now. And he's divorced. His wife left him for a Nobel prize-winning scientist. I swear stuff like this only happens in New York. I would have been thrilled if Elliot had left me for someone who won a Nobel prize. A Pulitzer would have been electrifying. If Midge had been awarded a MacArthur Genius Award, I'd be a proud divorcée. Hell, I'd even settle for someone who earned the *Good Housekeeping* Seal of Approval. Being left for a genius gives a breakup heft. It's a breakup that matters. I'd have been totally understanding, even supportive. "Go be with your genius, Elliot," I would have said. But no, Elliot left me for a phony dullard who talks babytalk to adults. How humiliating.

I suppose the next time we're in the elevator together I could ask him out for a cup of coffee, but I know I won't. I hate having the sophistication level of a 12-year-old, and not one of those precocious 12-year-olds that are everywhere these days. And I hate not being able to finish my play. I need to refocus. I can't get obsessed right now with a luscious-lipped man in an elevator. Once she wakes up, I'll have breakfast with Mom, then drive back home and get back to work.

(Laurie's house. LAURIE is slouched at the table eating while reading something on her laptop. GRACE is reading while sitting upright on a corner of the couch. The door-bell rings, followed quickly by a succession of knocks and bangs at the door.)

GRACE

Somebody's at the front door.

LAURIE

They sure are.

GRACE

I'll get it.

LAURIE

That's okay. I'll get it. You relax, Mom.

GRACE

You're eating. I'll get it.

LAURIE

It's just a snack. I can get it.

GRACE

I'm not an invalid. I can get up and answer the door.

LAURIE

Fine then, you answer the door.

> *(Laurie goes back to eating and looking at her laptop. Grace puts her book down on a table near her chair and gets up with a loud groan. She walks slower than necessary toward the front door, while the knocking continues.)*

                    LAURIE
Mom, are you okay?

                    GRACE
I'm still a little sore. That accident should
never have happened. It wasn't my fault, and
yet, you insist that I stop driving. What
happened was the fault of the auto industry.
You should be blaming Detroit for my accident, not me.

                    LAURIE
I don't want to blame Detroit. I like Detroit.
It's one of my favorite cities. And even if
what you're saying had a semblance of truth
to it, you still shouldn't be driving. Are
you going to answer the door or not?

                    (Grace opens door the door.)

                    GRACE
Larry?

                    (She   pushes   the   door
                    closed.   LARRY, standing on
                    the other side of the door,
                    pushes it back open. The
                    door remains open.)

What are you doing here? Laurie, did you
invite your father over?

                    LARRY
How are you, Grace? Don't answer. I really
don't care. I was driving by and thought I'd
stop in to see my daughter. Laurie mentioned
to me that you had imposed yourself on her
and taken up residence. I see she wasn't kidding. If you don't mind, I'd like to speak
to my daughter.

GRACE

Don't you have a phone, Larry? You should call
Laurie if you want to talk to her. Laurie is
excellent on the phone. She mastered the art
of speaking on the phone when she was a teenager. Of course, you weren't around enough
to have known that, but I assure you, she's
a pro. One of the best.

> (Grace cranes her neck to
> look beyond Larry.)

Is that your fancy car out there? I bet that
car has its very own phone in it. Why don't
you go back and sit in that nice-looking car
and call Laurie. I'll make sure she picks up.
Good-bye, Larry. Have a good call.

> (Grace tries to push the
> door closed. Larry is
> holding it open. They start
> pushing and pulling on the
> door while grunting and
> groaning, with subtle hints
> of orgasmic sounds as they
> scuffle. Laurie listens from
> the other room, shaking her
> head. She closes her laptop
> and walks to the front door.
> She makes umpire signals
> for TIMEOUT/FOUL BALL and
> SAFE while she walks toward
> them. Then she steps across
> the threshold and gives
> Larry a hug.)

LAURIE

Pops, what are you doing here?

GRACE
An excellent question.

LARRY
I should ask the same of you, Gracie. By the way, you look good. Did you get some work done?

LAURIE
Pops, be nice.

LARRY
Laurie, is there someplace private we can go to talk? Come for a drive with me. No offense Grace, but I want to talk to my daughter in private.

GRACE
Larry, give me the keys to that fancy car and I'll take it for a spin. You come in and talk to Laurie.

LAURIE
Mom,I don't want you driving.

GRACE
I won't go far. What kind of car is that any-way, Larry?

LARRY
It's a Jaguar. It reminds me of you, Grace. Beautiful on the outside.

GRACE
Our daughter is beautiful on the outside and the inside. I don't know how she got that way with us as her parents. Laurie, you're a miracle child.

LAURIE
I'm forty, Mom, hardly a child.

GRACE
Still a miracle that you came out so grounded
after all we put you though. With all you've
had to endure, it's completely understand-
able that you're a few pounds overweight.

LAURIE
Thanks, Mom.

GRACE
Larry, come in and let me take the car.

LARRY
And let you destroy my car too?

GRACE
If you want to be alone with Laurie…

LARRY
(Hesitantly and yet patronizingly) Don't
forget to look in the mirror before you turn,
and I don't mean looking at yourself. And the
accelerator is on the right. The brake is on
the left side….

(Larry hands Grace the car
keys, shaking his head, and
walks inside.)

Got any coffee, Laurie? The place looks great!

GRACE
(Gripping the car keys) Larry, our daughter
is a modern success story, buying her own
house before she was thirty. And she's beautiful. And kind.

LARRY
It's a miracle you didn't screw her up Grace,
with your rages, neuroses, and paranoid con-
spiracy theories.

                    LAURIE
Mom, I don't want you driving. Give me the
car keys.

                    LARRY
Well maybe you did mess with her brain a bit.
How could you not? I remember how you taught
her the alphabet. A was for Angry.

                    LAURIE
That's incorrect. A was for Anxiety.

                    LARRY
I stand corrected.

                    LAURIE
B was for Betrayal.

                    GRACE
I knew you were going to screw me over. C
should have been for that Cunt of a girlfriend you had.

                    LAURIE
Mom!

                    GRACE
I'm going for a drive. I don't want to be
insulted any longer.

                    LARRY
She'll be fine.

                    LAURIE
Pops!

                    (Grace walks out. Larry
                    plops himself down on
                    the chair.)

                    LARRY
She says she's done with me.

LAURIE

What?

LARRY

Nicolette. She kicked me out.

LAURIE

Of your new house?

LARRY

I don't know what happened. I need a place
to stay for a few nights.

LAURIE

Shouldn't Nicolette be the one who is moving
out if she's the one leaving you?

LARRY

The house is in her name. She wanted equality
in our relationship, so I gave her the house
to make her feel like an equal partner.

LAURIE

You did what? Pops, how could you think putting the house in her name was a good idea?

LARRY

(Picks up the book Grace was reading) She's
reading this? Why is your mother reading
The First Wives Club? I'd hoped she would
have moved on by now. She's had almost four
decades to get over me.

too obvious? cliché?

what should Grace be reading instead? Madame Bovary?

LAURIE

It's just a book. I'm pretty sure Mom's gotten over you. I thought you were so happy
with Nicolette? You were just telling me-

LARRY

I thought so too. She called me an uncompromising narcissist.

LAURIE
Well, there is that.

LARRY
I only wanted her to be happy. I need a little time to organize and recover. Laurie,
I was wondering if I could stay here for a
few nights?

LAURIE
Here? I think you should get a hotel room.
That's what husbands who get kicked out do,
they move into a hotel room.

LARRY
She froze my credit cards. She's out to get
me. Why didn't I see this coming?

LAURIE
You never see it. It's your blind spot. You
can use my credit card.

LARRY
That's generous, honey. But I don't feel
right about that. I'd like to stay with my
daughter. I'm not so young anymore, you know.

LAURIE
Normally I'd say yes, but Mom's still living
here. I can't kick her out.

LARRY
Maybe she can leave for a few days or a week.
Give me a turn.

LAURIE
I am not going to ask her to leave.

LARRY
How are you two getting along?

LAURIE
I'm not kicking Mom out.

LARRY
I understand. I'll sleep in my car.

LAURIE
Damn. You are uncompromising!

LARRY
If you won't help me out.

LAURIE
Pops, this isn't fair to me or Mom. But fine,
stay here. Please try to get things sorted
out quickly. I hope you kept notes from last
time. Your last divorce was a nightmare.

LARRY
The one before that wasn't bad though.

LAURIE
You were married to Honey-Bunny for less
than a month. That wasn't a real marriage.
It was a fling with paperwork. Pops, I don't
know-you're a hopeless romantic and a narcissist. Those traits are combustible. If
you stay here, you have to promise me you
won't let her drive again. In fact, sell your
car to get some money. Why am I doing this?
You two are going to kill each other.

(The front door opens and
GRACE walks in.)

GRACE
You're right, Larry. That fancy car of yours
does practically drive itself. Now, why don't
you take that fancy car and drive it home.

(Grace walks over to Larry,
holds her arm up in the air,
and drops the car keys in
Larry's lap, but they fall
on the floor.)

BLACKOUT

DAY 21

WHEN I GOT home yesterday, my clothes were scattered across the bedroom. They were congregating on the floor of my closet and piled up in a large heap on my bed. I was certain I saw the pile move. Marsden was supposed to be at Elliot's, but for reasons I can't now conceive of, I was absolutely certain he was hiding under the pile of clothes that I had left behind, and thinking about him being there, waiting for me, missing me so much that he had to fortress himself under my clothing, sent a mad rush of maternal love through me. I sat down on the bed and put my hand on top of the pile and started talking. I told this heaping pile of clothing about my trip to New York and asked how its college essay was coming along. The pile didn't respond. But since Marsden is a boy of few words, I continued talking. It was a lovely chat until I of course discovered that he wasn't hiding under the pile ruminating on the meaning of life while awaiting my return.

I picked up a pair of pants and asked them, "Why didn't you tell me he wasn't here? Why are you always so withholding?"

For as long as I can remember I've anthropomorphized my clothing. My socks compete with each other. The plain gray pair feels intimidated by the socks with patterns. I try to reassure them, "Don't worry, I'll wear you tomorrow," but they usually can't be appeased. They are prone to sulking and scheming.

Occasionally I move them out of the closet and put them in a bureau, but they aren't the instigators to the dramas, they're the foot soldiers and they maintain strong alliances with some of the more unsavory characters in my closet—I'm talking about you, teal silk shirt with the tiny stain. My closet is steeped in passion and fury, betrayals, secrets, affairs, and murder.

"I'm leaving you for a pair of skinnier legs, bitch."

Missing jacket. Hasn't been seen in weeks. Might have run off with a pocket full of coins.

My sole Dior dress has long felt threatened by the Anthropologie upstarts that began colonizing in 2008.

What I saw of my wardrobe when I got back from New York didn't look like a rift between two overpriced frocks—there had been a brawl.

How is it that I love doing laundry, but hate folding my clothes? Are we all just a series of contradictions in terms that we then qualify as complications?

I was putting my pants back in the closet when Maya called.

"You must be hungry. Stu's at a business meeting. Let's get dinner at Blue Ginger."

We met at the restaurant and after we got to our table, Maya said she had a gift for me. I'm not comfortable getting a gift unless I have a gift to give back, and I was relieved when I opened her gift and saw that it was a hand-bound notebook that I had once given to her.

When I told her, she looked embarrassed. It's not like Maya to screw up a regift.

"Don't worry about it," I tried to console her. "I was regifting it when I gave it to you. My agent had given it to me." We laughed over our first round of drinks and established a set of rules and regulations for regifting, which included the unwritten rule, which I am now writing, to never regift the crappy gifts that should never have been gifts in the first place. No one wants the regift shit. After a second round of drinks, we decided to open a store and call it REGIFT. It will be stocked with gifts to give again and again. It's a very contemporary, environmentally conscious, sustainable idea, although I suppose we will probably go out of business after a while, a byproduct of our success, because the market will be saturated with regifts, eliminating the need to buy a brand new regift.

After the third round I tried to talk her out of throwing the surprise party for Stu. "He's going to hate it," I kept telling her.

"I've already rented T.T. the Bear's for the night," she informed me. "And the boys in the band are all coming."

"The boys in what band?" I asked.

Until last night, neither Stu nor Maya had mentioned that Stu was a drummer in a band while at Macalester. Never once mentioned it! Stu doesn't seem like the college rock band type. He's the cute guy that was always in the library. The guy who took his girlfriend camping in the mountains for the weekend. The guy who graduated with a job lined up. Not a drummer in a hard-ass heavy metal punk-infused explosive noise machine band. And he played the drums like he was possessed? Hard to imagine Stu being intense about anything—other than Maya. He worships her, but I haven't seen evidence that he cares about much else. The kids and the dogs get some residual Maya worship showered down on them, but I doubt they generate any worship on their own.

Maya said the band broke up after graduation and Stu had fallen out of touch with his former bandmates, but she managed to track all three of them down. They were reluctant because they remembered how much Stu hated anyone mentioning his birthday, but she had convinced them to come play at the party.

"What band? How come I never knew Stu was in a band?" I remember that I kept asking her. Even after she answered I kept asking.

She's so Maya. Withholding but revealing. How does she do that? "I can't tell you everything. How boring would that be?"

It never occurred to me to not tell Maya everything. She is my everything person.

We ordered another round of drinks.

"But I want to know everything about you."

Why did I say that? I sounded more like a possessive lover than a curious friend. Even I admit it's a little creepy, but I actually do want to know everything about her—all her secrets. At least Stu is her husband. I'm just a friend with boundary issues.

Our fourth round of drinks arrived, and this is the one that I blame for my throbbing head. The topic changed to my precious divorce virginity. "I don't know what you're waiting for."

I keep having to explain this to her. It's not what, it's who. I'm not going to sleep with someone because Maya thinks having sex will get me over my writer's block. I will do almost anything for Maya, but I won't have sex with someone as a creative experiment. I'm not that blocked.

She persisted. "You need a divorce virginity deadline. I'll give you two weeks."

Maya was talking loudly and the people at the table next to ours turned their heads to look at us. The men turned back quickly, but the women lingered a moment longer, maybe in sympathy, maybe in judgment, we'll never know. Maybe they were drunk too. I think Maya was talking loudly on purpose, she wanted our conversation to be worthy of eavesdroppers. She does things like this. I attribute it to the publicist in her.

So with a rapt audience one table over, she told me about John, a new biker friend of Stu's. John is a civil engineer. Maya says he's funny.

But who isn't funny these days?

He rode his bike across the country after his wife left him. I do like that.

"Call him. Email him. Wait, I'll do it right now," she said, taking out her phone and shooting off an email.

"Stop, Maya, please." But nothing stops Maya.

Then she said, "You're divorced. He's divorced. You're both regifts."

The idea of us both being regifts sets us off in hysterics. I pointed out that we both crossed our legs at the exact same time to hold in the pee, which set us off again. And that was yesterday, Morning Pages.

This morning I woke up spooning the pile of clothes on my bed and my head feels like someone stuffed a wad of crinkled newspaper into it.

DAY 22

REGIFTED JOHN RESPONDED to Maya's email, and we now have a plan to get dinner at his favorite Thai restaurant. "Two thumbs up," Maya said approvingly. "And hopefully that won't be all that's up." Maya can talk about sex without saying, "Is this okay to say?" and questions like, "Elise, when was the last time you masturbated?" seem as natural to her as, "Elise, where did you get that shirt?"

When Maya and Stu have a fight, they have make-up sex. When they can't make a decision, they have make-a-decision sex. They have quickies and long experimental sessions. They are the married couple that messes up all the sexless marriage statistics.

Bobby once said to me that Maya feels comfortable in her own body. I told him that I think it's because she feels comfortable in her own brain. For her, the two seem to be connected. During her freshman year of college, she had a year-long relationship with her brilliant roommate who hadn't been kissed before Maya seduced her. She had what she called "the secret first marriage" to an insatiable and visionary Argentinian filmmaker that Stu doesn't need to know about. And then, there was the affair with the Harvard philosophy professor that Stu can never find out about.

I never could have had an affair while I was married to Elliot. The guilt I felt over for having a vicarious affair with Maya and the philosophy professor was more than I could handle. Every lustful moment she told me about was a thrill. I was enjoying sneaking around in her indiscretions so much that I couldn't focus on writing—or really anything—while waiting for her next salacious update. I tried to take time off from her affair. I even tried to break up with it. After all, what does it say about a person who is excited that her best friend is cheating on her husband? But I got pulled back in. I wanted to hear the details of every temptation and tryst. Every sexy shower and new position. I was devastated when the professor and Maya abruptly ended things. I couldn't stop crying. I couldn't sleep. I didn't know what to do with myself and, like a fool, I confessed to Elliot.

ME: I have something important to tell you and I'm not sure you're going to understand.

ELLIOT: Why don't you try me?

ME: Elliot, I'm having an affair.

ELLIOT: You're what?

ME: I'm not having sex with anyone. It's not like that. I'm having a vicarious affair, but it's over now, and I'm having a hard time dealing with it.

ELLIOT: Elise, what the fuck are you talking about?

ME: I can't tell you who it's with, but I have a friend who has been having an affair for a little over a year, but now it's ending. I'm sorry I didn't tell you about it sooner.

ELLIOT: Elise, I wouldn't have wanted to know then and I don't want to know now. I'm glad you kept it from me. Maybe you should continue keeping it from me.

ME: I can't function. I'm a wreck.

ELLIOT: I'm sure you'll get over it.

I wish I could pinpoint the moment when Elliot became disengaged and dismissive. Even though I know there wasn't an exact moment—that he didn't have a personality shift in a day—I am constantly trying to remember what the moment was. I spend my nights digging through the emotional wreckage to find a moment that I know doesn't exist.

It was the cumulation of moments in motion. His career was taking off and mine was tanking. I'm sure he could feel my envy. Elliot was trying to help people. Why couldn't I see that? Yes, I was proud of him, but dismissive of what he was doing, which meant I was envious of something I had contempt for. No, not contempt—that's too strong a word. I should have been more effusive and complimentary about the apps he was developing. I once said, "I guess I don't have an appetite for apps." And he said, "Well maybe you should find someone who feeds you what you want to eat." I apologized, but he didn't. He got in his car and took a drive. He didn't come back until late that night. "Where'd you go?" "I drove up to the North Shore." I didn't ask why. Sometimes I wonder if I drove him away. But the truth is, I feel like Elliot had been driving away for a long time. It just took me a while to realize he was driving off without me and I was going to be stranded on the side of the road.

I honestly don't think my writer's block has anything to do with Elliot. And getting laid won't suddenly get the creative juices flowing. If I were an athlete, Maya would be telling me to abstain. It's only because I'm a writer that she thinks I should be having sex. There are other obvious factors that are driving my inability to finish. The pressure to write a play that doesn't put people to sleep—not just a good play, but an important play. Mom's calls are a distraction. On the other hand, Dad never calls. My father's constant non-calls are as much of a distraction as Mom's incessant ones. And then there is Marsden. Always Marsden.

DAY 23

YESTERDAY, I DECIDED I'd return my commission and give up on *Deja New*. I didn't see another option. When I'm writing, I get interrupted, and when there are no interruptions, I can't focus. It's like I've developed an adverse reaction to playwriting.

And so I spent the day preparing for my date to distract me from my life and mentally composing a letter to Sammy Ronstein telling him that I wouldn't be finishing *Deja New*. I visualized a life without writing in it. I visualized a life with new pursuits, a new career, and a new man named John.

I wanted this man I had yet to meet to think I was a woman who quoted other people, smart people, philosophers, and comedians. I wanted him to think I remembered lines from movies and plays. If my divorce came up, I wanted to be Nora Ephron witty: "I have made a lot of mistakes falling in love, and regretted most of them, but never the potatoes that went with them."

I planned to introduce John to an aspirational me. If things clicked, I would work harder to maintain aspirational me, the me who quotes Shakespeare, and if he fell in love with aspirational me, I would have to become the aspirational me and I would no longer need to aspire to be who I wanted to be.

I memorized quotes by Emily Dickinson: "I dwell in Possibility."

Samuel Beckett: "Try again. Fail again. Fail better."

Joan Didion: "You have to pick the places you don't walk away from."

Charlie Brown: "Sometimes I lie awake at night and ask, 'Where have I gone wrong?' Then a voice says to me, 'This is going to take more than one night.'"

I put on my favorite pair of black jeans and my teal shirt, which acknowledges but doesn't accentuate my boobs and makes it appear that I have a waist. We met at the restaurant. I was surprised by how nice looking he was, and by nice looking, I mean he exuded a kind of benevolent hue. It's not that he was strikingly handsome, but he had a lived-in, relaxed appearance, with thinning brownish and rather non-descript hair that was offset by a great smile, beautiful eyes that didn't avoid making contact, but weren't aggressive contact makers, and a warmth in his body language. So many men keep their arms crossed, like they're erecting a gate between you and them, but John's arms were open, and he did this thing with his hands when he talked, it was almost like they were inviting you in. I felt comfortable with him immediately, which is unusual for me.

I ordered a glass of white wine, John got a beer, and we started chatting. It was easy. Our conversation popped along through the chicken satay. We seemed to have a lot in common. We both have Lance Armstrong obsessions—John, because he's an avid bike rider, me, because I'm fascinated by the fallen hero narrative.

We were talking and eating, and I noticed he had the remnant of a noodle on his cheek, and while deliberating whether I should mention the food on his face, a wad of pad thai secured itself around a bite of shrimp, and instead of slipping down my esophagus, got stuck. I tried to swallow to push it down, but it wasn't dislodging, so I took a gulp of water and attempted to swallow, but it still didn't go down. The water bubbled and bounced back up into my mouth. I tried to hold it in, but I couldn't. And that's when I started making quacking sounds, sounding like a duck in distress. I tipped my head back and pad-thai-laced water shot up in the air before falling back onto my chin and dribbling down my teal shirt.

I can remember hearing someone in the restaurant yelling out, "Does she need the Heimlich?"

And John saying, "No. She's coughing, so she's breathing."

The waitstaff formed a circle around me. I could feel water dribbling out of my mouth and down my neck. Someone asked, "Should I call an ambulance?"

I shook my head no.

Something shifted and the food went down. I took a breath and was able to say, "I'm okay. Thank you, everyone, for your concern." And then came the applause. It grew louder and louder. The diners in the restaurant stood up and clapped. They were giving me a standing ovation. Okay, maybe they weren't, but that's what I was imagining, and at that moment it became absolutely clear to me that I needed to finish my play. I am not going to give up on this. I will keep writing. I know what the play is about. I'm just not sure how to get there. But I will find my way. I will finish. In the words of August Wilson: "Your willingness to wrestle with your demons will cause your angels to sing."

DAY 24

DIVORCE VIRGINITY. WHAT a stupid concept. I hated the pressure I felt to lose my virginity the first time around. I was the last one in my friend group to have sex and all my non-virgin friends were there to help me. I became their project. They made charts and graphs and we roleplayed. And then, when the intense, brooding, gorgeous James came along and I had sex, all my friends disapproved. I'm still not sure if it was because they didn't like James or because they no longer had a fun project to work on.

I'm going to write about what happened last night with John—hopefully if I get it down, I won't be replaying it all day in my head. I want to be able to tell Maya the story without crying. I was up crying most of last night. It seems like I can't finish anything these days—I can't even finish fornicating.

I emailed John to thank him for a lovely evening and apologize for choking and making a scene. He was extremely sweet about it. "No apology necessary. I'm glad you're okay. I enjoyed talking to you. You're funny and sweet. You've got a great smile. So you choked. We all choke now and then. Do you want to get together for a cup of coffee?"

He drove to Dedham and we got coffee and walked around town. John had never been to Dedham before. He was intrigued that we still have an old-style movie theater here and he was excited that the bookstore is owned by the author of one his daughter's favorite picture books. "I can't believe I didn't know this place existed," he kept saying.

It doesn't take long to walk around downtown Dedham and after I had given him the tour, I invited him over. It's not my style. I'm not an inviter. I am too passive, I'm a passive-ist. I wait for invitations. I prefer the loneliness and insecurity of the wait to the adrenaline rush of assertiveness. That's the way I have long operated, but Maya's voice in my head was getting more and more insistent. And John seemed kind and interesting and easy-going and so I asked.

"Would you like to see my place?"

If only I hadn't asked.

He followed me home. I gave him a tour of the house. He asked questions about the theater posters hanging on the dining room walls. He wanted to know which ones were from plays I had written. He was curious about my furniture, wanted to know a lot of details about the Danish dining room table, and the backstory behind the faux-shaker rocking chair that I never sit in. And about the house. When was it built? What kind of wood are the floors? I started wondering if he was an asker, like Elliot.

I made tea. We sat down on the couch, with space for half a person between us. We were discussing whether Lance Armstrong's interview with Oprah last winter was a Shakespearean moment when he pulled me closer to him and kissed me. An actual kiss. With lips. I haven't felt lips on my lips in ages. If only we had stopped there. But we didn't. I sucked my stomach in and thought to myself, *Do something Elise. This is it. Do something.* The kissing was intense. I reached down to unzip his fly. I think I was on a mission for Maya. I searched for a hard-on, my fingers trolling around until they felt something. He wasn't as there as I thought he would be. I held his not-quite-hard penis in my hand, played with it with my fingers, and squeezed. I couldn't remember what to do. It'd been so long that I didn't remember if it was supposed to be harder than this. Maybe penises were supposed to be half-hard, hard-ish, kind of mushy and squeezy. Maybe I was misremembering what an actual erection looked and felt like. I didn't know if I should try to rip off his pants and give him a blow job or what to do. His arms went limp. His hands fell from my shoulders. Everything about him was now limp.

He apologized. I apologized. He apologized. We talked about his divorce. His wife had wanted it. Told him she needed to be with someone more emotionally present. He "didn't have more emotions to offer her," he said. She left. "She isn't the type of woman who looks back or frolics in indecision," he said. I can't identify. Indecision feeds me, it is my nourishment, my oxygen.

I didn't want him to feel bad, so I told him I wasn't ready either. I told him that Maya has been pressuring me to lose my divorce virginity.

"What does that mean?" he asked.

I explained.

He got up. Said he needed to go. I walked him to the front door in silence. We didn't kiss good-bye. I don't think we even said good-bye.

(GRANVILLE and LAURIE are in a bar, sitting on barstools with a high-top table between them—neon ads for beer can be projected on a large screen behind them. They each have a drink that they are sipping.)

GRANVILLE
It's weighing on me.

LAURIE
What's weighing on you?

GRANVILLE
Our pact.

LAURIE
What do you mean it's weighing on you?

GRANVILLE
I can't stop thinking about it. I don't stop
thinking about it. I'm obsessing. I've been
wondering if we knew something back then.
If our younger selves knew our older selves
would need protecting.

Do I need to explain the pact again?

LAURIE
I think our younger selves were scared of
the future.

GRANVILLE
I think our older selves are scared of
the future.

LAURIE
Is there a time in life when fear of the
future doesn't exist? Where you can soak it
all in and simply be fearful of the present?

GRANVILLE
We made this pact twenty years ago and I've
barely thought about it since. But now I
can't stop thinking about it. I want to do it.

LAURIE
You want to actually get married?

Add more from Laurie here?

> (A WAITRESS walks up to the table.)

WAITRESS

Ready for another round?

GRANVILLE

Why not?

> (Laurie looks at her glass and studies it.)

LAURIE

I think I'm all set. Thanks.

WAITRESS

You sure?

LAURIE

No. Never sure.

WAITRESS

(Laughs) I hear ya, honey. I hear ya. What will you be having, sir?

GRANVILLE

You know, I think I'll wait a bit.

WAITRESS

Just let me know when you're ready.

> (The waitress leaves.)

GRANVILLE

I feel like I should say that to you.

LAURIE

What?

GRANVILLE

Let me know when you're ready.

LAURIE

Ready for what?

GRANVILLE

Are you trying to be dense or simply trying to humiliate me?

LAURIE

Sorry, Granny. I'm not good at these kinds of conversations. You're asking me to look at my life. I work hard to avoid doing that. Literally working hard. All the time I can.

(Laurie stands up.)

And I've got other stuff going on right now. My father's wife left him and he moved in with me. My mother has been living with me for the past month. Yesterday, my father accused my mother of trying to poison him. And she hasn't denied it. My house is a war zone.

GRANVILLE

Are you leaving?

LAURIE

I should get back.

GRANVILLE

Stay. Come on. This is stupid. We're fucking forty. Yeah, we're both professionally successful but neither of us has figured the rest of it out. I'm so tired of being alone. I'm done with one-night stands and short, shitty relationships. Let's do it. Let's honor our pact and get married.

(Laurie walks around the
table to Granny's side
and puts her hand on his
shoulder.)

LAURIE

We haven't seen each other in ten years.
We've barely talked on the phone in five.
Getting married is a huge decision. I don't
do decisions well, Granny. I prefer indecision. When I'm indecisive, I can tell myself
that maybe I shouldn't be blaming myself for
the all the things I blame myself for because
they weren't things I decided to do.

GRANVILLE

I'm not following.

LAURIE

Do you think marriage needs a foundation of love?

GRANVILLE

We love each other.

LAURIE

I don't mean that kind of love. I mean the
other kind of love. And what about trust?

GRANVILLE

Do you trust me?

LAURIE

I don't understand where this is coming from.
Is there something going on that you haven't
told me? This doesn't compute.

GRANVILLE

Not everything has to compute.

(Laurie steps a few feet away from Granny and he stands up.)

Does this make sense if she's so indecisive?

LAURIE

Yes, everything has to compute. Making sure things compute is the only way I can get through the day. Granny, do you know the answer to $x^3+y^3+z^3=k$, with k being all the numbers from one to a hundred?

GRANVILLE

No Laurie, I don't. I have no idea what the answer is to that.

LAURIE

That was a trick question. Nobody does. It's unsolvable. I used to lose sleep at night, hoping I'd be the one to solve it. Of course I couldn't. Then one night at four in the morning, I realized I need to focus on things that I can actually figure out the answer to.

GRANVILLE

Does this compute? I've been fantasizing about you.

LAURIE

You must have the wrong person.

GRANVILLE

Oh, you're right. I've been fantasizing about your mom.

LAURIE

Ewww. Granny! Don't say that. Don't even joke about it.

(Granville puts his arms around Laurie.)

GRANVILLE
Think about it. I'm not kidding. Think about it.

> (Granville kisses her. Laurie
> pulls back instinctively,
> but then wraps her arms
> around his neck and kisses
> him back.)

BLACKOUT

DAY 25

Last night, I was part of a panel discussion called "Emerging Female Playwrights." I forgot I had agreed to do this until I got an email from Maya saying she was planning to come to the talk. I wish she hadn't sent that email. I wish this one had slipped by.

When they asked me eight months ago if I'd like to be a part of the stupid "Emerging Female Playwrights" panel, my answer was, "No, absolutely not." That was the answer I told myself. What I emailed back was, "I'd be happy to do it, although I don't know if I can still be considered an emerging playwright." They emailed back, "We are delighted you can join us for the Emerging Female Playwrights panel. We will send you an email with more details in the coming weeks."

Maybe "emerging" is better than being asked to be on a panel of "Failed Female Playwrights." Although a "failed female playwright" suggests you've done something. You've accomplished and you've fallen. With "emerging," I've been negated, rubbed out, sent back to "Go." They've given my virginity back to me—just like Maya has—but I don't want it back. I wish I were part of a panel with a topic like: "The Wendy Wasserstein Problem for Female Playwrights."

The other women on the panel were in their twenties. Even so, they seemed equally annoyed to be there. One of the women questioned if a panel on emerging female playwrights isn't in itself a sexist concept. She put it right out there and asked whether male playwrights—particularly white heterosexual male playwrights—have to emerge? My fellow emergelings were quick-witted and I suspect they will hatch and become fully feathered someday. And then, perhaps like me, the rest of their lives will take over and they will submerge. I'd happily take part in a panel discussion about submerging female playwrights.

Melinda Fulton, famous for going into universities and revitalizing theater departments, was moderating the panel, and since I'd been hearing about the so-called Fulton Touch for years, I was actually looking forward to meeting her. But she arrived late and there was no time to talk before—I had no interest in chatting after. When she introduced me, she noted that I've had 11 plays produced, and then, with what seemed like feigned outrage, added that in spite of that, I was still struggling to get my work out there. I'm sorry, Melinda, we've never spoken. How do you know what my struggles are?

I almost interrupted her introduction. But I held my tongue. If playwrights are holding their tongues, there is little hope that the rest of humankind will, as they say, speak truth to power. We have chosen this vocation to use our voices. I write to be heard! And yet, I sat there like a smiling emergeling. I was worried about my jowls, which are less saggy when I smile, so I kept smiling and nodding, while silently fuming that I had been introduced as a not-yet playwright.

And then she said, "Elise is also a part-time mother."

Excuse me?

Part-time mother. What does that even mean? I am a full-time mother with part-time custody and a full-time playwright who is no longer able to finish a play. Mothering and writing aren't part-time activities.

Imagine if mothering was a hobby. You pick it up one day, you are fascinated by it, spend an inordinate amount of time focusing on it when you could, and probably should, be doing something more productive, like laundry. But no, your child consumes you, like the best hobbies do. You collect all sorts of toys and books for this new hobby of yours, study it obsessively, take breaks from changing its diaper to gaze at it. You think about it when you should be thinking about other things. A part-time mother raises a son who, in spite of a warm and beautiful heart, is lazy, has been prodigiously messy since toddlerhood, and bangs around the house loudly, as if he has something to say, yet mumbles when he actually speaks. The hobbyist mother will not have the accomplished child that is president of his class, or captain of his track team. The hobbyist mother's son claims he wants to go to college following graduation, yet he has made it to his senior year without visiting a college or taking the SATs. The hobbyist mother never says, "My son is loaded down with too many AP classes and his lacrosse coach is breathing down his neck." She is forced to repeat words like "potential" when discussing her son.

Perhaps we've gotten it wrong. Maybe Marsden is living up to his potential. He is enrolled in a self-taught AP course on sleep. He's an AP stoner. The hobbyist mother's son will listen to music, eat an unfathomable amount of food, and sleep so much that you wonder how he was spawned from a family of insomniacs.

Things didn't get better after the passive-regressive introduction. Melinda asked the panel how we politicize the domestic in our work, and one of the panelists—LaShonda—shit, what's her last name? Whatever it is, she spent most of the discussion rubbing her forehead when she wasn't speaking, as if she was trying to rub off the skin in disgust to show us her brain because how else after all these years do you express, "You see, women have brains! In case you were wondering, here's mine!"—responded by saying, "Why would you ask us that? Is it that you think women playwrights are expected to tackle issues of domesticity, but to give domestic issues some heft, we feel obligated to politicize domesticity?"

Another fellow panelist said her work is all about giving voice to oppressed women and that she can't get produced anywhere except for tiny, underground feminist theaters because mainstream artistic directors aren't interested in giving a voice to oppressed women.

I brought up the princess archetype and the deleterious effect of the traditional three-act princess story and talked about structuring a scene around this idea. I described the scene in *Deja New* where Laurie's father calls her "Princess," and she lashes out at him. She tells her father that she felt like a princess fraud when she was growing up. How could she be a princess? She had a wart on her hand and freckles everywhere. She hoped that maybe her dad didn't know about the wart and maybe, somehow, he hadn't noticed the connect-the-dots of orangey-brown spots covering her body. She grew up terrified that he'd realize he was wrong, that she wasn't actually a princess.

I must have hit a nerve because the women in the audience started sharing their own princess trauma stories. There seem to be a lot of post-princess processing problems.

I will finish *Deja New* before my deadline. I never want to be called emerging again.

                    LARRY
Laurie, Princess-

                    LAURIE
Don't call me "Princess!"

                    LARRY
What?

                    LAURIE
I'd like you to stop calling me "Princess."

                    LARRY
But you're my little princess. You'll always
be my little princess.

                    LAURIE
I'm forty years old, Pops. My little princess
years have passed their expiration date.

                    LARRY
Ah, Princess!

                    LAURIE
Pops, do you realize how damaging it is to
call a little girl "Princess?" When I was a
kid, I suffered from what I now realize was
Princess Fraud Disorder. P.F.D.

                    LARRY
There's no such thing. That's nonsense.

                    LAURIE
It's not nonsense. Don't negate what your
little princess is saying. I knew I wasn't
a real princess because I had a wart on
my middle finger and frogs have warts, not
princesses. What I don't understand is why
you thought Princessery was something a
little girls should aspire to? It makes me

nuts. Do you have any idea how big the princess industry is in this country? It's a
multi-billion-dollar industry built to mess
with little girls' heads. And we aren't even
a monarchy. What's up with that?

LARRY
I was trying to build up your confidence.

LAURIE
Instead, you shattered it.

LARRY
You don't mean that. You loved it when I
called you "Princess." I don't know what's
gotten into you. Is it your time of the month?

LAURIE
Honestly? Are you kidding me?

LARRY
Is there something wrong with me asking? Is
it because I'm your father?

LAURIE
Pops, I don't have PMS. And even if I did, it
wouldn't matter. I am telling you that adults
should stop calling little girls "Princess."

LARRY
You're wrong. I don't believe you.

LAURIE
Why wouldn't you believe me? Why would I
lie about this? I'm not the one who lies
about things.

LARRY
Don't be mean to your father. I've never told
a lie that didn't need telling.

LAURIE
I have no idea what that means.

LARRY
I won't call you "Princess" again. You're
a grown woman now. You'd probably rather
be a queen.

DAY 26

MOM CALLED JUST after 8:00 yesterday morning to tell me that the government shutdown was over.

"Yes, I know," I told her. "It ended over a week ago."

"I wanted to make sure you knew," she said.

I thanked her and told her I needed to get to work.

She said she was planning to have a quiet day at home watching movies on TV. I didn't notice that her usual flurry of calls stopped after that. I was working on a pivotal scene in the second act. I was in the zone. That space where entry is usually denied, and it's only the rare occasion I get granted a visa. When I'm in the zone, time stops. It treads water. It levitates. It does all sorts of wonderful circus acts.

Aunt Rosemary called around 2:30 and yanked me out of the zone.

"Elise, something has happened. We need to talk. I know you're working on your play, but this is urgent. I have to pee. Can I call you back?"

Sure, Aunt Rosemary. Go ahead, use your bladder as a device to create dramatic tension. I waited for almost ten minutes before she called back. Peeing doesn't take this long unless you're Aunt Rosemary. She can turn a simple trip to the bathroom into a urinary tract infection. When she called back, she reminded me to whom I was speaking with.

"Elise, it's your Aunt Rosemary. The doorman called from your mother's building. You know the one I'm speaking of, the short one. Most doormen in the city aren't so petite. But what he lacks in size, he makes up for in charm. Every time I visit your mother, he asks how I am and whether I've been acting in anything recently. Of course, women my age have a terrible time getting cast in anything. We are secondary characters at best. We're either sassy old lady set dressing or fidgety and forgetful widows. Darling, I do hope you're writing a strong part for a woman my age in your play."

"I am."

"And I do hope you'll grant me an audition for it. Of course, I understand that you can't cast me just because I'm your aunt."

"I won't have any say over the casting, I'm sorry Aunt Rosemary. But why did Alan call you? I was around all day yesterday, so I don't know why he called you and not me."

"He's very discreet of course. He wouldn't have called if it wasn't time sensitive and urgent. We gave him my phone number after your mother had her incident. For emergencies. And between you and me, Elise, darling, he told me you looked awful when you were here last week. Of course, I wouldn't know because you didn't tell me you were in the city. But I understand, you're busy and you can't always fit me in."

"Alan thought I looked awful? But I'd just had a haircut."

"Elise, please, don't make this about you. We have an emergency situation."

Aunt Rosemary refuses to get to the point. She is an obsessive preluder.

"Did you know that I once rode in an elevator at your mother's building with the actress Diahann Carroll?"

"She used to live there. She was very nice."

"A magnificent talent and a pioneer. I asked her if she thought she might find a role for me in her next film."

"You asked her that in the elevator?"

"Elise, darling, I've learned to seize every opportunity and treat everything I do as an audition. I once saw Paul Newman walking down Fifth Avenue near 66th Street and I dazzled him by performing the dance scene from the *Three Faces of Eve*. Right there on the street. He was beaming. But my incompetent agent didn't have the nerve to follow up with him. She was useless. I hope you have a good agent, dear. You really can't get anything done without one."

"Aunt Rosemary, you said there was something urgent you wanted to tell me."

"You'll want to brace yourself. Your mother went out for a walk, you see. She put on her winter coat. I don't know why. It's October, for Christ's sake. Your mother is an extremist though. A spit of wind and she dresses for the Arctic. But of course once she got outside she realized she didn't need her coat. The doorman saw it all."

"Saw what?"

"Trudy took off her coat."

"But she didn't need a coat."

"She didn't stop with her coat. She continued to shed her habiliments."

"Habiliments?"

"Trudy took off her shirt."

"What? What did she do?"

"I'm not certain which shirt she was wearing. Did I mention that just a few weeks ago your mother and I had our yearly clothing swap? I don't know why we still partake in that exhausted ritual. Honestly, I already threw out the few antediluvian schmattas I took. I suspect your mother was probably wearing one of the shirts I gave her. They weren't one bit bad."

"She took off her shirt?"

"She released her bosoms."

"Aunt Rosemary? What? Fuck! Shit!"

"Try to refrain from such base vulgarities, dear. You sound like your mother. The doorman saw it all. He yelled out to her, 'Mrs. Hellman, do you need help with anything?' I think she must have been in a trance, and he broke her out of it because she put her shirt back on and sauntered back inside."

Aunt Rosemary's floral flourishes will withstand any emergency.

"The doorman called me. He really is a gem, and naturally I took a cab right over. I was so out of sorts after getting such a call, well you can imagine, that I left the apartment without my purse. He had to pay for my taxi."

"Alan paid for your taxi?"

"You'll have to reimburse him. Your mother was in an absolute rage when I arrived."

"I'm heading to the city now." I was already making my way toward the car when Aunt Rosemary clicked her tongue into the phone at me and said, "I don't know how to say this without sounding hurtful, Elise, but I think your mother needs real help, not you."

I reached down deep to pull out any zen-in-residence, and in an almost absurdly measured voice replied, "Okay, Aunt Rosemary. I understand. What would you like me to do?"

She took an exaggerated breathy moment before answering. "Hire someone to come over and be with her. Elise, I can't do it all anymore."

I held my tongue. Lassoed it up and wrestled it into submission and listened to Aunt Rosemary yammer on.

"Yesterday I was barely able to calm your mother down. She forced me to go home. Practically threw me out of the apartment. Wouldn't even lend me money for a taxi."

When we hung up, I called Mom. She downplayed the entire event, even suggested that Aunt Rosemary made it up, "You know how your aunt is. Everything is a crisis. I've been home all day and can't talk now. I'm watching *Gilda*. Rita Hayworth is absolutely marvelous in it. Can we talk later?"

But she didn't call back. And I didn't call her.

DAY 27

YESTERDAY, I HIRED a woman named Sue, who once worked for Maya's Aunt Mary, to help Mom for four hours a day. Aunt Mary was actually Maya's brother's best friend's aunt, but Maya likes to say that Mary was more of an aunt to her than any of her actual aunts, which I always tell her is an absurd statement as the only requirement for being an aunt is to be the sibling of your parent. But Maya insists she loved Mary like a niece loves an aunt—which is a particular kind of love, different from the love of a sister, daughter, or friend. I love Aunt Rosemary, thoroughly—but not totally; compassionately—but with complaints. Maya described Sue as "wonderful beyond wonderful as a caregiver and a person." I called and introduced myself as Maya's friend. Sue said that any friend of Maya's was a friend of hers and told me that her client for the past three years passed away two weeks ago.

"That's great news," I exclaimed.

Whoops.

"Of course, I'm sorry about your client's passing."

It feels fundamentally wrong to be happy about somebody's death, but I felt genuine glee, not to mention gratitude, toward Sue's client for dying. Sue said he was a kind man and I hope he had a long and fulfilling life and went without suffering.

I don't talk to dead people often, but after my conversation with Sue, I went outside and noticed a cloud that I thought might have resembled Sue's former client in his afterlife and I thanked him. I told the cloud about what's been going on with Mom and said I appreciated his timely passing so that Sue was available to help my mother, as I'm sure Sue had helped him. I waited for the cloud to respond with some sort of acknowledgement—a thunderclap or raindrops—but it remained evasively silent and essentially ignored me for the entirety of our conversation. I waited a while longer, communing with the nonresponsive cloud until I started feeling a bit snubbed, so I bade the cloud farewell, but made sure to thank it one last time before heading back inside.

Mom said she didn't need help with anything and wasn't planning to pay anyone for help she didn't need. So I told her that I had spoken to Elliot and in a display of kindness and generosity he said that he would pay Sue.

"Elliot has always had a soft spot for you, Mom," I said.

"Elliot was a wonderful son-in-law."

It's true that Elliot found my mother's eccentricities amusing, and I'll be paying for Sue's time out of my alimony money, so a case could be made that he will be in fact paying Sue. "Tell him thank you. I could certainly use some help around the apartment."

"I will, and I'm so glad this is working out. Sue is planning on stopping by at 1:00 to say hi and meet you," I said.

At 1:00 sharp Alan called.

"Hi Elise, it's Alan from 212. I'm sorry to bother you. A woman named Sue is here to see your mother, but when I buzzed your mother, she told me she didn't want to see anyone."

I told Alan I'd call my mother and call him back. I called Mom. She let the answering machine pick up and after the beep I hollered, "Mom, pick up the phone! Mom, I need you to pick up the phone right now! Pick up the phone! Mom, Sue is downstairs. Pick up the phone. Now! Pick up!!!!"

I hung up and called back right away. "Hi Mommy, it's me, Elise. Can you please pick up the phone? I miss you and want to talk to you." She didn't fall for it.

I called Sue on her cell and explained the situation. Lovely, gracious, kind Sue told me that Mom's behavior wasn't unusual, and that it often takes people a while to adjust to the idea of having someone in their house helping them out. She said she'd head home and that I could call her anytime.

An hour later Alan called to tell me that Mom had gone out. She told him that if she had any visitors, he should send them away and tell them to go to hell.

At 5:30, Alan called to let me know that Mom had just gotten back.

I started calling her, but she wasn't picking up. She was probably giving the finger to the phone every time I rang.

She finally answered. It was almost midnight.

MOM: Hello, darling.

ME: I've been calling you all night.

MOM: I didn't feel like talking.

ME: What if there had been an emergency?

MOM: No one needs me for emergencies anymore. No one who has an emergency is calling me. You are the only one who calls.

ME: That's not true. Aunt Rosemary calls you. Your friends call you. Telemarketers call you. Mom, what happened with Sue? Why wouldn't you let her up?

MOM: I didn't want her to eat my food.

ME: What?

MOM: She's going to eat my food.

ME: Sue isn't going to eat your food. I promise you she's not going to eat your food. If anything, she'll be making you food so you don't have to cook.

MOM: I don't want her in my kitchen.

ME: She doesn't need to be in the kitchen. We can make the kitchen off-limits to her.

MOM: If she's not going to cook for me, then why do I need her here at all?

ME: To help you out.

MOM: I don't need help and I don't want help. Elise, I've got to go now, *On the Waterfront* is about to begin.

I hung up, picked up a book, and read for a few minutes, but I couldn't focus, so I put it down and stepped outside to find the cloud. The night was moonless, starless, windy, dark, and menacing. It fit my mood. "Fuck you, cloud! Fuck you, fucking cloud!"

DAY 28

YESTERDAY WAS A good day. The pieces cascaded into place. *Cascaded*—that's a nice word. Nicer than *fell*—I don't know why we say the pieces fell into place. Falling seems a bit hazardous. Just look at what happened to Humpty Dumpty. Even with the resources of all the king's horses and all the king's men, Humpty Dumpty was screwed.

Mom allowed Sue into her apartment. Sue did Mom's laundry, tidied up, and had a lovely and peaceful day with Mom. "We had great conversations," Sue said. "Your Mom has lived such an interesting life with so much heartbreak."

How I wish I could meet this delightful woman whose life story is filled with interesting anecdotes about broken love and lovers she broke. Maybe I have met her. Maybe she's been there all along. Maybe it's me who has the issues, not her. I want to be a more compassionate and better daughter. I want to stop blaming Mom for things that happened decades ago. I want to get to a place where I can admire her. I've heard her stories, but they make me cringe. No. It's more than that. They set off my fight-or-flight instinct. Is it that I don't want to know about her sex life or that I have a cold and cruel heart?

I wonder if she told Sue about her lovers. Mom fell hard for an Israeli man when she was in her early 20s and moved to

Israel to be with him. But when she arrived, she found out he was engaged to another woman. She came back to the States broken and vengeful. She had a torrid affair with a married sculptor until an art school tramp, as Mom still refers to her when she recounts this story, stole him from her. After the heist of her married artist lover, she got engaged to a man whom everyone loved so much that he was widely referred to as "the mensch," until he broke off their engagement with a phone call and became widely referred to as "the schmuck with a shriveled schlong."

Did she tell Sue about how she met Dad? Dad was dating her now-former best friend when they met. They were on a double date and Mom's boyfriend at the time was arrogant and controlling. Dad saved her, and then tried to destroy her, she likes to say. Mom and Dad fell in whatever version of love the two of them are capable of. I suspect Mom and Dad started fighting immediately, but that didn't stop them from getting married and having a child. One child. "Darling, you took up so much time and energy, we couldn't possibly have another child," Mom used to say when I asked why I didn't have any brothers or sisters. When I was eight, Dad left Mom for younger, beautiful, and bubbly Lucy, who had a punk-rock haircut and piercing blue eyes. I met Lucy for the first time at the Russian Tea Room. Dad brought me there for a "special lunch." I had never seen such red and golden opulence. When the maître d' brought us to our table, I yanked on Dad's sleeve and informed him that there was a lady already sitting there, and Dad said, "I know. Elise, I'd like you to meet my very special friend Lucy." I recognized the name immediately and told her, "My mom calls you Douchie." Lucy laughed her big expansive laugh that eats up everyone else in the room. Dad referred to Mom by using a swear word. I informed him that he said a naughty word. He apologized. I ate chicken Kiev for the first time in my life. It was like nothing I had ever had before. I cut into the breaded chicken to find a treasure. I can still remember watching as golden butter oozed out and my first taste of the pure deliciousness that was hiding inside. Chicken Kiev was my favorite food until I was 18 and discovered lobster mac 'n' cheese.

I doubt she's already told Sue the stories of the lovers that followed the bastard ex-husband. "Your father was a boring lover. One of the worst I've ever had. I needed to make up for lost time," she'd told me. I never asked for or wanted details, yet I know that Ted had large balls, Bernie had a small cock, Edward was impotent, and Murry incompetent. I don't want to know any of it. When I ask how things are going, please don't tell me about Wally's saggy scrotum. Please don't!

But she did. It was like a compulsion. She was trying to shock me. But why?

She was in pain. She was being torn to shreds. She wasn't rational. She isn't rational. I want to feel empathy for her. I don't, though. I can't get there. Empathy is just another burden. Not only am I expected to look after Mom, I'm supposed to feel empathy for her. I can't. I won't.

I was feeling well rested and relaxed when I started writing this morning's Morning Pages, but now I feel like hurling flaming spitballs at Wally's saggy scrotum. Maybe that's not a bad thing. I can use my fury and write. I am on a roll. I am hearing it, seeing it, staging it; it's unfolding. My characters are telling me what they want to say, where they want to stand, what they are wearing, and whether they are having a bad hair day. Their hair is irrelevant, at least I think it is, but I appreciate their

KATE FEIFFER
complaining and their confidences. I want them to talk to me. And all I have to do is transcribe the relevant things they say, and I will have it. I feel like I'm getting close.

176

DAY 29

I'M NOT IN the mood for Morning Pages. I'll try, but I don't know how far I'll get. I'm depleted. The first time Mom called yesterday morning I didn't pick up. I was writing.

The second time she called, I answered.

MOM: Elise, I wanted to hear your voice. I think I'm going to stay home today and watch movies on TV.

ME: That's a great idea. Sue will be there soon.

MOM: That Sue is an awfully nice woman. Before you get off the phone Elise, tell me, what's new with you?

ME: Nothing is new. I should get back to work.

MOM: I understand. I'll never call you again. Good luck with the play.

ME: That's not what I meant.

MOM: I know what you meant. You don't have time for your mother. But before you go on with your busy life, will you at least remind me what your play is about?

I gave her the elevator pitch.

ME: The divorced parents of a single forty-year-old woman both unexpectedly find they need a place to stay and move in with her.

MOM: Oh that's right. It's a terrific play, Elise.

ME: You were really helpful when we talked about it a few weeks back. I appreciate it.

MOM: If there's anything I can do for you, Elise, just let me know.

ME: Thanks, Mom.

MOM: I'd like to see my grandson.

ME: Oh, okay. I'll bring him for a visit.

I remember when Marsden was little, Mom would take him to the Central Park Zoo. She brought him to *Mary Poppins* on Broadway and they loved going to the Broadway Diner for pancakes, just the two of them. It was so sweet. They giggled and had fun together. They were like two little kids conspiring. He brought out the best in her. And then after one spring break in New York, Marsden's second grade teacher called us and told us that Marden was teaching his classmates inappropriate words. "Where in the world did he learn the C-word?" she asked. And that was that. I chaperoned their time together from then on.

I was trying to get off the phone with her yesterday. As I do. Always trying to escape from her when she got more confused than usual. It started when she asked me if I was still married.

ME: I'm divorced. Remember? I was married to Elliot for sixteen years.

MOM: Was I married?

ME: What?

MOM: Was I married?

ME: You were married to Dad.

MOM: I was?

ME: For ten years. You split up when I was eight.

MOM: Yes, that's right. Of course. How is your father?

ME: He's fine. I'll tell him you say hello when I speak to him.

MOM: Please do. Send him my best.

ME: Really?

MOM: Of course.

(LAURIE and GRANVILLE are sitting on opposite sides of the same couch at Laurie's house. Laurie's legs move around as she talks—she pretzels them, she sits on them, and spreads them across the couch so her toes can tickle Granny.)

LAURIE

I was in line at the checkout counter at the grocery store yesterday and I turned around. I glanced into the cart behind me. I wanted to take a longer look, but I didn't want to be rude. I love looking into people's shopping carts.

GRANVILLE

I've never found other people's shopping carts particularly compelling.

LAURIE

Granny, you of all people—I'd think you'd be fascinated by what people have in their shopping carts. You can build an entire narrative about someone's life by what they eat.

> (Laurie spreads her legs out across the couch and starts rubbing Granny's leg with her foot.)

Wanna hear something embarrassing?

> (Granville runs his hand down Laurie's leg.)

GRANVILLE

Of course I do.

LAURIE

I've shopped for food I don't want because I want my shopping cart to look like I lead an interesting life. I don't want to always be that granola and yogurt person. I want to be more exotic.

GRANVILLE

I think you're overthinking shopping carts.

LAURIE

more riffing on this idea? →

Granny, I bet you could start a business connecting people with the food that matches their personality type. It would be easy. Single professional woman in her forties. Nonfat Greek Yogurt-Stonyfield Farm. Think about it. Introverts surely eat differently than extroverts.

                    GRANVILLE
You might be onto something. Come here.

                              (Laurie   crosses   over   to
                              Granny   and   their   faces
                              are   inches   apart   from
                              each other.)

                    LAURIE
The lady behind me didn't have grown up food
in her cart.

                    GRANVILLE
A selfless mom.

                    LAURIE
A lonely and defeated mom.

                    GRANVILLE
Not so. She has her kids to keep her company.

                              (Laurie returns to the other
                              side of the couch.)

                    LAURIE
Are you shitting me Granny? You sound like
my father.

                    GRANVILLE
I was joking.

                    LAURIE
You still sound like my father. Everything
offensive he says is a joke. Plus you have
food on your face. This is bad.

                              (Granville wipes his face.)

                    GRANVILLE
Is it gone?

                    LAURIE
Let me get it.

                         (Laurie reaches over and
                         wipes Granville's face. He
                         holds on to her, but she
                         forces a retreat to the
                         other side of the couch.)

                    GRANVILLE
What are you doing?

                    LAURIE
I think I heard my mother.

                    GRANVILLE
So?

                    LAURIE
I don't want her to walk in and think there's
something going on.

                    GRANVILLE
God forbid.

                    LAURIE
Seriously-she drives me crazy when she
thinks I'm seeing someone. Of course she
also drives me crazy when she thinks I'm not
seeing someone.

                    GRANVILLE
Okay, have it your way. So tell me. Why
do you think the lady in the grocery store
was lonely?

                    LAURIE
Okay-as soon as she saw that I was looking at
her cart, she started a conversation.

GRANVILLE
A sure sign of desperation.

LAURIE
"It's all they'll eat," she said. Like she
was apologizing for her cart. I looked at
it more closely to see exactly what was in
there. Just chicken nuggets, boxes of mac
and cheese, and juice boxes. And I said to
her, "I'm so sorry to hear that."

GRANVILLE
Did she take offense?

LAURIE
She asked me if I had children. Don't you
think that's too personal a question for the
supermarket?

GRANVILLE
You were checking out her shopping cart. You
made the first move. The gloves were off. How
did you respond?

LAURIE
I said, "Not yet."

GRANVILLE
And she felt sorry for you.

LAURIE
Exactly. At first, she gave me an "I'm sorry
for your loss" look. But then her expression
changed to an "I'm going to be your savior."

GRANVILLE
Whoa?

LAURIE
She started telling me about her IVF treat-
ments and said if I was interested, she could
recommend a great clinic.

GRANVILLE

And you said?

LAURIE

I told her, "Thank you. I appreciate it." I don't know why I said that. I guess I didn't want to disappoint her. She reached into this huge bag she was carrying, pulled out a notebook and a pen, wrote out the name of the clinic, and handed it to me.

GRANVILLE

You're still a people pleaser.

(GRACE walks into the room.)

GRACE

Laurie, these people are shysters.

(Grace notices Granville. He stands up and puts out his hand.)

GRANVILLE

Hello Mrs. Herman. I'm Granville, Laurie's friend from college. It's nice to see you again.

LAURIE

Mom, you remember Granny, don't you?

GRACE

Of course I remember him. He visited us once.

LAURIE

A few times.

GRACE

You slept on the sofa.

LAURIE
You remember where he slept?

GRACE
Why wouldn't I remember where he slept? A
handsome boy like this.

LAURIE
We're just friends.

GRACE
Are you married, Granny?

LAURIE
Honestly, Mom? Really?

GRACE
Have you ever heard of freedom of speech,
Laurie? I'm allowed to ask.

GRANVILLE
No, I'm not married.

LAURIE
Mom, can we talk about your car later please?

GRACE
Just tell me when you can give me a ride to
the garage. I'll take your father's car if
you're too busy.

LAURIE
Mom, your car was totaled. There is no car
for you at the garage.

GRACE
Then they'll have to give me a new one.

LAURIE
It doesn't work like that. You know it doesn't
work like that.

GRACE

Granny. They still call you that? Has that resulted in any problems. You know, down there?

LAURIE

Mom!

GRANVILLE

I think I better get going.

GRACE

Don't leave on account of me. It's a beautiful day. I think I'll go take a walk. Larry is napping. I can hear his roaring. That's what I call it. It's so much more than snoring-it deserves a different word. Is it okay with my daughter if I take a walk?

LAURIE

Mom. Really? Yes, of course.

GRACE

I'm not allowed to drive. My daughter thinks she's doing me a favor. But the truth is she's holding me hostage.

LAURIE

Good-bye, Mom!

GRACE

It's always nice to see Laurie's handsome friends. Come around any time.

> (Grace goes to leave the house. The sound of a door closing loudly and deliberately.)

LAURIE

What were we talking about?

GRANVILLE

Your mom's a character.

LAURIE

Oh, I remember-the lady in the grocery store, who wants me to do IVF.

GRAVILLE

You want to keep talking about the lady in the grocery store?

LAURIE

Do you have something else you'd rather talk about?

GRANVILLE

I do.

> (Granville moves over to Laurie's side of the couch and starts kissing her. Things get pretty heated. As they kiss, Grace tiptoes in from the front door and stands there silently, watching them making out. Granville is trying to lift Laurie's shirt up over her head when they notice Grace watching them.)

LAURIE

Holy shit! Mom, what are you doing? I thought you went out!

GRACE

I had a hunch.

LAURIE

You've been watching us. Ewww. Mom!

GRACE

Laurie, you're my baby. I get to watch you if
I want to. I used to give you baths, you know.

> (Laurie frantically puts her
> shirt back on and stands up.
> Granny rearranges himself
> and stands up too.)

GRANVILLE

It's nice seeing you again Mrs. Herman.
Laurie, I'll call you later.

> (Granny walks out the door
> and Grace continue to stare
> at Laurie as she moves around
> the house straightening up.)

BLACKOUT

DAY 30

SOMETHING IS GOING on with Maya. She assured me—three times, maybe four—that she's perfectly fine and that there's nothing at all to worry about. Maya has the kind of high-octane energy people often refer to as Energizer Bunny energy. I don't think I've ever seen her so much as yawn, so naturally I'm concerned about her. She's not the type to doze off on another person's couch at 3:00 in the afternoon.

When Sammy Ronstein's number came up on my phone, Maya was updating me about Stu's surprise party. She's invited 150 people and we're all supposed to arrive at T.T.'s before 7:30. She was telling me about Stu's bandmates. The lead singer lives in New York and is still in the music business. The bass player is a Silicon Valley dot-com millionaire and is flying in on his private jet from San Francisco, and the guitarist has a maple and Christmas tree farm in Vermont, and will what? Be driving to Boston in a beat-up pickup truck? Could this be right? It sounds a little too picture perfect. Or maybe that's our generation. We've set-designed our lives.

I popped into the kitchen to talk to Sammy Ronstein. Yes, part of me wanted Maya to overhear my call with him, to be looking at my face trying to read my expression, to watch me as I scribble down a few notes and stick my index finger in the air and circle it around to indicate that I'm listening to him ramble on. But I also wanted to be the type of person who leaves the room to take an important call. If I could have figured out a way to do both, I would have.

Sammy was calling to tell me that he had gotten Nancilla Aronie to direct the first reading of *Deja New*, which he's scheduled for December 12th, and he assured me that if the reading goes well, Nancilla will direct the play. Nancilla Aronie—as he told me and as I already knew—has won six Obies and four Drama Desk awards and been nominated for three Tonys. She has been lauded as a sensitive, intuitive, and brilliant director and is sometimes referred to as the Mike Nichols of her generation and other times as the Julie Taymor of her generation. She is one of the most sought-after directors working today and there's a chance she will be directing my play. A play I wrote. A play I am writing. A play I am trying to write. A play I need to finish. Today.

"Nancilla Aronie, are you kidding me?" I said to Sammy.

"Elise, you deserve this," he replied.

"Sammy, you're amazing. You're beyond amazing! I can't believe it!"

"Start believing it. Nancilla and I have been discussing working together for a while. We were just waiting for the right project for her, and I think *Deja New* might be it. She saw *Stealing Obituaries* at Williamstown and loved it. She's a fan of yours."

"I can't believe Nancilla Aronie knows my work. This is so exciting, Sammy. Thank you!"

And then, before we hung up, he said, "Elise, if we get Nancilla attached, *Deja New* is going to have the eyes of the world on it."

I happy-danced into the living room singing, "I've got Nancilla on my mind," only to find Maya on the couch with her eyes closed and mouth open.

Confusion.

Panic.

I walked over to her and put my hand in front of her face, like I used to do to Marsden when he was a baby, and the warmth of her breath filled the palm of my hand.

Relief.

"Did I fall asleep?" She seemed as surprised by the possibility of this happening as I was.

"Are you okay?" I asked.

She assured me and reassured me that she was fine. "Just having a bit of insomnia these days."

"Join the club," I said. But I don't believe her. Sure, she might be having insomnia. No one I know sleeps anymore. But Maya wouldn't let a bit of pedestrian-grade insomnia get to her. When I told her the news about Nancilla Aronie, she jumped up from the couch and wrapped her arms around me. "This is it, Elise! This is going to be it! I'm on it."

Within minutes she came up with about ten ideas for how to generate early buzz for the play.

A play I haven't yet finished writing.

I hardly need to write that I barely slept last night. Lesser days have kept me awake. The Ambien I took made me restless. One of my pillows was stuffed with thoughts of Nancilla and the other one was stuffed with thoughts of Maya. At 2:00 in the morning, I got up and googled Nancilla Aronie. Her Wikipedia page is filled with the acclaim that comes with being young and extraordinary. The youngest female director to direct a play on Broadway. The youngest to get nominated for a Tony Award.

She's been profiled in *The New York Times* and interviewed in *O Magazine*. She said she came from a large working-class family and that she and her sisters and brothers would pretend they were princesses and princes, kings and queens, court jesters and confessors, and that she spent much of her childhood in character as Mary Queen of Scots. After googling Mary Queen of Scots, I now know that Mary became Queen of Scotland when she was just six days old and that her husband died a violent death in a suspicious house explosion. I was not a bit sleepy so I googled Maya. Like a good publicist, Maya gets publicity for others, but keeps a low profile for herself. So I googled Stu, who had an even slimmer online presence. Practically nothing at all. I kept trying different iterations of his name, but he barely existed. I thought about starting a Wikipedia page for him, Stuart Davis, born on the day JFK was assassinated, but I didn't. Instead I YouTubed the biggest hits from 1963—"Puff the Magic Dragon," "Be My Baby," and "It's My Party."

DAY 31

IT'S SUNDAY MORNING and Marsden's alarm is blasting "Girl on Fire" by Alicia Keys.

I love the sounds the house makes when he's in it.

He turned off the alarm. Does he remember it's Sunday and he can sleep in? I can hear the sliding and thumping of his feet. He never fully picks them up. This little fact, his feet shuffling in the morning, is one of the few things I still know about him. It's like I have no idea who my son is even though I gave birth to him, nursed him, read him bedtime stories, cheered with him when he learned to swim, and brought him to the ER when he broke his arm. I took him to see Broadway musicals— *Shrek*, *The Lion King*, *Wicked*. He loved them, couldn't wait for the next one. "Marsden's already a theater geek," I'd tell anyone who asked me about him.

I know what has shaped him. The good and the bad, the memorable vistas and the emotional litter. You think that since you gave birth to someone, since you raised someone, you should be granted access into their brain. You should understand your child better than anyone you've ever met, so why is it that I feel like I don't know him at all?

He moves slowly through the world, as if he's not terribly interested in getting from one place to the next. His eyes are half shut most of the time, like it's too much work to open them all the way. And his hair is greasy and too long. He can't be bothered to shower. I don't know what he thinks about or cares about. I don't even know if he thinks or cares, but I suspect he must do both. His friends talk when they stop by. They are syllabic positive. I wonder if he breaks out more words for them, shows up with an inflection or two, if he makes them laugh, makes them think, or if he is their silent stoic friend? Tall and handsome. I would never expect that to be the son I raised. No, my son is supposed to be a chatty theater geek. How did my lap-sitting, babbling, sly jokester turn into a riddle wrapped in a mystery inside an enigma rolled up in a teenager devoted to the practice of concise sentences and monosyllabism?

Last night I asked him how he's doing on his college essay.

MARSDEN: Good.

ME: That's great. What is it about?

MARSDEN: Stuff.

ME: Can you be a bit more specific?

MARSDEN: Nup.

ME: Have you really started it?

MARSDEN: Yup.

ME: You know you don't have to go to college.

MARSDEN: Yup.

ME: And if you don't want to go, you don't have to write this essay.

MARSDEN: Yup.

ME: So what do you think?

MARSDEN: About what?

ME: Going to college. I'm not trying to be intrusive. I just want to talk.

MARSDEN: Okay.

ME: So....

MARSDEN: What?

ME: What do you want to do?

MARSDEN: Mom, can you please leave?

But that was last night. Now I hear his feet shuffling and he's calling for me. I love it when he calls for me! I love the sound of—
"Mooooom!"
"What is it, Mars?"
"Can you make me breakfast?"
"I'm writing something. I'll do it in a minute."
"Can you write later?"
"Just give me a minute. I'll be right there."
"Moooom."
"Mars, can't you make yourself breakfast?"
"No."
"What do you mean no? You're eighteen. You can surely make your own breakfast?"
"I'll skip breakfast."
"You need to eat breakfast."

"There's nothing in the house to eat. I got hungry and had
a snack in the middle of the night."

"You ate everything?"

"I was hungry."

"Were you high?"

"No, Mom. People get hungry without being high."

"Marsden, you know it's Sunday, right?"

"It's Sunday?"

"Yes."

"I forgot."

DAY 32

I JUST HAD a nightmare about Marsden's divorce ferret. The ferret was lost. I was running around frantically asking people if they'd seen a ferret, then I spotted it under a parked car. I squatted down to grab it but couldn't reach it, so I rolled under the car and the car's engine started. I screamed, but the driver didn't hear me, and the car ran over my legs, like they were a speed bump. Miraculously I wasn't hurt, but the ferret was. I picked up the long limp ferret and put my ear next to its little ferret heart and could hear beating that sounded more like bongo drums than a heartbeat. With my free hand, I opened its mouth and started breathing into it, I gave the ferret mouth-to-mouth resuscitation until it bit me with its sharp little fangs and that's when I woke up.

Of all the animals we got for Marsden to try to fill this or that void, the divorce ferret is the one that haunts me in my dreams. Maya once pointed out that she adopts rescue dogs, and I adopt creatures to rescue me. Most of them weren't up to the task.

The first one was the snail we got after Marsden told his pre-school class he had a baby sister and her name was Snail. We decided to get him a real snail and he named the snail Turtle, and we thought that was so clever that we got him a turtle, which he named Iguana, and we pretended to be playing along when actually he was manipulating us, or more specifically, me, as Elliot had no real interest in expanding the menagerie and I was overcompensating for feeling guilty that Marsden never was going to get a real sister or a brother, because one child was starting to feel like one too many, but of course he can never know that and so I got him an iguana, which he named Hamster, and we moved into the rodent years, with a hamster named Gerbil and a gerbil named Rat and then a rat named Puppy, which is how Sinatra came into our lives when Marsden was in second grade. Marsden wanted to name the puppy Monkey, but I put on the brakes before we moved into primates and named him Sinatra. He had bright blue eyes and started to croon as soon as we got him home. Beautiful, sweet Sinatra. My other son.

Marsden started asking for a ferret as a friend for Sinatra. I don't know why he got hung up on a ferret. But I put the kibosh on that one. No ferret. Marsden was crushed. Years later, when Elliot said he was moving out, I told him we should get Marsden a ferret before breaking the news to him.

Marsden was in high school by then, but I wasn't thinking straight. There were a lot of things I did during that time that I now wonder about. I was desperate. I would have pierced my nipples. I almost did. Well, I thought about piercing them but got a second hole in my ear instead. And sexy lingerie and a Brazilian wax. I wrote a one-man show for an audience of one and tried to seduce Elliot back. How many marriages have been saved by someone trying to riff on a marriage while wearing sexy lingerie? Certainly not mine.

We gave Marsden the ferret before we told him that we were getting divorced.

"What's this for?" Marsden asked when we presented it to him.

"It's a ferret. You always said you wanted a ferret."

"I wanted a ferret when I was like eight years old," he said.

"Well, now you have one." I handed Marsden a little studio apartment of a cage with the ferret and Elliot told him that he's working with an architect friend to design a Victorian castle worthy of such a fine ferret.

A week later, Elliot and I told Marsden that we needed to talk about something important. We were advised to present a united front and not to start blaming each other or fighting.

"It's not your fault."

"Yeah, I know," Marsden said.

"We both love you very much."

"Cool."

"You'll get through this."

"Yup."

"Do you have any questions?"

"Nup."

"Are you worried about where you'll live?"

"Not really."

"Don't be sad."

"Okay."

"Do you want me to talk to your teachers?"

"Mom, I'm in high school."

"Are you sure, honey? Divorce can affect your grades."

"It won't affect mine."

He was right about that. Marsden has been a strong C student throughout high school. Consistent. That's what my son is. He's consistent. It's a good trait to have. Marsden named the ferret Divorce Ferret. Divorce Ferret traveled back and forth each week between Elliot's new house with Midge—four streets down from our old house—and our new house—twenty minutes, two towns, and what felt like a time zone away. Four months later, when Marsden was staying at Elliot's, Divorce Ferret disappeared, and we were a family divided without any animals.

DAY 33

MY PHONE CONVERSATIONS with Aunt Rosemary can feel like a one-act play. Or something.

ME: I hope it's not too late to call.

AUNT ROSEMARY: Of course not, dear, but you shouldn't be taking time out of your busy writing schedule. Tell me, how's the play coming along?

ME: It's okay. Not really. I've got too much going on to focus.

AUNT ROSEMARY: We've got everything covered here. Go back to work, Elise. We all know you're on deadline. It's important for you to remember that you're an artist first.

ME: I don't know about that. Everything going on feels a bit overwhelming now. I'm struggling trying to figure out the ending of the play.

AUNT ROSEMARY: You'll come up with something brilliant. You always do. As an actress, I know good writing, and you are a magnificent writer.

ME: You're sweet for having so much confidence in me, but I'm not so sure.

AUNT ROSEMARY: Darling, don't be hard on yourself. Being hard on yourself is a family curse. You must try to throttle it. You should be working, not on the phone with me.

ME: I wasn't writing. I'm getting ready for bed. I'm calling because I can't reach Mom. She was saying terrible things to Sue today. She kept calling her a fat C-word.

AUNT ROSEMARY: Concubine?

ME: No, not that C-word. The C-word Mom uses. You know which C-word I'm talking about. I told Sue she should go home and take a few days off. I said I'd pay her and that Mom would be fine. She sounded really rattled. I've been calling Mom to talk to her about it, but she hasn't picked up once.

AUNT ROSEMARY: I suppose that's because your mother went out for a walk to get some air and she had a fall.

ME: She fell? Is she okay?

AUNT ROSEMARY: Well, to be honest, she's now claiming that someone pushed her. She won't admit to having fallen. You know your mother; she thinks everyone's out to get her.

ME: So is she okay?

AUNT ROSEMARY: Darling, she's fine. She's at Mount Sinai. They're taking X-rays to make sure nothing is broken. There's nothing to worry about. They're just being cautious.

ME: I'm glad she went to the hospital.

AUNT ROSEMARY: She would never have gone to the hospital on her own. We're lucky that someone called an ambulance.

ME: What? Why are you just telling this to me now? Why didn't you call to let me know? Why didn't Mom call?

AUNT ROSEMARY: Your mother didn't want to bother you. She knows you're on deadline.

ME: Dammit!

AUNT ROSEMARY: Darling, please, don't be bitter. It clogs you up and gives you wrinkles.

ME: It's just that she's always calling when she shouldn't be and never calls when should.

AUNT ROSEMARY: Maybe you could show up for her now and then. You know Julie is always here for me and she's got such a high-pressure job.

ME: Julie is a great daughter. I'll drive to the city in the morning.

Hang up. End of call. Blackout.
And off to the city I go.

DAY 34

MOM FELL.

Mom says she was pushed.

Nothing's broken.

Aside from her memory.

Her fury at the world remains intact.

It's been a long time since I was in a hospital and I had forgotten how many sick people there are. It's humbling seeing so many people in one confined space, suffering and in pain. Floor after floor stacked on top of each other with hospital beds, operating rooms, recovery rooms, machines beeping and monitoring, blood flowing through tubes, drips dripping. How does a building sustain all the pain—the buzz and hums and silent sobs and screams? Doesn't any of it seep into the walls? Why don't they sag with the weight of it all?

Mom's doctor reminds me of Harrison Ford—*Indiana Jones* Harrison Ford. He looks like he should be on an archeological dig, picking at and sifting through dirt, not in a city hospital excavating with tests and scans. But there he was, eyes with a hint of squint and sandy scruff, digitally sifting through layers of skin and membranes and muscles to get to the old bones to make sure nothing was broken and try to figure out why they gave out. He wants Mom to stay in the hospital. He explained that her oxygen level is at 85 percent, a good 10 percent below what they'd like to see. He's concerned that there may be a clot in her lungs and wants to run more tests and administer a CT scan. He also wants her to see a pulmonologist for more digging and sifting, even though in spite of the low oxygen, she's proven that she's quite capable of using her lungs for a good yell.

When I arrived, she was verbally abusing a nurse who was trying to take her blood pressure. "Stop it, you bitch!"

And then. Oy! Let me write the scene.

INT: hospital room. Two beds: each bed is a temporary resting place for a woman hovering around the age of 80. Neither of these women is accustomed to sharing a room. They do not converse, yet they have composed full narratives about each other, neither of which is particularly charitable.

MOM: They're holding me hostage.

ME: They're not holding you hostage.

MOM: I'm calling my lawyer. Do you remember my lawyer's name?

ME: I don't know who your lawyer is. You don't need a lawyer though. You need to find out why you fell.

MOM: I fell because I was pushed.

ME: You weren't pushed.

MOM: Elise, you weren't there. You didn't see. I was pushed.

ME: Okay fine, who pushed you?

MOM: I don't know, but somebody did. Maybe it was that woman.

ME: You mean Sue?

MOM: Sue pushed me.

MOM'S ROOMMATE: Can you be quiet? I'm resting.

ME: Sorry. (Whispering) Sue didn't push you. Nobody pushed you.

MOM: (Not whispering) I know I was pushed.

ME: I don't think you were pushed.

MOM: Why do you always argue with me?

MOM'S ROOMMATE: Be quiet or I'm going to call a nurse.

MOM: Tell that bitch to shut up.

ME: Maybe I am always arguing with you. I'm sorry. I'm not telling her to shut up and don't call her a bitch.

MOM: (Yelling) I'm talking to my daughter. (Whispering) Bitch. Why do you always argue with me? I'm telling you that my doctor is holding me hostage.

ME: Mom, stop it! Your doctor is not holding you hostage. Why would anyone hold you hostage? Certainly not for your delightful disposition.

MOM: Stop yelling at me Elise!

ME: I'm not yelling at you.

MOM'S ROOMMATE: Yes, you are.

MOM: I'm running away.

ME: What?

MOM: If you don't take me home right now, I'm running away.

MOM'S ROOMMATE: That's a good idea.

(I pull a notebook out of my bag and hand it to Mom with a pen.)

ME: If you're going to run away, you have to write a runaway note.

(She takes the pen and paper from me, as if this statement was a greater truth. As if all runaways penned notes. It was in the runaway rule book.)

MOM: I don't know what to write. What should I say?

ME: Figure it out yourself. I'm not going to ghostwrite your runaway note.

MOM: But I don't remember how to write.

ME: What?

MOM: I don't remember how to write. I haven't written anything for a long time.

ME: I get it. I don't remember how to write either.

(LARRY, LAURIE, and GRACE are sitting around the dining room table in Laurie's house, each eating a large bowl of bouillabaisse. A French baguette with slices cut, but not all the way through, is in the center of the table.)

LARRY

Mmmmmm. Is that lobster?

LAURIE

Lobster, cod, clams, mussels, shrimp, and scallops.

GRACE

Laurie, darling, you've outdone yourself.

LAURIE

This is nice. The three of us having dinner together. Don't you think?

what does Laurie want? Does she know what she wants?

GRACE

Who would have imagined that the three of us would be sitting around a table eating bouillabaisse?

(Larry reaches for a piece of the bread. He struggles as he rips the slice from the loaf. Grace watches him. The expression on her face is one of disdain and annoyance.)

LAURIE

Want some help, Pops?

LARRY

Not necessary.

(He successfully liberates
the slice of bread and he
dips it in his soup. He
then starts chewing and
sucking on it. Soup is
dripping off of it.)

LARRY

Delicious!

LAURIE

Thanks, Pops.

GRACE

Larry, you have food on your face. Over here—

(Grace points to her cheek.
Larry wipes the wrong side
of his face).

No, the other side.

(She pushes her finger into
her cheek.)

LARRY

If you don't like the way I eat, don't look
at me when I'm eating.

GRACE

Wipe your face off.

LARRY

If food on my face bothers you, I'd like to
keep it there.

GRACE

I can't eat while you have food on your face.
It's making me sick.

LAURIE

Mom, just let him be. Pops, this side.

> (Laurie points to Larry's
> cheek. Larry wipes his
> entire face in a dramatic
> fashion with a napkin.)

Let's talk about something else. You know,
it would be really great if...I'd like it
if you two could try a bit harder to get
along. I've been thinking we should set some
ground rules.

LARRY

Do you hear that, Grace? Our daughter wants
to set ground rules.

GRACE

It's her house, as she keeps reminding me.

LARRY

Because you've overstayed your welcome.

GRACE

At least I was welcome. You've barged in on
a guilt trip.

LARRY

Grace, try to control your temper. Laurie
just said she doesn't like it when we fight.

LAURIE

I've been trying to make peace between you
two for most of my life. I'd really like it
if you could get along.

GRACE

Your father put us through a lot.

                    LARRY
Your mother didn't leave me any choice.

                    LAURIE
You know, I'm starting to understand why you
two want to kill each other.

                    LARRY
Your mother was impossible to live with.

                    LAURIE
Have you ever considered what kind of impact
your nonstop bickering has had on me?

                    GRACE
It couldn't have been that bad. You came
out terrific. Larry, we have a magnificent daughter.

                    LAURIE
Who made bouillabaisse for her parents
for dinner.

                    GRACE
You're a marvel. Our daughter is a marvel. No
thanks to you, Larry. I think I should get
some credit for raising a marvel.

                    LARRY
Take the credit, Grace. If that's what you
need to feel good about yourself.

                    GRACE
Even when you're trying to sound nice, you're
an ass. How long are you planning to stay
here Larry? Don't you have some side dish you
can stay with?

                    LAURIE
Mom. Honestly. Both of you-listen to me.
This is what's going on. Pops is staying

here at my invitation. It's sometimes hard
to imagine that you were ever married-

                    LARRY
Your mother was very beautiful.

                    LAURIE
Please stop saying that. You know, when you
split up, I didn't understand what was going
on. I wanted you to get back together more
than anything. I cried myself to sleep every
night for, I don't know how long, maybe a
year, hoping Daddy would come home. Praying
Daddy would come home. Making deals with
God, or anyone out there who might be able
to help. Promising every day to be a better girl if Daddy comes home. What did I
do wrong? What could I do to fix this? I
remember my ninth birthday party. I made my
wish. I remember Mom saying, "You did it.
You blew out all your candles. You can stop
blowing now." But I didn't stop. I couldn't
stop blowing.

                    LARRY
And look what happened. Your wish came true.
I'm back.

                    LAURIE
I know. And I'm really happy about it. But
I'm starting to think that wishes should
have a statute of limitations.
Pops, you do know that when you left, something in Mom snapped. Or maybe she was always
like that, and I hadn't noticed.

                    GRACE
Laurie, I'm right here.

LAURIE

(To Grace) You critiqued every move I made and watched over me like a KGB agent. (Pointing to Larry) When he married Robin, you screamed at me for a month.

GRACE

You liked her more than me. I couldn't stand it.

LAURIE

Robin was fun and nice to me.

GRACE

No she wasn't. Trust me. I remember.

LAURIE

Pops, I don't know why you let Robin go.

LARRY

Robin wanted to have children. I never wanted children.

LAURIE

Thanks.

LARRY

I meant more children. I loved having you. I thought Robin accepted that stipulation when we got married.

GRACE

If she made a deal, she made a deal. She should have honored her deal. Larry, I agree with you for once.

too much of Larry's eating issues?

(Larry takes a big slurpy mouthful of bouillabaisse and starts coughing.)

LAURIE

Are you okay?

GRACE

Let him be.

LARRY

(Talking through his coughs) Did you hear that, Laurie? You mom wants me to choke to death. (Still coughing) How do you like dem poached eggs.

GRACE

I'm sitting here and I'm thinking. That's what I do, I think. I'm always thinking. Analyzing the flip side, the dirty underside of mixed motivation and selfish intent. No one makes bouillabaisse for a regular family dinner. It's a very complicated dish. And I'm wondering what's really going on.

LARRY

Give it a rest, Gracie. Sometimes a bouilla-baisse is just a bouillabaisse.

LAURIE

Mom's right. This bouillabaisse kind of has an agenda. Not a big one. But like a minor agenda.

GRACE

I knew something was fishy.

LAURIE

Not fishy. Agenda-ishy. I'm worried about leaving the two of you here by yourselves, but a friend has invited me to go away with him for the long weekend coming up and I told him I'd go if it was alright with you.

LARRY

Did you hear that, Grace? Our little girl has a guy. You don't need my permission to go away.

LAURIE

He's an old friend from college. Granny. I
don't think you've ever met Granny, Pops.

LARRY

Isn't Granny a girl's name?

GRACE

Larry, don't be such a schmuck. Granville is
very handsome. And I bet he can perform even
with that name.

LAURIE

Mom, what are you getting at? Pops, Granville
is his real name. His old friends still
call him Granny though. So is it okay with
you if I go?

LARRY

I like a man named Granny. Go! Have a great
time. We'll be fine here.

LAURIE

I'm worried about leaving you two here
together.

LARRY

Don't worry about us. Your mother knows how
to handle me.

LAURIE

Please, while I'm gone, no slinging of
insults. Try to keep the passive aggressive jabs to a minimum. Maybe don't spend
time together. Pops, please don't let Mom
use your car.

LARRY

I wouldn't think of it.

LAURIE
Try to be kind and courteous to each other.
Or if that isn't possible, maybe just don't
speak to each other. I'll only be away for
three nights.

BLACKOUT

DAY 35

MOM'S PULMONOLOGIST WAS a stunningly beautiful Asian woman. I'm starting to wonder if the doctors who work at Mount Sinai are hired by a casting director. I have yet to meet one without movie star looks. Mom's pulmonologist exuded care and compassion and unbelievable patience. She ran a series of tests, none of which Mom could complete. The first test should have been simple enough—put your lips together and blow. What came out was a putter, a wisp—dead air. So much nothing that the candles on her next birthday cake should celebrate. They will not be victimized by another gusty birthday reveler nor tormented by an aging yahoo desperately trying to extinguish them. It's a wonder that someone with so much bluster has so little blow.

Mom looked small and fragile. She rubbed her nose when the pulmonologist talked to her and told her she didn't understand the tasks that she was being asked to perform. Mom apologized about not having the breath to blow, and instead of venting her frustrations, she continued to apologize for messing up. She went so far as to thank the pulmonologist for her time and help.

The pulmonologist said to me, "Your mother is a lovely woman. You're very lucky."

The doctors haven't yet figured out why her oxygen level is so low. They think she may have a small hole in her heart and want to do a transesophageal echocardiogram, which, as Mom's pulmonologist explained, would require sticking a probe with ultrasound capabilities down her esophagus to examine her heart. When she said this to me, I reflexively responded, "But I don't think she has a heart."

As soon as the words came out, I wanted to eat my face. Only my mouth is part of my face and does not extend around it. Someone should fix that. If there is a species that is capable of eating its own face, I would like to be reincarnated as that species.

After the appointment, I wheeled her back to her hospital room. Mom insisted that she felt better and that she wanted to go home. I told her she'd be going home soon, but that she had to stay in the hospital just a while longer. While I was talking, I started to feel dizzy. I couldn't catch my breath. I needed fresh air. I needed to get out of the hospital. I understand why Mom wants to leave. It can be hard to breathe in here even if you don't have low oxygen levels. Marsden had texted to ask if I could buy some acne cream for him. I had an excuse to leave. I had a mission. My son needed me.

MOM: Are you coming back?

ME: I'll be back a little later.

MOM: I'll be here. They're holding me hostage.

ME: Mom, are you back to that? We just had such a nice morning.

MOM: Maybe you had a nice morning. I didn't.

I rode down in the elevator with an ageless-looking rumpled man: while his face was free of wrinkles, his shirt was full of creases and crinkles. I left the hospital and walked across the park. Once on the West Side, I popped into a Duane Reade, but instantly felt overwhelmed and walked back out. I passed a CVS, then another Duane Reade, and kept walking down Broadway. I sped past the Apthorp pharmacy, but right after passing Fairway, I got trapped behind an elderly couple who were eating while they walked. At first I tried to blow past them, but I couldn't find a clearing and eased into a slow pace behind them. I started listening to them argue and then recognized their words. How was that possible? This elderly couple on Broadway were saying lines I had written.

"Larry, you have food on your face. Over here. No, the other side."

"If you don't like the way I eat, don't look at me when I'm eating."

"Wipe your face off."

"If food on my face bothers you, I'd like to keep it there."

Was it a sign? Coincidence? Synchronicity? God showing off? It's exactly what Julia Cameron writes about in *The Artist's Way*. This is it. This is that thing that happens. These Morning Pages are actually working. I had an epiphany, an insight, a vision.

Laurie will find her inner strength—no, that's too-cliché and overdone. I don't want her riding off into the glow of an inner strength sunset. But she leaves. Why does she leave? Is leaving really the only solution for a woman? Must we always Thelma and Louise it off a cliff or walk out into the water for a final swim? What if Laurie stays? What if she makes Larry and

Grace leave? Maybe she locks them out. That could be both funny and poignant. What if staying is her leaving?

I turned around and headed back to Duane Reade. The toothpaste aisle was empty, so I squatted down and wrote three pages of notes. One doesn't often get a good look at the lower shelves at a Duane Reade. One should. They are impressive. Everything has its place, and the flow of products is masterful. I hadn't realized just how many alternatives are available to help us obtain white teeth and fresh breath; there really is no excuse for gingivitis and halitosis anymore. Over on the pimple products aisle, I found an overwhelming selection of astringents, scrubs, creams, gels, pads, washes, and masks dedicated to the noble cause of zit eradication. The wrinkle reduction creams were shelved right next to the acne cures. What brilliant shelf stocking! I hope whoever it was that woke up one morning and decided to put the acne medication next to the wrinkle reduction products got a raise. The mothers that are buying their teenagers acne medication just take one step to the right to rid themselves of the worry lines that the teenagers they are buying the acne medication for are causing. I decided to try a wrinkle reduction cream that promises to eliminate my fine lines. (Hopefully not the ones I will be writing!) Soon Marsden and I will have faces as smooth as the man in the elevator with the wrinkled shirt.

And because my day was suddenly blessed, I got back to Mom's building and found my handsome, engaging, slightly mysterious elevator crush waiting for the elevator and I ele-flirted with him for 15 glorious floors.

DAY 36

S̲ammy R̲onstein i̲s not more excited about *Deja New* than he's been about a project in a long time. In fact, he has concerns about the play. Concerns wasn't the word he used. "Considerations." That was the word. I had told him I was in the city because my mother was in the hospital and he insisted we do lunch. Do lunch. What is that? When did lunch become something that got done rather than eaten? He said to meet at Orso at 12:30. I arrived at 12:25 and he was already there. I spotted him as soon as I walked in. Sammy has a large head, expressive features, and a compact body that is hardly worth mentioning because you can't help but focus on his face.

He barely said hello. Jumped right in—with feverish enthusiasm. "Elise, *Simple Syrup* was gold. Pure gold! Joleen brought the disappearing middle-aged woman to the stage. No one sees her. And no matter how many mirrors and reflective glass windows catch her gaze, she can't even see herself. You created a character who resonated."

"Thank you, Sammy," I smiled with my new Crest White-strips confidence. All teeth, no glee. I didn't know where he was going, but I knew he was going somewhere I didn't want to go.

Sammy Ronstein does that self-deprecating thing that people do when they want you to know how important they are, but they also want you to think they have too much humility to brag. "I admire playwrights like you, Elise. I could never write a play." He leaned in across the table. I leaned in. We were forehead-to-forehead. He wanted to tell me something important. I was important. He used my name, sprinkled it into the conversation to make sure I was paying attention.

"Elise, I don't have the discipline or the empathy or the gift with language, but I love the company of creatives. I get off on listening and I try to do my small part to support the playwrights whose work I care about. I want them to have a safe space for their work. Don't think I don't get a lot out of it. I have been honored to work with so many brilliant women in theater and I bow to them—Anna Deavere Smith, Eve Ensler, Sarah Ruhl, Annie Baker, Paula Vogel, Fiona Gunderson, Lynn Nottage, and dear Wendy, how we all miss Wendy. Such an unimaginable loss."

He pulled back for dramatic effect. Now sitting upright in his chair, he smiled and shook his head. "I sound like I'm namedropping. I hate namedroppers. Don't you? I don't care what your name is, Elise." He shook his head from side to side as he said those last words—I (head to the left) don't (over to the right) care (back to the left then centered and looking directly at me) what your name is. Elise. Still making eye contact—"There are considerations. We have Nancilla Aronie ready to direct and I know you want her blown away by *Deja New* as a groundbreaking piece of social commentary about the failure of feminism and the modern American woman."

Is that what my play is about? Why didn't I know that? Is that what I'm supposed to be writing?

I'm going to try to get down what Sammy said, word for word to the best of my potholed memory:

"Elise, I want you to hear me out. I am only saying this for the strength of the play, so I don't want you to overreact or to take what I say personally. My notes are just that, notes in the service of making great theater. I've been doing this for a hell of a long time, and I have some experience in what works and what doesn't. I want you to recreate the magic you did with *Simple Syrup*. I know it's in you. But from what you've sent me, I'm asking myself, is it too obvious? Too simplistic and reductive? And then I thought, what if you turn it on its head, shift the focus away from Laurie. Start the play as Granville's story. Let Laurie's character be revealed first through Granville, and then through her mother and her father. You can use those around her to shape and form her, as she feels they have.

I tried to moderate my voice, to keep it from cracking or upticking or doing any of those things that women's voices get criticized for doing. "So you're asking me to write a play about a woman from a man's perspective? And then from her parents' perspective?"

"I'm not asking you to do anything. I am exploring opportunities to make your play punch with the impact of a heavyweight fighter in a welterweight match. This is how the process works. You surely remember that, don't you?"

"I understand where you're coming from and I value your notes and your experience and will, of course, consider your ideas, but I don't really think that's how this story should be told. I feel that the other characters are there for Laurie to push against, not to be revealed by." I kept my Whitestripped-smile on display as I responded to Sammy, so as not to appear confrontational, smiling, Julia-Roberts-toothy, through my fury.

DAY 37

THE FIRST TIME I woke up was 2:22 in the morning. It almost always happens like this. I get catapulted out of a dream, a full-on expulsion from sleep, and when I look at the clock, I discover that it's either 1:11 or 2:22 or 3:33 or 4:44. The numbers 2:22 were green and glowing, piercing through the darkness of my childhood bedroom. I watched the clock and waited for a new sequence of numbers to appear. At 2:23, I realized I couldn't move my arms. Sammy Ronstein had snuck in while I was sleeping and tied me up. At 2:24, I realized it was the blanket that had wrapped itself around me. I was swaddled like a 48-year-old baby. By 2:30, I managed to unroll myself from the blanket and I rolled off the bed. It hurt like hell. I don't know when I drifted off again, but at 4:44, I woke up gasping for breath. Sammy Ronstein was standing over me. His big face was breathing into mine. "Don't breathe at me," I said. "I'm giving you oxygen. You'll die if you don't have oxygen," he replied. Maybe it was a dream. It's 5:55 now.

I am awake. I don't want to be awake today.

Yesterday, Mom's doctor confirmed that her memory lapses are due to cognitive decline, which he said may have been triggered by a series of Transient Ishmael Attacks. No, not Ishmael. Ishmael is *Moby Dick*. I wrote it down like a hundred times so I wouldn't forget. They are mini-strokes, appetizers before the main course. Ischemic. That's it. Call me Ischemic! Transient Ischemic Attacks.

I am grateful for her Harrison Ford look-alike doctor. He wants to start her on a drug called...oh damn...what was it? Aricept. Yes, Aricept. He says it might help slow down the memory loss she is experiencing. I should have been paying more attention to what was going on. All her calls, and I just wanted to get her off the phone. The signs were there. She's been asking the same questions over and over. She suddenly wanted to know about Dad. Why was she so interested in Dad? She hates him. I'm a playwright. I understand dramatic fore-shadowing. I saw the signs, but for some reason I can never spot the foreshadowing in my actual life. Chekhov's gun may be prominently displayed on a wall, but I won't notice it, or if I do notice it, I don't stop to think, *Look, there's a gun, it must be there for a reason, I bet someone is going to get shot.* No, I glide by the gun, thinking: *Nice gun, what should I eat for lunch?*

Like with Elliot. I should have noticed that Elliot had stopped asking questions. When I met him, he was an asker. Not a lot of men are askers, and I loved that Elliot asked questions. Sure, some of his questions were things like, "What do you use your toaster oven for?" But he also asked other questions, like, "What have you seen that's interesting lately?" and "What's the play you're writing about?"

On our first date, he asked me what my favorite color was when I was a kid.

"Why do you want to know?"

"I want to know about you," he said.

"Fuchsia," I told him.

"Bold and cheery. I like that," he said and smiled, revealing the dimples. "What's your favorite band? Do you like eggplant?

Have you ever spent the night on a sailboat? Will you spend the night on a boat with me?" He asked questions and he smiled. And flirted with his dimples.

I can't remember if the questions stopped suddenly or if they dripped dry. He was surely getting curious about Midge, asking her about her favorite color, the bands she liked, and whether she preferred a classic GE range or a JennAir? Even now, it's painful to think about the questions he must have asked her. I'd actually rather think about them having sex. Midge stole my fucking questions and I want them back.

No, I don't. I really don't. I think I'm just so stuck in the habit of thinking I do. I don't actually miss him. I think I'm mostly missing the thought of him. The thought of him is much better than the reality of him. Everything about him would be better if he didn't have to be a part of it. His success story is a great story, until he shows up and ruins it. Elliot is a visionary entrepreneur, a self-made man, who created a business that matched people with their perfect appliances, because Lord knows before Elliot, people were hooking up with disastrous dishwashers and toasters from hell. Elliot Sherman, founder of the Appliance Alliance App, enticed millions of Americans to connect with their perfect appliance by taking an Appliance Alliance Quiz, so people can move forward in a confusing world of mass appliances, confident that they have the right appliance just for them. The Appliance Alliance was a niche that didn't need to be filled, yet Elliot had a hunch that people wanted to have a deeper and more meaningful relationship with their appliances, so he created a way for people to pick appliances that best matched their personalities and suburban America was hooked. Everyone needed new appliances. It seemed utterly amazing that so many people had survived for so long with appliances they were fundamentally incompatible with. Thank God Elliot came along and saved the day. He embraced his success with a knowing entitled smugness and his damn dimples.

I know how a marriage ends, mine did, but I can't seem to figure out how a relationship ends. Maya's right, I am still in a relationship with Elliot—problem is we're divorced and he's living with another woman.

DAY 38

MOM BARELY HAS any wrinkles and the specks of gray in her hair look more like highlights than decay, and when I walked into her hospital room yesterday, the light streaming in through the window had formed what looked like a halo above her angelic-looking face, and I thought that maybe this was a sign. Maybe she's changed. Maybe we can move on. Maybe things will be different now.

"Elise, is that you?" she asked.

"Hi Mamma," I said. I rarely call her Mamma.

"I'm glad you're here. I have something to tell you. I'm dying,"

"You're going to be okay," I assured her and sat down on the bed. I took her hand in mine and ran my index finger over the topographical landscape of her veins.

"I'm dying," she repeated.

I suggested we ask her doctor for his opinion. I spoke in a soothing, reassuring tone. It was morning. She looked like a living angel. I had worked on a scene of the play before heading over to the hospital and had meandered through Central Park. I felt good and wanted her to know I cared about her. "Mom, I'm sure you're going to be okay. Your doctor is just trying to figure out why you fell."

"I don't care what the fucking doctor says. I'm not dying because I'm sick. I'm dying because they are trying to kill me and I don't want to die right now because if I die you will use an ugly photo of me for my obituary. I know what you're planning. It will be your final revenge."

"They are not trying to kill you and I am not looking for a final revenge," I assured her.

She yanked her hand away from mine.

"If I get out of here, I'm going through my photos and only keeping the ones I sanction for my obituary."

"You don't need to do that. I promise I will use a great photo. Anyway, I don't think there are any bad photos of you. You're gorgeous, Mom."

"I am throwing out all my photos and I want you to throw out any photos you have of me."

"Why do you think I'm after revenge? And if I were, why do you think I would do it posthumously?"

She turned her head from me. The halo had been replaced by a flood of blinding light.

"You're right, Mom. I'm going to use a shitty picture of you."

I certainly thought it. I may have said it. I'm not sure.

DAY 39

YES, I LEFT Mom in the hospital and came home. I had to get back. The doctors still can't figure out why her oxygen level is so low. Before I left, I apologized to Mom. I shouldn't have reacted the way I did. She's frightened and confused. I should have let her vent. She's the patient, but I need to be patient.

I decided to walk across the park to the hospital. Handsome Elevator Man was in the elevator when I stepped in. It was the first ride we'd had to ourselves in a while. First there were a string of people—from the ninth, seventh, and fourth floors—who intruded on us, then two days ago he was riding up with someone who looked strikingly like Laurie Anderson. I kept trying to look/not look. Since Lou Reed just died, I offered my condolences. Elevator condolences must suck. During our last ride down to the lobby, a toe-gazing visitor from the 14th floor stepped into the elevator and the three of us descended in silence. I tried to catch my handsome elevator man's eye. He seemed to be contemplating something. What was it? Was it me? I've found that our clipped conversations in the elevator literally elevate me. They carry me through my time visiting Mom. I look forward to them, they energize me—these travels in a box without windows, without natural light or life's scenery to look out on. Somehow, it's different spending vertical time with someone—moving up and down instead of forward or backward. I can't shake the feeling that we've shared something. And yet, I don't even know his name.

HANDSOME ELEVATOR MAN: Where are you off to this morning?

ME: To the hospital to see my mother before heading back home. It's so nice out, I thought I'd walk across the park.

HANDSOME ELEVATOR MAN: How's she doing?

ME: They're concerned about her memory, and they can't figure out why her oxygen level is so low. All the tests they're running are coming out terribly inconclusive.

HANDSOME ELEVATOR MAN: It's hard not having answers.

ME: And where are you off to?

HANDSOME ELEVATOR MAN: Just out for a walk. Mind if I walk with you?

It turns out he's lived at 212 for 13 years. He and his wife and their kids moved from LA to the city. He works with musicians, managing their careers. It *was* Laurie Anderson in the elevator. We started talking about the building.

HANDSOME ELEVATOR MAN: Do you find it odd how much the doormen know about our lives, and how little we know about theirs?

ME: I think about that a lot. When I was a teenager, I used to ask Alan all sorts of highly personal and inappropriate questions.

HANDSOME ELEVATOR MAN: I don't know anything about him. I don't know where he lives, if he's married, what he likes to do when he's not working, although it seems like he's always there, opening the door, day and night. Does he ever not work? What did you find out?

ME: He's gay.

HANDSOME ELEVATOR MAN: I didn't know that.

ME: It seemed like a big deal back then.

HANDSOME ELEVATOR MAN: What about the other doormen? Did you inquire about their lives beyond the building?

As we crossed Central Park, I launched into stories of doormen past. My arms flail when I talk, not with the choreographed restraint of a conductor, but with wild twirls and grand improvised gestures. Sometimes my wrists look like windmills and astute listeners may notice the cracking sounds they make as they whirl around. Maya and I were once taking a walk on a bike path, and while telling her a story, I violently threw my fisted hands out to the side at the exact moment a biker was attempting to slip past us, and my fist landed like a punch on his face.

My arms flung and dipped and cast about as I told Handsome Elevator Man about Tony, the doorman who ducked down and talked to himself when he didn't think anyone else was in the lobby. There were a lot of kids around my age who lived in the building back then and we all figured Tony was reliving his war days—we never talked about which war, but Tony looked ancient so I'm pretty sure I thought it was the Revolutionary

War. And there was Paul, who was a retired cop and never opened the door for anyone under the age of 15. I'd scurry in and out as fast as I could and always say thank you to him. I never asked him anything. And Bob. All the kids in the building loved Bob because he'd chase us around the lobby. But then Lorene Liman, who lived in apartment 4A, popped down to the lobby in the middle of the night because she had forgotten to pick up her dry cleaning, which had been delivered earlier in the day. The front door to the building was closed and there was no doorman at the door. Later on, after everything went down, Mrs. Liman told my mother that she figured the doorman had gone to the bathroom and would be back in a few minutes, but she didn't feel like waiting for him, and besides, she was nervous being in the lobby all alone in the middle of the night. So she walked across the lobby, which felt darker and scarier than usual, and pulled open the door to the mailroom to look for her dry cleaning.

I was getting into the story, and did a dramatic full arm rotation, from front to back and moving fast, as if I was pointing to the building's mailroom, where dry cleaning and packages and mail were kept.

My arm was spinning fast, and my hand slammed into his. And when it did his fingers closed in around mine, only I'm not sure if he was holding my hand in a flirtatious way, or if he was protecting himself from further assault, so I kept telling my story. His hand holding mine.

Blathering on.

ME: Lorene Liman opened the door to the mailroom and discovered Bob in there. Bob didn't usually work the overnight shift, so she was probably confused, but there he was—with a prostitute, pants down around his knees.

Since I can't separate my arms from my mouth, I pulled my hand away from his and put it back into rotation. I should have held on to his hand. I should have stopped and looked at him. I should have said something. I should have turned to him and kissed him. Passionately.

Instead.

I rambled on about how Bob the doorman got fired and the kids who lived in the building learned what the words *prostitute* and *whore* meant.

When we got to the hospital, we said good-bye. It was casual.

"Thanks for joining me."

"I enjoyed chatting."

Nothing more. I still don't know his name. I could ask Alan. But I want to hear it directly from him. Whispered from his lips into my ear.

While riding the elevator.

DAY 40

THE LANDLINE WAS ringing when I walked in the house yesterday. I almost didn't answer. I'm sure I sounded exasperated when I picked up.

"Mrs. Hellman, this is Mrs. Yule, Marsden's guidance counselor. Is this a bad time?"

"No," I lied. "Is everything okay?"

Mrs. Yule had called to let me know that she had just spoken with Marsden and was deeply concerned. The emphasis she put on the word *deeply* was drenched in judgment.

I don't trust or like Mrs. Yule. I think she's more interested in her own achievements than actually helping the kids. When we met with her last spring, she was all smiles, but the authenticity of her smiles was betrayed by the road map of chiseled frown lines around her mouth. "It's come to my attention that Marsden hasn't visited any colleges," she said. "This is very unusual for our students who are planning to attend college next year."

She told me that some of their students start visiting schools when they are freshmen in high school, a few even in eighth grade, although she said she discourages starting that early, but you can't quell some of the more eager and ambitious students. You know how it is. Most of their students start seriously looking during the second half of their junior year. By November of senior year, they should be culling their list and working on their essay. Mrs. Yule then "refreshed my memory" of the deadlines that she suspected Marsden would miss and had missed and queried as to why he hadn't taken the SAT or the ACT yet. She rattled off a list of prestigious colleges and universities her students have gotten accepted to. Mrs. Yule informed me that she's not only placed students in American colleges, but in schools around the globe including Abu Dhabi University. She sounded like some frat boy bragging about sexual conquests. I hope Marsden doesn't brag about his sexual conquests. I doubt he's had any sexual conquests to brag about. He surely doesn't have the energy or time for sex. Between school and naps and smoking, his schedule is rather full.

Mrs. Yule is deeply concerned about Marsden's grades. "A rather lackluster transcript," she sighed. "What about extracurriculars?"

"Is sleep considered an extracurricular?" I asked Mrs. Yule. I could feel the tension rising. Marsden was going to be the one who screws up her sterling record of getting students placed at prestigious universities. I was thinking about how frustrated she must be. I was honestly more concerned about how Marsden's lassitude was going to affect Mrs. Yule than how it was going to impact him.

"Maybe he should consider taking a gap year," she suggested. "There are some terrific gap year programs that I can recommend."

"He said he wants to go to college next year," I replied. Then I explained to her that I can't push him. I told her that Marsden is a self-starter, he just takes a long time to get started.

"Then perhaps he isn't actually a self-starter. Most of the self-starters I see are much more proactive than Marsden," Mrs.

Yule said. I could hear her trying not to sound condescending. I hate the sound of someone trying not to sound condescending. I started to get reactive. I wanted to condescend to her condescension and sound less condescending than she did while doing it.

I paced my words and explained to Mrs. Yule that there are different kinds of self-starters—yes, of course there are the proactive, motivated self-starters, who fit the conventional self-starter mold, but there are also the slow-to-start self-starters. "They are the slow cookers of self-starters." I explained that "Marsden just needs a bit more time to marinate."

But she misheard me and asked, "Did you just say he needs more time to masturbate?"

What? No! Did I?

I denied it in full. I tried to make a joke out of it and place the blame on her. "Mrs. Yule, I most certainly didn't. Excuse me for asking, but where is your head at?"

She was not amused and ended our conversation abruptly. By the end of the school day, I suspect Mrs. Yule had had told her fellow administrators about our conversation. She's probably working on a book: *Parents Say the Darndest Things.*

The truth is Marsden has been a slow-to-start self-starter. It took him longer than most to join the post-utero world and from his first hour of life, he has looked drowsy. Beautiful, tired boy that he is. It seems like a genetic impossibility that I ended up with this sleepy mono-syllabic son. There is nothing in my DNA that doesn't scream chatty insomniac. Even Elliot, for all his faults—if he actually has faults other than leaving me for Midge—is engaged and talkative and energetic. Somehow the two of us created this silent, sleepy, gorgeous giant, whose motto in life seems to be "the path of least resistance." How can

4

there be so few words in that six-foot-two body? What is in there if not words?

"Yup." "Nup." (Not even a full "Nope.") "Sure." And recently, "Dunno."

When Marsden got home from school, I told him Mrs. Yule had called.

"Marsden, do you want to go to college next year?"

"Sure."

"Do you want to look at some schools?"

"Okay."

"Are there schools you're thinking about?"

"Not really."

"Do you think you'd like to go to a large university, like UMASS, or a small more intimate school?"

"Dunno."

"Someplace rural with cows or in a city with cars?"

"Dunno."

"Close to home or far away?"

He shrugged.

"In states that begin with an A or an M?"

"Yup. Sure."

"A and M or A or M?"

"Mom!"

"Should I set up some school visits?"

"Okay."

"Okay."

He will get there. I have confidence in him. My beautiful boy is a self-starter.

DAY 41

ELLIOT LEFT ME a voice message yesterday. He said he wants to get together and talk. Mrs. Yule must have called him too. I secretly—maybe not so secretly—wish—but wish I didn't wish—that Marsden was more like the overachieving kids at his school. Why is he doing this whole Deadhead in Dedham thing?

I get it. I do. I'd be doing it too if I were him. I just wish he had more consideration for me and my deadlines. What am I writing? I should have more consideration for him and his teenage apathy.

After Elliot's call, I took a long walk with Maya at Cutler Park. We haven't walked in Cutler Park since I moved to Dedham and walking there made me feel like I was back in my old life, my real life—my real fake life. I didn't know where I wanted to go when my marriage ended, all I knew was that I wanted to leave Wellesley. I decided on Dedham because the wide streets and brick buildings felt unpretentious, and I liked that the town has a theater that's been around since before the Depression. I wanted to be in a town that has survived depression, that felt permanent while everything else in my life felt uprooted and uncertain. Plus, it seemed meaningful that the town was originally named "Contentment"—isn't that what we all want? And yet that got taken away and they got stuck with "Dedham"—so it goes.

On our walk, Maya told me I shouldn't get together with Elliot. She said, "It takes you a minimum of two days to recover after you see him." This is true. She said, "You are stressed out you need to focus." This is true. She said, "If you want to actually finish your play, which I am beginning to doubt that you do, then you shouldn't get together with Elliot." She's wrong here. I want to finish. It's just that I don't know how. And right now, I don't know if I should start all over again or finish for the first time.

Sammy Ronstein emailed me yesterday: "Checking in, Elise. I feel like a kid on the days leading up to Christmas. I think about *Deja New* all the time. I hope our conversation was helpful. If I can be there for you in any way, let me know. Nancilla Aronie would like to have a character breakdown to her by tomorrow."

I'm overwhelmed. I'm breathing funny. My inhales and exhales don't seem to be the same length. My inhales are too long and exhales too short. My face looks round and bloated. I think I'm inflating myself with inhale. I need to write. But maybe the truth is that I'm not really a playwright at all. I'm just someone who managed to write a few plays.

I think I should get together with Elliot. He's Marsden's father and Marsden needs help. I'll call him instead. We can talk on the phone. That'll be better. Maya is right. I shouldn't see him. She wants me to go out with her new client instead.

"Elise, I'm sure he told me that he's recently divorced for a reason."

"Probably because he wants to sleep with you," I said.

"Only because he hasn't met you yet," she replied.

I told her about my crush on the man in my mother's elevator and insisted that I'm a one-crush woman.

But Maya persisted. Maya's client is promoting his animal rescue business. Raj's Rescues. "Call him right away because he's going to get snatched up quickly."

I told her I am not interested in men who get snatched up, that I prefer men with a longer shelf life.

She didn't laugh. I can usually make her laugh.

We took a few steps in silence before she started speaking again. I might be the playwright, but she knows how to structure the beats for an interesting conversation.

"You need to get over Elliot."

"But I don't want to lose my divorce virginity. I like it."

I agreed to email Raj of Raj's Rescues because that's what I do.

> Hi Raj, this is Maya's friend Elise. I'm a playwright
> on deadline, but Maya insisted that I reach out. You
> know Maya, she's always promoting something.

I didn't send the email.
Maybe I'll send it today.
I don't think I will though.

DEJA NEW

CHARACTERS

LAURIE—40, personable, professionally successful, smart, attractive, and yet perpetually single. As to why? Could it be the psychological hold that her narcissistic divorced parents have over her, even though they split up thirty-two years ago when she was eight? Laurie admittedly is more comfortable dealing with the complexities of mathematical equations than navigating emotional and interpersonal problems.

GRANVILLE "GRANNY"—40, Laurie's best friend from college. Also single, personable, professionally successful, smart, and attractive. Granny wants to honor the pact he made with Laurie in college that they would get married if they were both still single at forty.

GRACE—70s, Laurie's complicated, passive-aggressive, aggressive-aggressive, needy, angry, boundary-crossing, beautiful, and loving mother.

LARRY—70s, Laurie's charming, narcissistic father and the ex-husband to her mother, as well as numerous ex-stepmothers, and the current husband of Nicolette.

NICOLETTE—40s, Larry's current wife. Looks like a younger version of Grace. She is a lost soul who has found an older man when she should have found herself.

(Additionally, all waitresses should be played by the same actress who plays Nicolette, aside from the waitress in the final scene who is actually Nicolette. The other waitresses should be wearing wigs that are hair-appropriate to the types of venues they are working in. For example, the waitress in the first scene could have short, spiky hair.)

DAY 42

I SENT CHARACTER descriptions to Sammy, but that's all I got done yesterday. I spent the rest of the day compulsively checking my email for Sammy's response. Three thousand refresh clicks and nothing of interest aside from penis enhancing spam. Sammy's "considerations" have poisoned me.

Everything I write feels shallow and contrived. I try to find my inner Chekov, but there's no inner Chekov there, so I search for my inner Wendy Wasserstein, but she's missing too. I seek Beckett. It doesn't matter. I can't find him either.

Every writer who inspires me also intimidates me. Everyone I try to grab at dissipates as soon as they see my hands heading their way. Yasmina Reza. Gone. Noel Coward. Gone. I know somewhere there's an inner me lurking that is insightful, comical, and full of big ideas. Or maybe I don't have big ideas. Maybe my ideas are small. Why do we have to assign sizes to ideas anyway? Must everything be so competitive?

I don't want to get caught up wallowing in my insecurities. Well actually, maybe I do. I zealously embrace my insecurities. I want to bathe in them and imbibe them, and wrap myself in an insecurity blanket.

Marsden got off the bus yesterday and headed into the kitchen, where I was standing, snack in hand, and wearing a closed-lipped smile, so as not to look too eager.

"How was your day?"

I examined his face while waiting for his answer. What might he say? What was he thinking about? What was he going to tell me? His mouth opens. My smile broadens. I'm about to find out.

"Good."

I try again.

"How was school?"

"Fine."

"How were your classes?"

"Okay."

"What about Geology?"

"It rocked."

"Good one. What are you reading in English?"

"A book."

"Which book?"

"Can't remember. Can I go now?"

It's true that Marsden drives in the slow lane and all his classmates are passing him by. As Mrs. Yule confirmed, they have toured colleges, worked on their essays, taken the tests. They're preparing for next year and they surely know what book they're reading in English class. I should have insisted that Marsden switch schools. He shouldn't be going to a private school with students whose parents have private chefs and private jets. He should be enrolled in Dedham High School. But Elliot convinced me that Marsden should go to one of the best schools in the country. A school whose motto is "Where mind over matter matters."

"You want to take that away from him?" he asked.

"Yes," I replied.

But only to myself.

"I guess not," I said to Elliot.

I wonder what would have happened if I had taken Marsden and moved somewhere else. Maybe New York. Maybe Nebraska. Moving Marsden to a different school could have changed everything for him. It would have changed everything for him. Doesn't every action cause a reaction? You see it every day.

When I was in New York I watched a line of pre-school kids walking down West End Avenue in red vests tethered together. They were crossing 92nd Street and at the urging of one of their teachers, the front of the line sped up, but the back of the line wasn't prepared for the change of pace. The boy at the very end of the tether fell. This set off a chain reaction. One by one, they toppled. Down they went, little heaps in the crosswalk. A chain reaction set off by one action.

I recently read about a woman on a plane who scrolled through her sleeping husband's texts and found a series of intimate exchanges with someone named Annie X.

I can't wait to get inside you.

She shook her husband awake. "You motherfucker!"

"Shhh," he said.

She handed him his phone.

"Not here. We're on a plane," he pled.

She screamed. Wouldn't stop.

"What's going on?" asked a passenger seated in 28C.

The flight attendants descended. An infant in row 18 started to wail. The woman couldn't be pacified, and the pilot diverted the plane and landed so the scorned wife and her cheating husband could be escorted off. As a result, connecting flights were missed. One passenger missed a wedding, another didn't get to say a final farewell to her mother.

KATE FEIFFER

What we did and didn't do has shaped Marsden into the man he is or isn't yet—all those actions had reactions and now Marsden is disappearing because of them.

DAY 43

WHAT SHOULD I tell Sammy Ronstein if I can't finish? What about Nancilla Aronie? I have a setup for success, serious success, that could catapult me into the realm of playwrights who matter, but I'm never going to matter because I still can't figure out my ending. I know if I don't finish this play, my career will be over. I guess that's fine. I was never going to be a serious playwright anyway. Who was I kidding? Just myself.

Self-delusion is the sweetest nectar.

Maybe I should have been a poet. Most writers are driven by deadlines. But apparently not me because yesterday was wasted researching sandwiches.

I miss the straightforward, no-nonsense sandwiches, the ones I ate when I was a kid. Peanut butter and jelly, tuna fish, bologna, grilled cheese—all on white bread. Did these utilitarian sandwiches reflect a simpler time? Absolutely not. The '70s were soaked in strife. Vietnam, Nixon, women's lib, civil rights. The sandwiches of the '70s had an ungarnished raw authenticity. Since then, sandwiches have evolved into fussy, pretentious, vainglorious affairs. A sandwich is no longer just a sandwich, it's an art project.

The 4th Earl of Sandwich was a big man with big appetites. Did I really just write that? How dreadfully cliché. Would you ever describe someone as a small man with small appetites?

How would I describe Marsden? Maybe as a lanky lad with still undiscovered appetites. But that's not our portly Earl of Sandwich. He ate, drank, womanized, and gambled profligately. He was a big man with big appetites.

As the story goes, the 4th Earl of Sandwich refused to break for food during a marathon game of cards and ordered his minions to bring him a meal of salted beef stuffed between two slabs of bread, paving the way for the fast-food revolution and eating lunch at your computer. I was saddened to learn that this perfectly packaged meal was named for a rakish asshole with a gambling addiction. Not only did he get the world's most convenient lunch food named after him, he managed to get a set of islands. And if that's not enough to give someone indigestion, Lord Sandwich had a talented and beautiful mistress, an opera singer, who was killed by another one of her lovers after leaving the opera one evening.

The year after her murder, a book came out about the entire affair with the brilliant title: *Love and Madness: A Story too True: in a Series of Letters between Parties Whose Names Would Perhaps be Mentioned Were They Less Known or Lamented.* I wish books still had titles like this. I love the title so much I made myself memorize it. I downloaded the book and couldn't believe how full of passionate purple missives it was. *When will tomorrow come? What torturing dreams must I bear tonight?* Every time a soft *s* is written, it is printed as an *f*, so the book reads like you're listening to a small child with a slight lisp who says paffion for passion and conreffion for confession. *Shall I have your foul, and shall he have your hand, your eyes, your bofom, your lips, your...*

Yesterday, I also found out that for a brief period during World War II, selling sliced bread was illegal, due to a shortage of steel, wheat, and wax paper, which bread was packaged in. The earliest bread slicers were manufactured in the 1860s, but pre-sliced bread, a tenet of a true sandwich, wasn't widely sold until Wonder Bread came along in the 1930s and turned sliced bread into the greatest invention since sliced bread. Then, during World War II, a decade after prohibition ended, the prohibition of sliced bread began. Public outcry was fierce, savings were minimal; the ban was lifted after three months.

I hadn't realized that the term Sandwich Generation has been around for 30 years already. I salute the other sandwiches out there, the women feeling the squeeze from two generations. We are in this together. I think I may abandon playwriting and open a sandwich shop called Sandwich Generation Sandwiches, which will only sell peanut butter and jelly, grilled cheese, and tuna fish sandwiches. My sandwich generation intuition tells me it could be big.

(GRACE and LARRY are in Laurie's living room, which is now filled with large cardboard boxes. Grace gestures at the boxes and the furniture, then she points at Larry.)

GRACE

Is this necessary?

LARRY

I needed to get my things out of the house before Nicolette got rid of everything.

GRACE

So you bring it here? I thought you didn't have any money. How'd you pay the movers?

LARRY

That's none of your business, Grace.

GRACE

None of my business. Nothing is ever my business. Laurie is going to be upset when she sees all this. And she'll probably take it out on me. You'll get a pass. You always get a pass.

LARRY

I'm looking into getting a storage bin.

(Grace walks around the boxes, sighing and shaking her head.)

GRACE

I've been wondering about something lately, Larry. Why did you marry me?

LARRY

What kind of question is that?

GRACE

I'm curious. Why did you marry me?

LARRY

Grace, that was a long time ago. You want me to remember why I did something forty-five years ago?

GRACE

Forty-two years ago. Larry, I'm not asking why you didn't want to go to Laura and Charlie's New Year's Eve party in 1973 and insisted I go alone. Or why you wouldn't wear a suit to your sister's wedding. I'm asking you why you married the first of the five women you married? I get it. I understand that it must be hard to keep us straight in your head, along with all your business dealings and man-about-town philanthropy and

philandering. But now, after another one of
your wives saw through you, you're retired
and alone and have time on your hands to
reflect. And I'd like it if you could think
back and try to remember why you married me.

LARRY
Grace, what are you looking for? Is your ego
feeling that fragile?

*make this
a monologue?*

GRACE
What ego? I have no ego. You suck up all the *Let*
ego in the room.

← *Grace
really
unload!*

LARRY
All right then, why do you want to know?

GRACE
I told Laurie you never loved me. That I was
just a conquest.

LARRY
Why the hell would you tell her that? What
the hell is wrong with you, Grace? Are you
trying to poison her against me again?

GRACE
Again? I never tried to poison her against
you. You were the one who played up the fun
dad role and left me with having to discipline her. Of course she loved you more. You
did everything in your power to sabotage me.

LARRY
Laurie never needed to be disciplined. She
was the best-behaved kid I ever met. If you
believe you had to take on the role of dis-
ciplinarian, you're fooling yourself. Your
failings with our daughter were your failings alone.

GRACE

It made my blood boil. The more I hated you
the more she loved you, and after a while I
started to hate her for loving you. And you
have no idea how much I hated you for making
me hate my daughter. Larry, you have no idea.

LARRY

Grace, I did what I needed to do.

GRACE

Abandon your family?

LARRY

Save myself.

GRACE

You act like I was trying to kill you.

LARRY

Weren't you?

GRACE

Go fuck yourself, Larry.

LARRY

Come on Grace. Why are you bringing this up?

GRACE

I want to know. Did you ever love me? I mean
it, Larry. Did you ever love me?

LARRY

Of course I loved you.

GRACE

I don't believe you. You want to hurt me.

LARRY

By saying I loved you?

GRACE

You should have told her you were going to
do this. Have you seen how Laurie keeps this
place? She's impeccably neat, and you've
turned it into a junk yard. Larry, you're
still as selfish as you always were. I can't
talk to you anymore. We promised Laurie we
wouldn't fight.

> (Grace walks around the
> room looking for a place to
> sit and finally positions
> herself on a somewhat
> precarious stack of two
> boxes. The doorbell rings,
> followed by knocking.
> Neither of them moves.)

Aren't you going to get it?

LARRY

I'm not expecting anyone. Are you expecting someone?

GRACE

No, Larry, I'm not. But when somebody is
at the front door, convention dictates that
the person closest to the door gets up and
answers it. Since I have found a seat on this
side of the room, and since you are standing not four feet from the door, I would
think you might take it upon yourself to see
who it is.

> (She sighs. Larry walks
> to the front door without
> saying anything. He opens
> the door and NICOLETTE, who
> looks like a younger version
> of Grace, bursts in.)

LARRY
Nicolette.

That's called stealing Larry. I should have you arrested.

NICOLETTE
Larry, you emptied out our house. ʌ

LARRY
(Gesturing) I hired some movers to pick up a
few things.

(is he defensive? angry?)

NICOLETTE
You can't just do that. I want to talk to
Laurie. I want to explain my side of the
story to her.

LARRY
Laurie's not here. She went away for
a few days.

> (Nicolette pushes past Larry
> and walks into the house.
> She scans the room and sees
> the piles of boxes. Then
> she notices Grace.)

NICOLETTE
Oh, hello, sorry, I didn't see you there. I'm
Nicolette, Larry's wife.

GRACE
I'm Grace. Also Larry's wife. The first one.

> (Nicolette walks over to
> Grace and the two women
> stare at each other.)

Take whatever you want. And make sure that
includes Larry.

                    NICOLETTE
He's all yours now. My lawyer will be in
touch about the boxes Larry.

                    (Nicolette leaves and Larry,
                    seemingly unfazed, walks into
                    the kitchen.)

            BLACKOUT

DAY 44

I DON'T. I can't. I'm not. I don't know what to do. I don't know what to write.

Here goes.

I lost my divorce virginity.

I'll start there. I had sex. This is what Maya has been encouraging me to do to push me out of my writer's block. She should be happy. I want her to be happy. Only I had sex with Elliot, so I doubt it'll count.

I finally told him he could stop by to talk about Marsden. I offered him a cup of tea, which he took. He asked about my appliances, about the play, about Maya. He wanted to know what I was reading and what I had seen recently, and he told me he had been invited to the opening night of the revival of *The Sisters Rosensweig*.

I've wanted to be a Rosensweig sister ever since I first saw the play when I was in my 20s. I particularly wanted to be Pfeni, because she is eccentric and changed her name from Penny to Pfeni and is a globe-trotting journalist with a bisexual boyfriend. And she has a sister named Gorgeous and a sister named Sara, and I am an only child who would have loved to have sisters with mellifluous names like Gorgeous and Sara. The sisters have interesting men flitting in and out of their lives, providing color and commentary while they clash and bond. Why the hell did Elliot get invited to the opening night instead of me?

We went into the TV room and sat on opposite ends of the couch. The platter of Trader Joe's spring rolls that I placed on the coffee table in front of us made sitting on the same couch feel manageable. They provided us with a task we could do while sitting and talking and gave us something to look at so we weren't forced to look at each other. Elliot was making idle conversation and we fell into the kind of back and forth that happens when people who actually like each other talk. Elliot is quick-witted and laughed, probably to flash his dimple. We started reminiscing about Sinatra when he was a puppy, that time when he ran away and we couldn't find him for two days, when my father and Lucy came to visit and Sinatra peed on Lucy's purse, and the time Marsden had the flu and Sinatra loyally slept by his side for a week, only leaving his bedroom to eat and for mandatory walks.

"He was so handsome," I said.

"Yes, I guess he was," said Elliot.

"You are too," I whispered.

"I heard that," he replied.

I could feel my face turning red, as if Elliot wasn't the man who left me for another woman, but was a new crush. What was I doing? I needed to stop whatever was happening and get to the point. "Let's talk about Marsden."

"Mrs. Yule has called a few times. She's concerned," he said.

"Are you?" I asked.

"I'm not terribly concerned, but I figured you were," he said.

He was right, of course. I told him that Marsden barely talks to me, that he seems to be high all the time, that he's directionless, and unmotivated, and that I am scared of further alienating him. I told him that I'm trying not to have expectations but it's hard when Maya's kids—hell, when every kid around—makes run-of-the-mill overachievers look like underachievers, leaving little room for the actual underachievers to shine. I complained about how much pressure there is to have the perfect kid, and how much I wished I was competing in that forum and throwing out names of schools like Amherst and Vassar and how upset I am because I will never get to tour those schools with Marsden because he's a lazy stoner, and I feel like a bad person and a bad mother admitting that I'm disappointed. And I started crying, while I was saying all of this, and Elliot moved across the couch and put his arm around me, and I fell into him. It felt so natural, so comfortable, so easy, until he started kissing my head. I thought about pushing him away and saying, "What the fuck are you doing asshole? We're divorced. Get out of my house!" But instead I let him kiss the top of my head and caress my neck and I held my breath as his hand moved down to my shoulder and across my clavicle, and under my shirt, which I purposely had left unbuttoned enough to tempt him but only so he'd feel regretful, and under my bra, and I exhaled and practically came at that moment when his hand touched my nipple.

I lifted my head to look at him.

"Is this okay?" he asked.

"NO!"

That's not what I said. I don't think I said anything.

He took off my shirt and kissed me. I undid his belt. He tasted the same as he used to. I always loved the way Elliot tasted. He was inside of me before I could stop myself from wanting him inside of me. We came at the same time. That rarely happened when we were married.

"Are you going to tell Midge about this?" I asked afterward.

"Probably not. Midge and I are having problems," he confided.

"I'm sorry to hear that," I said.

Why did I say that? I am thrilled they are having problems. Even if Elliot and I don't get back together. Did I just write that? We are *not* getting back together. I am not falling back in love with him. I am not letting him dick me around anymore. I will be the one in charge this time, and so what if I want them broken up, and so what if I am the cause of their breakup. Oh, sweet justice! I want her to be heartbroken. And even if they don't break up, I will not let him destroy me again. I shouldn't have slept with him. But since I did, I'm going to make sure it counts. Having sex with Elliot will get me over my writer's block.

DAY 45

SUE BROUGHT MOM home from the hospital yesterday with her new appendage, a portable oxygen tank that she's supposed to use whenever she goes out. Later in the day a large not-portable oxygen tank for home use was delivered. One day she falls. She thinks she's pushed. Her memory is sketchy, her oxygen low. A week later she is a person who will need oxygen pumped into her system for the rest of her life. I know she doesn't want to be that person. She wants to be the strikingly beautiful woman who turns heads when she walks into a room.

I was supposed to hire someone to stay with Mom overnight, but I didn't get around to it. Sue offered to stay with her, but I was worried Mom would start abusing her again, so I told her that if she could just do the daytimes that would be wonderful.

As soon as Sue left for the day, Mom called. She wanted to tell me about the two nice men who stopped by to drop off the oxygen tank and how they showed her and the lady who comes over how to use it. She invited them to stay for lunch, but the men were too busy. Mom managed to find out that one of them was single and she got his number for me, only she's not sure where she put it, but when she finds it, she'll give it to me. He was, according to Mom, very handsome.

"Thanks Mom, but I'm not dating now," I told her.

"Why not? Did you get married again?" she asked.

"No, I'm still divorced and still not married."

"What about me, am I married?"

"No, you're divorced too," I said.

"That's right. I was married to your father. How is your father? Do you think I should give him a call?"

Less than an hour later she called again to tell me she was watching *The Long, Hot Summer* starring a young Paul Newman. She wanted to know if I had ever seen the movie.

"I haven't."

"You should," she told me.

"Okay, I'll watch it when I can."

"It's on now," she said.

"I'll watch it now." I got off the phone and turned on Turner Classic Movies.

I was falling madly in love with Paul Newman when the phone next rang.

"Elise, I have to pee," she said. "I have these things stuck up my nose. I don't know what to do. Am I allowed to get up?"

"Take them out and go pee," I said.

We hung up and I returned to Paul Newman and felt connected to Mom in a way I don't think I ever had before. We were both in our bedrooms watching the same movie, no doubt falling in love with the same actor. I lifted my legs and bent my knees the way she does. I wanted to stop running from her. I realized I can be with her and feel strong feelings of love as long as I am 200 miles away from her.

Then she called back to say the oxygen tank was broken.

She found a phone number for emergencies and asked me to call it.

"I'll call during a commercial," I told her.

"Well, I might be dead by then," she said.

So I turned down the volume and spoke to a cheery woman who informed me there was an on/off button on the top of the machine that Mom should try pressing. I called Mom back to tell her about the button. The one she must have pressed to turn it off when she went to pee.

"I don't know how that got turned off, but it's working again," Mom said, and we hung up.

Two hours later, Aunt Rosemary called. She wanted me to know that she is a saint. "Someone should have explained to her how this thing works. We're lucky that I live a twenty-dollar cab ride away and don't mind schlepping out in the middle of the night."

Mom was yelling out in the background. "We're all set here, Elise. Your Aunt Rosemary figured it out. She's a genius."

"Your mother says I'm a genius."

"You are a genius Aunt Rosemary. I'll send you a check for the cab fare."

DAY 46

I CONVINCED MAYA to cut out of work early and come to Dedham for a walk. She showed up 25 minutes late because she had issues wrangling her three rescue dogs. Simon refused to get in the car. She couldn't coax or bribe him with treats and he's far too heavy to lift.

Simon, who is the newest to the group, has a glass eye, is the size of a pony, and is as stubborn as a mule. Quite a contrast to Harpo, the Corgi-German Shepherd mix, and even Jeanie, who is some sort of labra-rigamarole. When Maya talks about them as a group, she refers to them as "the rescue dogs." It doesn't matter that they've assimilated into their suburban lifestyle with plush dog beds and organic chewies, they will always be "the rescue dogs."

My walks with Maya are my sanity and the winding trails around the magnificent rocks of Wilson Mountain usually bolster my mood, but yesterday I was stressed out about having slept with Elliot and I was pissed at Maya for showing up late. Not only did I not tell her about Elliot, I lied to her about Marsden. I was feeling testy and competitive and annoyed. And now I feel regretful and ashamed. Why did I not confide in her?

Maya has been saving my ass since I met her—literally—in Terminal C at Logan Airport. I remember the moment we met. I felt a tap on my back. I turned around and this stunning woman on the short side of short said, "I'm sorry if this is inappropriate, but I thought you'd want to know that your skirt is tucked into your underwear." I reached back and felt my skirt wadded up and stuffed into my undies. "Oh my God, this is so embarrassing," I screeched, to apparently draw more attention to myself.

Maya said, in her raspy voice, "Don't worry, it happens to me all the time."

I could tell by looking at her that wasn't the case. She was luminescent, even in airport lighting.

A week later, I was in Trader Joe's and felt a tap on my back again. "Excuse me," said a woman who looked like she popped into the supermarket for a few healthy snacks on her way home from the gym, "Didn't we meet last week at the airport?" I instinctively reached back and to my ass—pants on. No wadded-up skirt stuck into saggy mom-undies this time.

We chatted in the chips aisle and figured out that our kids went to the same school and that she had done publicity work for a theater that had produced two of my plays. We exchanged phone numbers and got together the following week for coffee. We had people in common, favorite books and movies. We had endless things to talk about and became instant confidantes. It was friendship at first sight. That's a thing. I'm sure of it. I bet it happens more frequently, and can be more powerful, than love at first sight. Maya is my rock. She got me through Elliot's affair and my divorce and now she's pushing for full restoration, personal and professional. But for some reason I am resisting. I'm not only resisting; I'm finding that I'm getting annoyed with her. I don't know why.

Maya's one of the smartest people I know. She's got a photographic memory, but unlike a lot of people who have access to encyclopedic amounts of information, she isn't constantly letting you know all the things that you don't know. She knows you know what you don't know, and she never says, "I can't believe you didn't know that." She understands there are different types of intelligence, and she is equally game to gossip, play shrink, give unsolicited advice, as she is to discourse on 19th-century Russian playwrights.

She does brag about her kids though. She was telling me about their family dinner. That's another thing she does, she always calls it "family dinner." Why can't it just be dinner? Her *rescue dogs* are dogs and *family dinner* is dinner. I don't know why she feels the need to qualify everything, to sweeten the pot. Her pot is already so sweet. Sam and Marina, two of the most interesting, talkative, engaged teenagers I've ever met, cooked an authentic Medieval dinner—described as chicken with cameline sauce, venison in sorrel verjuice. I could practically taste the tart flavors mixed in with the ginger and cinnamon, and I kept saying, "This sounds amazing. They are amazing."

Marsden is not amazing. Not like that. And I want him to be. I want to see how it feels to not be the one with the struggling son, the failed marriage, the complicated mother, the otherwise involved father. I wish Marsden would regale me with his brilliant ideas about comprehensive immigration reform and tell me that he was thinking he'd like to study public policy in college.

I lied to Maya while we walked yesterday. I rationalized it to myself while we were walking. I'm a storyteller and storytellers tell stories, and that's what I was doing. But shouldn't I be a truthteller? Isn't that really the point of storytelling—to get to the truth?

I told her that Marsden and I had a family dinner together last night too, and I pronounced "family dinner" so slowly and loudly, it was as if I was talking to a non-English speaker. I told her that Marsden was talking again. That I couldn't get him to shut up.

The truth was that Marsden and I drove to Panera Bread, picked up sandwiches to go, and chowed them down on the car ride home. Our conversation didn't get beyond, "How's your sandwich?" "Good." "Mine's good too."

I blame the Kennedys for creating a family dinner crisis in America. The mythology that's developed around their dinners—those beautiful, brilliant, strong-jawed Kennedy kids debating geo-politics over dinner, as matriarch Rose and patriarch Joe peppered them with questions, has screwed up the very American ideal of dining alone. Aren't we supposed to be a country built on self-reliance and individualism? Shouldn't we promote eating alone in front of the TV or computer screen?

We used to have family dinners, but even back then they were fraught. We'd claim our seats at the table, always the same seats, and I struggled to create a conversation worthy of a Kennedy. Maybe these dinners were the first signs of Marsden's retreat into a petulant silence.

ME: Marsden, did you learn anything interesting at school today?

MARSDEN:

ELLIOT: Mom asked you a question. Did you learn anything interesting at school today?

MARSDEN:

ME: Marsden?

MARSDEN: Oh? What?

ME: Did you learn anything interesting at school today?

MARSDEN: Nup.

ME: Nothing? Really?

MARSDEN: It's school, Mom. We don't do a lot of learning. They just want you to think we do.

ME: Aren't any of your classes interesting?

MARSDEN: English is good, I guess.

ELLIOT: What spices did you put in the tomato sauce?

ME: I'm glad you like English. So, who here knows the name of the president of South Africa?

MARSDEN:

ELLIOT: Here's a hint. It's not Nelson Mandela anymore.

ME: Marsden, do you know who the president of South Africa currently is?

MARSDEN:

ELLIOT: Marsden, Mom asked about the president of South Africa?

ME: Marsden?

MARSDEN: What?

ELLIOT: Mom asked you a question.

MARSDEN: I know.

ME: About the president of South Africa.

MARSDEN: I told you.

ME: I didn't hear you.

MARSDEN: Maybe you should get your hearing checked.

ME: Marsden, do you know who the president of South Africa is?

MARSDEN: Why do you care so much about South Africa? Are you planning on moving there?

And so it went. Night after night. Me always asking about the president of South Africa. Marsden never looking it up. Never answering.

Our fraudulent family dinners were a metaphor for my fraudulent marriage. I hate that I lied to Maya. And right now, I hate doing these Morning Pages.

DAY 47

WHEN MARSDEN GOT home from school yesterday, he slipped into his room without saying a word. I knocked on his door, but he didn't answer, so I opened it, just slightly.

"What are you doing?" He sounded accusatory.

"I knocked but you didn't answer," I explained.

"I said, 'Don't come in.'"

"I didn't hear you." I opened the door all the way and stepped into his room with one foot. This was my approach to asserting parental authority while respecting his personal space. He was sprawled on his bed with headphones on and he seemed to be writing something.

"You didn't say hi to me when you got home from school," I said.

"Hi," he blurted out dutifully. "Are we done?"

"No, we're not done. I want us to have dinner together tonight, sitting down at the table."

"Why?'

"Because that's what families do," I said.

"Yeah, but that's not what we do."

"It's what we used to do."

"When I was like ten."

"That's not true, we had dinner together until Dad left."

"Okay."

"Okay, what?"

"Okay, we did."

"And I'd like us to have dinner together at the table tonight."

"I can't."

"Why not?" I was trying not to raise my voice. Marsden has accused me of yelling at him when I'm talking slightly louder than my normal decibel. He has told me to stop screaming at him when I've talked through clenched teeth. He inflates well-modulated anger into hysterical rage. I have never let him see hysterical rage because I know what that looks like, and I refuse to show him, but sometimes I think I should, just so he understands what it really means to yell and scream at someone. And so I knew exactly what my voice was doing when I said, "Why not?" I repeated. Curt and sharp, but not yelling.

"Stop yelling at me," he said.

"You can't accuse me of yelling at you whenever you don't like what I have to say."

"Can you leave my room?"

"No."

"Will you leave my room?"

"Good grammatical fix. But no, I won't. I want us to talk."

"Then I'll leave."

"You're not going anywhere," I said, then put my foot down, while simultaneously giving in. "Dinner is at 6:30. I want you seated at the kitchen table then. Now I'll go."

I closed the door to his bedroom and went to the kitchen to prep for dinner. I decided to make homemade chicken nuggets because he used to love chicken nuggets—he'd call them chicken snugglets—and I wanted to recreate something from his childhood that might inspire him to think about who he was and who he's turned into.

At 6:30 p.m. sharp, Marsden entered the kitchen, plopped down onto a chair, and started intently staring at something. I tried to discern what he was looking at, but there didn't seem to be an end point to his gaze. His look didn't appear to be that of a poet staring off into the abyss, a philosopher contemplating entropy, or a scientist wondering about the thermodynamics of the universe. I followed the path of his eyes, which, as far as I could tell, seemed to be settled on the corner of the couch. His gaze was that of a teenager temporarily trapped by his mother's prying eyes. I put dinner on the table and Marsden looked down at his plate.

MARSDEN: What's this?

ME: Isn't that fun! You used to love it when I made your food look like a face.

MARSDEN: Nice asparagus hair.

ME: Do you like it?

MARSDEN: Yeah.

ME: I know it's silly, but I was thinking about when you were little.

MARSDEN: Yeah.

ME: How are things? How's school going?

MARSDEN: Okay.

He opened his left hand and looked at something written on his palm.

MARSDEN: Jacob Zuma.

ME: Excuse me?

MARSDEN: Jacob Zuma is the president of South Africa.

ME: You wrote crib notes on your hand for dinner?

MARSDEN: I thought you might ask. You used to always ask.

ME: But that's cheating.

MARSDEN: Why?

ME: You can't have the answers written on your hand. You'll get expelled.

MARSDEN: From dinner?

ME: No, from school. Marsden, you don't cheat on your tests, do you?

MARSDEN: No, Mom.

ME: Are you sure?

MARSDEN: Yes.

ME: Because you shouldn't cheat.

MARSDEN: I know.

ME: Good. How do you like the chicken nuggets?

MARSDEN: They're good.

ME: You haven't eaten many. Are you sure you like them?

MARSDEN: I don't feel well.

ME: I wasn't criticizing.

MARSDEN: Okay.

ME: I'm sorry.

MARSDEN: I'm not hungry. Can I be done?

ME: But we haven't talked.

MARSDEN: What do you want to talk about?

ME: You.

MARSDEN: Okay.

ME: Is everything okay with you?

MARSDEN: I told you I don't feel well.

ME: I don't mean like that. I mean in general. I don't feel like things are okay.

MARSDEN: Maybe that's your problem, because I'm fine.

ME: Define fine.

MARSDEN: No Mom, I'm not going to define fine.

ME: Have you thought more about what you want to do next year?

MARSDEN: Yes.

ME: What are you thinking?

MARSDEN: Can I be excused?

ME: Right now?

MARSDEN: Is that okay?

ME: I guess.

MARSDEN: Thanks.

ME: You're welcome.

And that was my attempt at reinstating our family dinner. Just to confirm what I already knew: family dinners are not meant for any family that I'm a part of.

DAY 48

ELLIOT CALLED FIVE times yesterday. Mom called six times. Mrs. Yule called twice. The first time she called was because I forgot to call the school to tell them Marsden was staying home sick. The second time was because a teacher passed Tommy Kane in the hallway and noticed he smelled like pot and hauled him into the principal's office. At first Tommy denied he was high, but then he admitted it and played the "things are really messed up at home" card. They pressed him on who he was smoking with, and he told them Marsden because he knew Marsden was out sick—he was probably thinking he wouldn't get in trouble and figured his friends would applaud him for duping the dopes in charge with a few rounds of "Awesome Dude." I didn't smoke much when I was in high school, but when I did, at least I knew to chew on a piece of gum and splash myself with Jean Nate afterward. How is it that Marsden's sophisticated stoner friends don't carry around Listerine or something or other to cover the reek? Since Mrs. Yule is out for Marsden, she assumed Tommy was telling the truth and that he'd snuck out of school to meet Marsden in some suburban drug den. Mrs. Yule probably thinks I am the den mother who supplies pot and seduces susceptible teenagers.

"No, Mrs. Yule, I am not turning a blind eye and I will get you a doctor's note to prove it. Marsden is sick, like I told you before…. No, he's not getting high with Tommy Kane or anyone else…. Yes, I will get you a doctor's note….Yes, I understand what will happen if Marsden isn't really sick."

To be honest, I was terrified Tommy was telling the truth and confronted Marsden. He didn't answer when I knocked on his door, so I barged in, which I have been trained not to do, and found him curled up in his bed. I so wanted to hold him like I used to when he was a little boy and he'd let me wrap my body around his, but I didn't dare. Instead, I called out his name.

ME: (Whispering) Marsden. (Slightly louder) Marsden. (Normal voice) Marsden. (Yelling) MARSDEN!

MARSDEN: Hunh. What? WHAT!

ME: Mrs. Yule called.

MARSDEN: Who?

ME: Mrs. Yule. She said that Tommy Kane said he was smoking pot with you.

MARSDEN: What?

ME: Tommy got caught high and said he got stoned with you.

MARSDEN: What? How?

ME: I don't know, by smoking with you. Are you really sick?

MARSDEN: What the hell, Mom. Yes.

ME: Did you sneak out and meet Tommy?

MARSDEN: Can you leave?

ME: May I take your temperature?

MARSDEN: No!

ME: Why not?

MARSDEN: Because I'm not five years old.

ME: You're being accused of skipping school and getting high with Tommy.

MARSDEN: I'm sick.

ME: The school wants a doctor's note. I want to take your temperature.

MARSDEN: I can take my own temperature.

ME: I'm taking your temperature.

MARSDEN: No!

ME: Yes!

The two of us sat in silence listening to the slow methodical beep...beep...beep of the thermometer that would determine my son's fate. I reached over after the fast flurry of beeps to take the thermometer out of his mouth, but he got there first. He held onto the thermometer for a few breathless moments, and then handed it to me. I wondered, was this a sign of defeat or fevered confidence?

I stared at the numbers on the thermometer. 101.2. It was the thrill of winning a Tony Award.

ME: You're sick!

MARSDEN: I know.

I called Marsden's doctor. We missed the walk-in hours so I had to beg for a doctor's note. I told the receptionist that Marsden's entire future depended on a doctor's note and swore he had a fever. I told her we'd be happy to come in, but if she couldn't fit us in, we'd both be willing to take lie detector tests to prove he had a fever if we had to.

The phone rang all afternoon, but instead of being the distraction that it usually is, instead of pulling me away from writing, it was driving me deeper into my scene. It was like I was running a marathon, and the ringing phone was everyone cheering me on from the sidelines. All these people wanted something from me, and my withholding was giving me the creative drive I've been lacking.

> (LARRY walks out of Laurie's kitchen into the living room, smacking his lips, while eating a piece of quiche. GRACE is in the living room rearranging Laurie's things.)
>
> LARRY
> This isn't bad, Grace. You're a better cook than you used to be. You know, you're a better mother now than you used to be too.
>
> GRACE
> What does that mean?
>
> LARRY
> You're more relaxed. I couldn't stand the way you mothered. You were a smother, not a mother.
>
> GRACE
> That's clever, Larry. Did you come up with that yourself? The Dr. Seuss of slander. I'll be honest, Larry, mothering didn't come

naturally to me. It would have been nice to have your support rather than your contempt.

                    LARRY
Honestly, Grace, I wasn't equipped back then to do what I should have done.

                    GRACE
And what was that Larry? What should you have done?

                    LARRY
I should have gotten you some help. I should have been more available. But you.... You were impossible to be around. You were neurotic and suspicious of everyone.

                    GRACE
I knew you were going to leave me. I saw you eyeing the younger girls.

                    LARRY
Only to confirm what I already knew; they couldn't hold a candle to you. Grace, you had so much going for you, but you allowed your demons to take over. Why the hell did you teach her B is for Betrayal?

                    GRACE
I was angry and scared of the world. You could leave, but I was stuck with me.

                    (Larry looks at Grace up and
                    down and his tone softens.)

                    LARRY
I should have stuck with you. If I had been a real man, a real father, I would have stayed. You raised a great girl.

                    GRACE
We're lucky to have her. We're lucky she puts
up with us.

                    LARRY
Do you know why I've gotten married so
many times?

                    GRACE
You have a low tolerance for human frailty
and you're superficial.

                    LARRY
I wanted you, but the you without all your
issues. The truth is none of those marriages
lasted because I never loved any of them like
I loved you. I tried. I convinced myself that
I did. But I didn't.

                    GRACE
What are you saying, Larry?

                    LARRY
Grace, you were the love of my life. I just
couldn't stand you. It's a terrible burden
to despise the love of your life.

                    GRACE
Go to hell!

                    LARRY
I should.

                    GRACE
Should what?

                    LARRY
Go to hell.

                    GRACE
Don't start getting apologetic and reflective. It's too late and it doesn't become you.

LARRY

The first time I met you, I knew I wanted to take you to bed. I couldn't take my eyes off of you.

GRACE

I was dating your best friend. And you were dating someone he set you up with. What was her name?

LARRY

Sally Rushkin. We went on a double date. I was trying to pay attention to her, but all I cared about was what you had to say. I kept seeing Sally Rushkin so I could keep double dating with you. But then you broke up with Ben.

GRACE

Because you and I went to bed together.

LARRY

Ben didn't take that well. I didn't realize he'd be so upset about it.

GRACE

(Shaking her head and looking around at the boxes) It'll be nice for Laurie when things here are back to normal.

LARRY

Normal. What's normal? There is no normal. We should do away with the word normal. It's outlived its usefulness.... Do you still hate me, Grace?

GRACE

Not hate. More of long-simmering loathing.

LARRY

Gracie.

                    GRACE
Larry.

                    (Larry puts his hand over
                    his eyes and starts to cry.)

                    GRACE
Larry, stop that. Stop that immediately.

                    (Larry looks up at Grace.)

                    LARRY
How come you never remarried?

                    GRACE
You want to know why, Larry? You always said
I worried too much. You were brilliant and
charismatic and I was madly in love with
you, but I knew deep down it wouldn't last.
Only I let my guard down. And then you left.
But you didn't just leave. You flaunted your
fabulous freedom in front of me with one
woman, then another. Well, I didn't want it
to happen again.

                    LARRY
I'm sorry Gracie.

                    GRACE
You know what they say, fool me once, shame
on you. Fool me twice, shame on me. I wasn't
about to make that mistake again. I knew
you'd leave me, but I let myself stop worrying. What people don't realize is that there
are benefits to being a worrier. I always
found it odd that the non-worriers amongst
us are so worried about the worriers. There's
really nothing to worry about. They should
go on with their not worrying. We worriers
are just fine. Worrying is our way of adapt-

ing to the dangers around us. Not worrying is another way of adapting, but it's not the worrier's way. Have you ever noticed the only difference between the words *worrier* and *warrior* is two vowels? We worriers and worry warriors. We're on the frontlines: fighting the good battle against salmonella and E. coli, automobile accidents, tripping and slipping, rip tides, skin cancer, breast cancer, colon cancer, pancreatic cancer, and the rare forms of cancer that are difficult to detect and harder to treat. We're out there, worrying for the rest of you, about robbers and rapists, drug use and abuse, vitamin deficiencies, radiation from microwave ovens, children with short attention spans, global warming, the unemployment rate, whether the air traffic controllers have gotten enough sleep, lightning strikes, climate change, and nuclear weapons. We worry that husbands will cheat, pregnant daughters will miscarry, and marriages will end. We take this on for the rest of you to be free, to live in health and sickness, to be happy and suffer, to enjoy your life or to hate it, whatever your inclination, just don't worry about it. Leave that to us.

LARRY
Thank you for your service.

GRACE
You're welcome.

LARRY
You know Grace, you are the most interesting, exotic, and beautiful woman I've ever met.

GRACE
I used to be a catch.

LARRY

I wasn't talking about then. I'm talking about now. You were the love of my life. Every woman I was with after you I was with for one reason: I wanted you. I was trying to find you, only a version of you I could tolerate.

> (Larry stands up and walks over to the CD player and puts on music. He then walks over to Grace and puts out his hand.)

Dance with me.

GRACE

What are you doing?

LARRY

I'm asking you to dance with me.

GRACE

But. We can't.

LARRY

I still love you, Gracie. Let's forget all the other crap. Dance with me.

GRACE

(Sighing) Larry, you've lost your mind.

LARRY

Have I?

GRACE

I'm certain you have.

LARRY

Okay, so what if I have? Is that so bad?

GRACE
I'm not sure. I've despised you for the past
three decades. It's hard to let go of all
that well-fed hatred.

LARRY
I was a terrible husband to you.

GRACE
And an even worse ex.

LARRY
I wish I could do it again.

Bullshit
GRACE
You'd do it differently?

LARRY
Grace, dance with me. Please.

GRACE
Sit down Larry. Don't be an ass.

LARRY
I'll beg you if I have to. Grace, please. My
beautiful Gracie.

GRACE
Why are you doing this, Larry?

LARRY
One dance.

                    (Grace slowly gets up and
                    walks over to Larry. The
                    two of them start dancing
                    and continue dancing for up
                    to two minutes.)

LARRY
Would you mind if I kissed you?

                    GRACE
What are you saying?

                    LARRY
I'd like to start over again. I'd like to
kiss you, Grace.

                    BLACKOUT

DAY 49

YESTERDAY, THE PHONE rang hourly, like church bells, only not like church bells at all. Unlike the day before, each ring was an unwelcome interruption that jolted me out of my *Deja New* world and into a world that feels like it is trying to eat me alive. Mom called. Mom called again and again. Elliot's number came up twice on the caller ID. I don't want to talk to him. I don't want to discuss what happened, and I don't want to talk to him about Marsden like we used to talk about Marsden before we slept together. What's there to say anyway? Marsden is no longer talking to me. He still had a fever so he stayed home from school again. His door remained closed all day and as far as I know, he didn't leave his room. Not to eat, not to brush his teeth, not to go to the bathroom. I tiptoed by his room every few hours and listened to the silent anger pouring out of it. Finally, last night I knocked on his door until he said, "Whaaa?" I often joke about Marsden's monosyllabism. I shouldn't have joked. I prefer the monosyllabic words to the grunts.

ME: How are you feeling, honey?

MARSDEN: Unh.

ME: Do you want some soup?

MARSDEN: Nuh.

ME: Tea?

MARSDEN: Nuh.

Marsden's remoteness is making me think about how young I was when I started pulling away from Mom. Marsden started shutting me out five years ago. I've been shutting Mom out since I was eight. That's four decades of punishing her. She doesn't deserve four decades.

She deserves two decades. I should have started punishing her later in life.

To make up for my selfish behavior, I answered the phone every time she called yesterday.

"Elise, is this you?" she said each time I picked up.

"Of course it is." I tried not to sound irritated. I was going for chipper. "How are you today, Mom?"

Our conversations started promisingly enough.

But then:

MOM: Elise, I don't want that fat bitch coming into my house anymore.

ME: Mom, I don't know who you're talking about. Sue is not fat and she's not a bitch, so it can't be her.

MOM: I'm talking about that thing you send over every day. She's not welcome here anymore.

ME: Mom, Sue is helping you.

MOM: I'm not letting her in again. I hope she dies.

ME: Mom, don't say that. You shouldn't say that about people. Especially not about Sue.

MOM: Okay, I don't hope she dies. I hope she gets shingles. Or herpes.

ME: She's just trying to help you out. You should be grateful.

MOM: I don't want to be grateful. I want to be alone.

Mom's rage crept toward paranoia and by last night, she was accusing Sue of stealing her *Madame Bovary*. Everyone wants Mom's *Madame Bovary*.

DAY 50

LAST NIGHT, I had a terrible sex dream. I was married to Elliot but I was having bad sex with Stu? Why was I having bad sex with my best friend's husband? I must subconsciously want to betray her. Consciously, the idea makes me sick. Nauseatingly sick! And I'm not being overly dramatic or hyperbolic—I woke up feeling like I might puke. My subconscious and conscious are so incompatible it's amazing they reside in the same hemisphere, much less the same head. Maybe Maya's obsession with my divorce virginity led me to sleep with Elliot and I am punishing her in my subconscious by sleeping with her husband. Or maybe I feel guilty that I haven't told her that Elliot and I had sex. Or maybe I'm seeking subconscious revenge because she hasn't been returning my calls. Why is she blowing me off? Why now? I have two weeks until my deadline. I can't deal with another distraction. All I know is my nocturnal betrayal feels like a real betrayal and this isn't who I am or what I do. Except it is, since I just had what felt like very real and very bad sex with Stu.

He kept yelling at me, "This is the worst sex I've ever had." And I kept trying to make it better, but I couldn't. I pushed my pelvis into him and asked, "Is this better? Is it good now?" I couldn't figure out what to do with my legs. Should I wrap them around him? My legs felt like two long vaginal appendages that were overcomplicating everything, so I tried to give him a blow job, but I couldn't find his penis, and every time I thought I captured it in my mouth, it was gone. I was snapping around like a little Pac-Man. It all felt so real. My body is tingling and my breath smells bad. I think I have bad sex dream breath.

I was still married to Elliot in the dream. Was that wish fulfillment? No. I was betraying him too. I like the idea of betraying Elliot. I never once cheated on Elliot, not even in my sleep. He cheated on me. Then he cheated on the woman with whom he cheated on me. He deserves to be cheated on, even if it's dream-cheating.

DAY 51

YESTERDAY I BAKED a batch of lemon squares and dropped them off on Maya's front porch with a note:

> Haven't spoken to you in a while. Can't wait to tell you about the weirdest sex dream I had last night. Stu was in it. Let's walk. I miss you!
>
> 🤍 Elise

I kept my phone close to me, waiting for Maya to call. I checked my email incessantly looking for her name to pop up in my inbox. I drove back to her house to grab my note before she saw it. Or Stu saw it. I can't imagine what led me to tell her about my sex dream in a note. I was panicking. Thinking about how I can't even write a note to a friend without humiliating myself. I was too late. The lemon squares and the note weren't on the deck. I drove home crying.

At least my angst was productive. Yesterday I did some of the best writing I've done in weeks. I was digging into the tensions between Laurie and her parents—so much of what people think about gets left unsaid and the things that are said probably shouldn't be said.

I was writing with a kind of distracted fury. The phone didn't stop ringing and each time it rang, I jumped up to see if it was Maya calling. It never was. Mom called three times.

Elliot called once. Sue called twice. Aunt Rosemary called once. And Sammy Ronstein called.

"Checking in, Elise. When will you be sending the play over?"

I felt like a spurned lover. I kept telling myself, *She's got a busy life. She'll get a kick out of the sex dream. Maya gets it.* But what if she doesn't. Why hasn't she called?

For a while, I distracted myself by looking up quotes about maternal love. The best one was credited to a serial killer.

"I miss my dog more than I miss my mother. Dogs offer unconditional and nonjudgmental love. Mothers don't."

I hope I'm sad enough when Mom dies. I hope I am sadder than I was when Sinatra died. She did the best she could. Isn't that what I'm supposed to say? I have never lacked for clothes or fresh food. I grew up in a beautiful apartment. Sure, she tried. But was that the best she could do? In spite of her constant screaming and blistering temper, I know Mom loves me unconditionally. Well, unconditionally with conditions. And about her rages, even when they were directed at me, they were never really about me. They were about her unhappiness. She has never physically hurt me. She spent 48 hours in labor with me. I should be grateful. She was sliced open for me, and yet I was embarrassed when she wore a bikini with all her scars on display. The scars that were there because of me. I begged her to cover up, to wear a one-piece, to pretend she didn't know me. I hated those scars. Selfish child. I wouldn't be alive were it not for those scars.

Dad once said to me, "I don't know what I was thinking marrying your mother. Worst mistake of my life." I felt sympathy for him and blamed Mom for his bad behavior. Maybe Mom isn't the monster I've made her out to be. She is frail and forgetful. I think I need to recalibrate and think of her temper

as a tic, or a disease. I shouldn't judge her for having a disease.
Rage flu. Cantankerous cancer. Hemorrhoids of hate. Scream
seizures. She is sick. I will be there to take care of her.

I'll call Maya this morning. Or maybe I should give her
space. I don't want to be that hovering friend who has sex
dreams about her husband. Maybe we both need space.

DAY 52

SUE IS LEAVING. It's a title for a play. *Sue Is Leaving*. The play takes place over the course of an eight-hour day and is based on actual events.

Scene 1:

Late morning.

Int. a two-bedroom apartment in New York City's Upper West Side. MOM, an 81-year-old aging beauty wearing a light blue stained cotton nightgown, is sitting in a chair next to a large oxygen tank is. SUE, an attractive woman in her mid-30s or 40s, is standing a few feet from Mom and talking into a phone. Downstage right, ELISE (48) has a pen in her hand and gesticulates excessively when she talks. On a table next to Elise is a computer. Behind the computer is wall covered with different colored stickie notes.

SUE: (Holding the phone) Elise, I'm sorry to bother you. Your mother is having a difficult day. She's very angry and she's trying to fire me.

ELISE: She can't fire you.

SUE: She's insisting I leave her apartment. She accused me of stealing from her. I tried to calm her down, but she threw a vase at me and called me a—I'm sorry, I'm not comfortable repeating those words.

ELISE: Yes, I understand. Are you okay? Can I talk to her?

SUE: If you could calm her down, that would be helpful. (To Mom) Mrs. Hellman. I'm on the phone with Elise. She'd like to talk to you.

MOM: I didn't give you permission to call my daughter. Give me the phone. (Under her breath) Fucking cunt. Elise, is this you? Hi, darling, how are you? I miss hearing your voice.

ELISE: Mom, why are you talking that way to Sue?

MOM: I don't want her here. I didn't invite her over. She's trying to take over my life. I want her to leave.

ELISE: But you were getting along with her so well.

MOM: I was faking it. We weren't really getting along. I was pretending to get along with her for you. Everything I do is for you, Elise. But I can't do it any longer. The bitch is stealing from me and I don't want to see her again.

ELISE: You need her help. And don't call her names.

MOM: I'm fine by myself. I don't like people in my apartment. Except for you. But you never come visit anymore.

ELISE: I was just there and you're not fine by yourself. You can't even figure out your oxygen. You need to use the oxygen.

MOM: Will I die if I don't use it?

ELISE: You might.

MOM: Good. I'd rather die than have this person in my apartment. She bothers me.

ELISE: Sue doesn't bother you.

MOM: You're not here. You don't know what goes on.

ELISE: Sue is fantastic. She is one of the most fantastic people who has ever lived.

MOM: She's stealing from me.

ELISE: She's not stealing from you.

MOM: My *Madame Bovary* is gone. It was a first edition and is extremely valuable. Elise, I have to pee.

ELISE: Please be nice to her and don't fire her. Do it for me, Mom. Please.

MOM: Fine. She can stay. I'll do this for you. Good-bye darling.

Later in the day. The afternoon light throws an orange glow over the room.

SUE: (Phone in hand) Hi Elise, it's been a bad day. Your mother can be terribly mean.

ELISE: I know. I grew up with her.

SUE: I'm afraid I'm not going to be able to work here any longer. I don't say this lightly, but I think your mom may be the cruelest person I've ever met.

ELISE: Well, yes, she's difficult, but I'm sure you've met people who are worse. Weren't the kids in your middle school worse than my mother?

SUE: Can I confide in you as a friend?

ELISE: Sure. I was hoping we'd become friends. If you stay, I think we would become friends. So go ahead.

SUE: There's something about your mother. She can be kind and wonderful and her life stories are fascinating, and you start to think that she really likes you, but then she snaps. It can come out of nowhere. And she says things. Elderly people often lash out, and I'm a professional and understand that, but it's different with your mom. No one has ever gotten under my skin like she does. I've gone home and cried because of the things she's said. I'm having trouble sleeping. She's the first client I've worked with who has affected me like this. I'm sorry to leave you in a lurch, it's just that—

ELISE: Please don't quit. I really need you. I'm on an important deadline. Just stay for another two weeks. Please!

SUE: I'm sorry Elise. I hate to put you in this position. But I'm not going to be able to stay.

ELISE: But I don't know what to do. I'm on deadline. I need you. Please, Sue. Just two weeks. You're supposed to give two weeks' notice.

SUE: I can't be with her anymore. It's bad for my health. I think you should come down to the city tomorrow.

Blackout.

DAY 53

DURING MY DRIVE to the city, I started pounding on the steering wheel and cursing the highway. The traffic felt like a bad metaphor for my life. I was near tears while creeping along in a snarl of cars. Driving past the severely mangled minivan that caused the traffic jam, I could no longer hold them back. Cars started moving again, accelerating past the accident scene, trying to make up for their lost time. It all seemed so inhumane, and I was part of the inhumanity because I wasn't sure if I was crying for the wrecked lives on the side of the road or for the inconveniences in my own life? I didn't know and I hated myself for not knowing.

I arrived at Mom's with a splotchy face and red eyes, and naturally, the handsome man in the elevator was waiting for me. Waiting for me. It does sometimes seem that way.

HANDSOME ELEVATOR MAN: Are you okay?

ME: My mother's aide quit. The drive to the city was harrowing.

HANDSOME ELEVATOR MAN: I'm sorry to hear that. Let me know if there's anything I can do. I'm no James Taylor, but please know that you've got a friend.

Does he want me to close my eyes and think of him? Like in the song? Because I do.

Clumsy. I'm so clumsy. When the elevator door opened and I stepped out my left foot got lodged behind my right ankle and I tumbled over myself and landed on my knees, half in the elevator and half in the hallway. I was scrambling to get up before the elevator door closed on me when I felt Handsome Elevator Man's embrace. No, wrong word—it wasn't an embrace. He bent down and, with what I will call a warm and tender touch, helped me up.

"Why won't you just kiss me?" the me who isn't me asked. The me who is me said, "Just checking the view from down here. Not much to see. Thanks for the lift."

I can't tell if my flirtometer is calibrated wrong. Have I misread authentic kindness and compassion for flirting? I gathered myself together and unlocked the door to Mom's apartment. Sue was sitting at the kitchen table waiting for me. "I'm sorry to leave you in a lurch," she said.

I told her I understood and wished her well and she left without saying good-bye to Mom.

I walked into Mom's bedroom and tried for calm, even though I was furious.

ME: Hi Mom, I just got to the city.

MOM: I can't talk to you right now Elise, I'm busy.

ME: I wanted to say hello.

MOM: I'm watching *Laura*. It's one of the greatest films ever made. Sit down and watch with me.

ME: I'm not in the mood for watching. I just had a long drive.

MOM: Can you come back later then?

I left Mom watching *Laura* and wandered around the apartment. The oxygen tank was in the living room, sitting unused. I opened the fridge. It was stuffed with food. Sue must have done a big shopping trip before she left. I searched Mom's bookshelves for some kind of enlightenment or at least the missing *Madame Bovary*. Mom's bookshelf is not organized by an obvious or consistent driving principal. Biographies are together with biographies, but not necessarily alphabetically. I think she may have shelved them as one might decide a seating arrangement for a dinner party. Who will get along? Who would like to meet? Diane Arbus, Eva Braun, Anaïs Nin, and Zelda Fitzgerald— perhaps for a ladies' night out. She has Charles Darwin rubbing up against Marylin Monroe. She was setting them up no doubt. Philip Roth is with Jacqueline Suzanne. Nabokov's *Lolita* is next to L. Frank Baum's *The Wonderful Wizard of Oz*—what if Dorothy and Lolita went to school together? The way her books are shelved is provocative and outrageous and curious. I can't count the hours I've spent staring at her bookshelf, but I'm sure I've spent far more time gazing at, admiring, admonishing, and analyzing her book arrangement than I have spent looking at any painting in a museum.

When Mom finally emerged from her bedroom, I could hear her walking deliberately and slowly toward the kitchen. She used to walk faster. The hallway from her bedroom to the kitchen has become a journey. I waited. She opened the door to the fridge. I could hear her standing in front of the fridge chewing and called out to her from the living room.

ME: Hi Mom.

MOM: Elise, is that you?

She was eating a slice of bread, chewing loudly while she walked into the living room. She sat down on the couch, away from the oxygen. I moved the tank closer and held the tubing out for her.

MOM: I don't want to use it.

ME: You have to use it.

MOM: I didn't know you were coming to the city. I was watching *Laura*. It's one of the greatest films ever made. Have you ever seen it?

ME: I don't think so.

MOM: We all wanted to be Gene Tierney. Did you know your Aunt Rosemary and I got our noses fixed on the same day? We wanted to be actresses.

ME: Aunt Rosemary is an actress.

MOM: Aunt Rosemary isn't a real actress, Gene Tierney was a real actress. Gene Tierney had raw talent. Aunt Rosemary has a good nose, but no talent.

ME: I think you're being too critical.

MOM: You have talent. You are a talented playwright.

ME: Thank you. Will you please start using your oxygen now?

She delicately picked up the cannula, handling it like a strand of pearls, and inserted the little nibs in her nose. She looked at me with watery eyes. She sat slouched on the couch next to the oxygen machine in her stained nightshirt. How is it that she is still so beautiful? My mother gets under your skin, with her needy love, her venomous rage, her lip-smacking snacking, and her haunting beauty.

DAY 54

MOM WANTS TO move. She claims she's been thinking about it for a while and came up with what she called "a sensational plan for the rest of my life. You know, I'm eighty-one, Elise. I probably only have about five years left. I have to make the most of them. I'm lonely here," she said.

She told me that Monique moved to an assisted living community in Massachusetts and is deliriously happy there. "I've known Monique since we were in high school," she said. "That's over sixty years. Can you imagine? Monique always finds the most interesting people in the room to talk to. You knew if someone was friends with her, you'd want to be friends with them too. I asked if the people living there were a bunch of old dullards and she assured me that they were very interesting. The place is packed with retired college professors and Monique says she's going to talks all the time and learning Russian with a former KGB agent who defected to the United States in the seventies." Mom closed her eyes and seemed to retreat into her thoughts. I wanted to ask if she was thinking about high school with Monique, but I also wanted to let her have those memoires if she was, so I didn't say anything. When she opened her eyes, she looked at me and said, "Massachusetts sounds like a wonderful state. Have you ever been there?"

"Yes, Mom, I live in Massachusetts."

"Of course you do. I don't know where my memory is going these days. I must be getting old. By the way, Elise, I've decided I'm selling the apartment. I'll need money to move. I called a realtor."

"How did you find a realtor?"

"I don't remember. I think someone told me about them. Maybe your Aunt Rosemary. I think it was Rosemary. I want to sell this place as soon as possible. I'm not getting any younger."

"None of us are."

"Yes, but I feel like I am getting older faster than I used to."

I picture Mom as a rock, cursing as she rolls down the side of a cliff—she starts tentatively, but picks up speed until she can't be seen, only heard. Screaming. Swearing.

"I think you should find a place to go before you start calling realtors," I said.

"What I do with my apartment is none of your business," Mom replied. Of course she was right. But she was also wrong.

"I'm just saying that you shouldn't sell the apartment until you know where you're going."

I could see the future. She'd sell her apartment and have nowhere to go. She'd have to move in with me. After Mom moves in, Lucy will finally get fed up with Dad and kick him out, and he'll have nowhere to go and he'll have to move in with me. And then I'll be a single, middle-aged woman with both my parents living with me in a prime example of life imitating art. Only there will be no art, because I will never have finished *Deja New* because I'm too busy dealing with all this shit and don't have time to write.

"Let's find a place for you to go before you sell the apartment," I pleaded.

"Elise, you're being a pain in the ass. This is my apartment and I'll do what I want with it," she insisted.

Until she got it all switched around and became paranoid.

"Elise, are you trying to get me to move out, so you can have my apartment? Is that what you want, to stick me in a home so you can take my apartment?"

"No." I assured her I was very happy living in my own home and that I had no intention of moving back to New York.

"Then why are you forcing me to leave?"

"You're the one who said you wanted to sell the apartment as soon as possible. I am suggesting that you don't act rashly."

"I was?"

"Yes, you were, Mom."

I could tell she was thinking. Probing her brain. Connecting the missing dots.

"I think I should go visit Monique first. I'm going to go call her and tell her I'm coming for a visit."

It was during this conversation that Monique told Mom that she has a boyfriend. A man named Chester, or something like Chester. I couldn't hear what she was saying, and I didn't know if she said he's a nice man named Chester or a nice man with chest hair.

"They're all fucking. Everyone is having sex there," Mom said gleefully when she hung up.

I didn't respond. Or maybe I gasped.

"Don't be such a prude, Elise. I want to move there. I don't need to visit."

DAY 55

MONIQUE CHANGED HER mind. She doesn't want Mom to move there. She scolded Mom for calling her too many times yesterday and told her that she's feeling smothered. She also told her she never wants to see Mom again and that Mom's not welcome there. She said the place she's living in is extremely exclusive and hard to get into and they wouldn't even accept Mom. I didn't realize the admissions process was so competitive, but I think if they accepted that jackass Monique, they'd surely accept Mom.

"Fuck Monique," I said.

"Fuck Monique," Mom agreed.

I spent the afternoon researching independent living, assisted living, lifecare living, Eden alternatives, and the very many euphemistic gradations of what could be called last-stop housing. Most of the places I found have names that make them sound more like day spas than nursing homes. Atria. Avita. Sunrise View. The Esplanade. Many of them are situated on scenic campuses, and offer cultural opportunities—concerts, movies, lectures, art classes. You can dine in elegance and get rowdy at game night. You'll age with a smile and take exercise classes, or swim in the pool, and still have quiet moments for alone time, often on a bench near a stream, to relax and reflect. But not about death. And no one is screaming obscenities, which may be a problem for Mom. These places look like colleges for the geriatric set, only instead of going to graduate school, you graduate to a nursing home, and instead of earning a PhD, you leave with your RIP.

When I was a kid, I had to walk past a nursing home on my way to and from school. The old people didn't talk, they sat in wheelchairs that were pushed up against the side of a building. They had sunken faces, collapsed mouths, and defeated necks. There was one lady whose eyeball was no longer engaged in the socket and it rested on her cheek instead. I had a daily ritual of passing by the almost dead, slumped like spineless vertebrates spackled onto their wheelchairs. I knew the old people weren't being treated the way they should be, but it wasn't until the *New York Times* wrote an exposé about abuse in the city's nursing homes that the adults on my street took notice and the nursing home got shut down. That was the first time I recognized that grownups see the same things as kids but don't look at them in the same way. The adults turned their heads away from the old lady with the eye on her face. We kids turned toward it, to stare and be frightened by it, to make up stories, to feed our nightmares. The adults accepted the senescent souls wilting in their wheelchairs as part of the city's stench and decay until the *New York Times* woke them up.

Nursing homes have gone upscale since then. I particularly liked the looks of the Avita in Connecticut and decided to call. I spoke to a woman named Eleanor, who asked me a few questions about Mom and listened patiently as I gave her far more information than she could have possibly wanted. Eleanor was very gracious, and said, "Sure, sure," just the right number of times for me to know she was listening. Unfortunately, Eleanor said that at the moment there weren't any available residencies at Avita, but that Mom should come for a tour and apply to get on the waiting list. I asked her when they were expecting availabilities and she said she couldn't be sure, so I asked her if somebody had to die before there were availabilities, and she said that was often the case, and I thought about asking her how many of their residents currently seemed to be homing in on death, but even I, the person who has a reputation for saying the wrong thing, knew better.

I'm worried that getting into assisted living has gotten too competitive. It's like getting into college, everything is so competitive these days. And I don't really know where to start. Do I call all the Atrias and Avitas and Sunrise Villages and get Mom waitlisted? Will she have to visit and tour? How would she possibly do that? I would need to go with her. I don't have time to start touring assisted living homes, I'm on deadline. Why don't I have siblings? Now is the time a sibling would be very helpful. How am I supposed to figure this out, finish a play, and fend off Mrs. Yule? At least Marsden has a guidance counselor. I wonder if they have guidance counselors for people interested in moving to assisted living? If I could find a guidance counselor for Mom, that would be helpful. Although honestly, Mrs. Yule makes it clear that she'd rather be working with the top kids in the class. She's one of those guidance counselors who only wants to guide the kids who don't need guidance.

DAY 56

I WONDER IF people are born with one defining trait—one powerful aspect of their still undeveloped personality that will drive who they become. If the other parts of their personality adhere themselves to the powerful trait along the way. If all the many traits that make us who we are, the parts that make sense together, and the parts that seem like inconsistencies, position themselves to that one driving trait and react to it, like a chemical compound, by becoming stronger or weaker in its presence. What if Mom's powerful trait was her rage? Gram used to say that Mom came out screaming and never stopped. All the other parts of her had to find a place to settle in with all that anger. Mom tells me that when she was pregnant, I didn't want to come out. When she went into labor, I stalled and refused to finish the job. The doctor had to finish it for me, and I was born by Caesarian section. Caesarian section—what in the world did Caesar have to do with women having babies? It occurs to me that my defining trait, since birth, might be my resistance to finishing things. If I didn't even have it in me to finish being born, how am I going to finish this play?

For my fifth-grade science project, I constructed a volcano out of clay, but I never put in the lava. My volcano didn't puff smoke or spew lava, for no reason other than I didn't finish it. A volcano without smoke and lava is like a brain without thoughts. How many books have I started reading and not finished? How many meals have I taken out of the oven before they had finished cooking? How many jars have I put the lid back on but not twisted closed? How many thank you notes have I written but never sent? If I go through the exercise of writing a thank you note, why can't I be bothered to get it into an envelope and address and send it? Because I don't finish things.

The only thing I consistently finish is the laundry. It's not that I fold my clothes all the time, but there's something about doing the laundry. Sure, I complained about it when Marsden got head lice. But that was boot camp. Pillowcases—clean! Sheets—clean! Clothes—clean! Now start again! It felt like a Sisyphean task, but then, when the daily loads finally ended, I felt empty. I missed doing laundry. It nourished me. It made me feel like a productive person.

I wouldn't want to be a 1950s laundress with an impossibly tiny waist, perfectly applied lipstick, and a new Maytag. I don't want to be waiting idly, with my lips puckered, and my hair sprayed to perfection, for my washing machine to break down so the Maytag repairman can come over. If I had created the Maytag Man, I would have cast him differently. Why did they make this elusive figure so milk toast? Maytag lost an opportunity to create some serious dramatic tension. He's a mythic figure and could have been more like the Marlboro Man—strong, bronzed, swaggering, and benevolent. Or slightly deranged. He has dark circles under his eyes and is temperamental. He probably has shit-stained underwear, even though he has a working washing machine. It's his little rebellion.

I want to be the kind of laundress who has a slightly awkward repairman with an encyclopedic knowledge of how machines work, not just washing machines, but all machines, and he'll come weekly to repair my overpriced, but poorly engineered, washing machine. And then we'll have sex on top of it. And it won't be my tiny waist that seduces him. I will be more like the hunched laundress from the Honoré Daumier painting. My forearms will be formidable. Or I'll be Picasso's woman ironing—sensual, penetrating, with an alluring androgyny. My repairman is turned on by the scent of a true laundress. I'd like to legitimately lose my divorce virginity with my Maytag Man. It would be sweet retribution if the ex-wife of the man who created the Appliance Alliance had sex for the first time since her divorce on the appliance that was chosen specifically for her with a man who was not. This probably will never happen, but I can write about it in a play that will no doubt never get finished.

I did finish my divorce. That was completed. And I wrote 11 plays—more than 11—but 11 that had full productions: five of them were off-Broadway, two have had multiple regional productions. Maybe I can finish things, and my defining trait is that I have a finishing complex. I am a finisher who doesn't believe I can finish things, which means I walk around with my shirt half-tucked in, my belt is buckled but my fly is unzipped.

(LAURIE and GRANVILLE have gone somewhere scenic for a long weekend. They are sitting on Adirondack chairs or recliners, but do not look terribly relaxed, in spite of the breathtaking view of a glistening lake-scenic vista can be projected on a large screen behind them. Granny is looking at Laurie, who is looking out over the audience as if she's looking for something.)

                    GRANVILLE
What are your thoughts on dinner? Maybe that
cool looking Italian restaurant?

                     LAURIE
Okay.

                    GRANVILLE
Or that funky diner we walked by?

                     LAURIE
I guess-

                    GRANVILLE
What are you looking at?

                     LAURIE
Nothing really. It's beautiful here. I was
just thinking.

                    GRANVILLE
About your parents? Will you look at me?

               (Laurie turns to Granville.)

                     LAURIE
You know. I'm just—

                    GRANVILLE
I know you're just. You haven't stopped
talking about them.

                     LAURIE
I'm sorry. I keep thinking...I don't know,
with them at the house...It's bringing up
all this stuff for me. I feel like—

                    GRANVILLE
We've been here for almost two days.

LAURIE

I know. But I didn't realize leaving Tom and Jerry alone would be so stressful.

GRANVILLE

They'll be fine.

LAURIE

Granny, your parents are still in love with each other. I don't think you can understand what it's like to have parents who actively despise each other. They've tried destruction by lawsuit and character assassination. They tried the I-can't-hear-you-I-can't-see-you-you're-dead-to-me thing. That didn't last long though, because it deprived my father of the joy of incessantly telling my mother that he'd be legitimately dead if he hadn't left her.

GRANVILLE

Laurie, you don't have to play diplomat to your warring parents. You don't have to be the one to broker a peace deal. And you don't have to play the role of little girl who wants her parents to get along, and I don't know, maybe even back together again. Whatever hold they have over you, you can break free from it. In fact, I am offering you my help to do so.

LAURIE

I just wish they would stop fighting, and, I don't know, maybe pay some attention to me for once.

GRANVILLE

I understand that. (Pause.) Kind of. (Pause.) Maybe I don't. I don't understand it actually. Just let it go.

                    LAURIE
Okay. I'll let it go.

                    GRANVILLE
It's beautiful here.
(Laurie looks out over the audience. She
wants Granny to think she's taking in the
natural beauty of the place.)

                    LAURIE
Look, swans! Have I told you that I love the
name MatchIT? I'm excited for you. Maybe
what people really need to feel content is to
be truly compatible with their stuff. I know
I'll be using MatchIT Style to help me find
the right clothes for different occasions.

            (Granville stands up.)

                    GRANVILLE
I don't want to talk about work. Let's do
something.

                    LAURIE
Okay. But I want you to know that I think
you're onto something big. What do you
want to do?

                    GRANVILLE
I think we need to hang out and be like we
used to. I feel like I can't even talk to
you anymore. Let's talk like regular people
talk. Like old friends talk.

                    LAURIE
That sounds good.

                    GRANVILLE
So....

(Laurie looks out into the
audience.)

LAURIE

Do you think it's going to rain?

GRANVILLE

I don't want to talk about the weather. (Pause)
Shit. Have we already run out of things to
talk about? The kids haven't even been born
yet and we have nothing left to talk about.
I guess if we get married, at least we've got
a jump start on all those empty nesters with
nothing left to talk about.

needs more
starters +
stoppers

LAURIE

Okay. How about this? Did you know that something like twenty percent of marriages end up
sexless? So if we do go ahead with this and

show
tension

get married, we've already taken care of the
sexless part of our relationship, and maybe

Body
Language.

we'll have great sex for the rest of our lives.

GRANVILLE

Now you're taking. This is the kind of conversation I'd be delighted to engage in.
Shall we get started?

(Granville walks over to
Laurie and pulls her up
from her chair. They start
to kiss, but then Laurie
steps back.)

LAURIE

I'm sorry. I can't stop thinking about them.
What if they're saying terrible things to
each other?

                    GRANVILLE
So what if they are? They're adults. They can
take care of themselves.

                    LAURIE
I know. But they're in my house.

                    GRANVILLE
And?

                    LAURIE
I feel bad about them fighting when they're
in my house.

                    GRANVILLE
Would you care if they were fighting if they
were somewhere else?

                    LAURIE
I think that would be okay. I'm used to that.
But I want them to get along if they're in my
space and I know that's not going to happen.
My father will say something that will set
my mother off, and then she'll say something
that he'll mock, and then he'll do something
hideously passive aggressive, and then she'll
scream at him, and then he'll shut down and
refuse to engage or do something even worse
which I don't want to contemplate.

                    GRANVILLE
Can you try not thinking about them?

                    LAURIE
You're not being terribly understanding.
This is real for me.

                    GRANVILLE
I get that. But you're forty years old and
we went away for a long weekend to be alone.
And we were just getting started with the

fun stuff. But we're not here alone at all. Your parents have been here hovering over us since we arrived.

LAURIE

I know. I'm sorry. (Her voice cracking) I want to be with them.

GRANVILLE

What?

LAURIE

I miss them. I want to go home.

GRANVILLE

We have this place for another night.

LAURIE

I know. I don't care. I'm sorry. I want to go home. Can we leave? Please.

BLACKOUT

DAY 57

THIS MAY BE a mistake. How is it not a mistake? I should have taken Aunt Rosemary up on her offer. Why didn't I say yes?

It was the *finally*.

She got me with the *finally*.

"I'm finally going to see my grandson."

I wanted to say, "Actually, Mom, maybe you should stay in New York. Aunt Rosemary said she'd be delighted to stay over for a night with her big sister."

But instead I said, "What do you mean by *finally*?"

"You're always trying to keep me away from my grandson. You don't want me in his life."

"That's ridiculous."

"You don't trust me."

"You taught him the word 'fuck' when he was five."

"Is that what you think? I wouldn't teach a child to curse. He's very bright and picked it up on his own."

"And you taught him the C-word when he was in second grade. He said it at school. At least none of the other kids knew it was a bad word, but his teacher went ballistic."

"What C-word?"

"Mom, you know what C-word."

"For God sake's Elise, say it. Say 'cunt.' It won't kill you."

319

"I don't want to say it. And I don't want you saying it in front of Marsden.

"I won't say anything to him. I won't say a word. I will remain silent."

"You're not going to talk to him?"

"You'll be angry with me if I do."

"That's not true."

"I'm just glad that I finally get to see my grandson."

And that's how the conversation went. I don't know how I'm going to find time to write in the next few days. My deadline is beginning to feel like hot lava coming at me. These Morning Pages are a waste of time. I should be using this time to work on *Deja New*, not to be regurgitating yesterday's news. Although yesterday's news was pretty sweet. Aunt Rosemary—bless her—came over for dinner in what she described as a Cyclopean cyclone. She was indeed drenched when she arrived. We got her dried off and into some of Mom's clothes. Mom doesn't seem to get dressed too often anymore, so she told Aunt Rosemary to keep them. She even told her she looks ravishingly stunning. High praise coming from Mom.

I had picked up a rotisserie chicken from Citarella earlier in the day and Mom and Aunt Rosemary gnawed on chicken bones and reminisced about their childhoods.

Mom was a young rebel. She started running away when she was eight; at thirteen she painted her bedroom walls black. She shoplifted, smoked, adopted a stray cat that she named Dammit, wore tight sweaters, tried to emulate Lana Turner, and left home to go to Los Angeles for college.

Aunt Rosemary confessed that she wanted to be rebellious too, that she secretly coveted all the negative attention that Mom got. That's why she dropped out of school and followed

Mom to LA. She was breaking up with her good-girl self to reestablish herself in the mold of her deeply troubled older sister, but then she met Uncle Bill.

When Mom and Aunt Rosemary talk about their childhood, their faces lose the strain of age and their eyes glisten. Mom has command of insignificant details, which, had they happened yesterday, would already be lost. Aunt Rosemary giggles and snorts like a young girl. They cut each other off and cut each other down.

"Your mother was a real beauty, but I had the talent," said Aunt Rosemary.

"Your aunt always believed in herself," replied Mom.

"Trudy, the truth is I always wanted to be more like you."

And then Mom said, "Rosie, the truth is, from the day you were born, I envied you."

They cuddled up together like kids until the rain tapered off and Aunt Rosemary went home. It was a pretty remarkable evening.

I guess I better get Mom up and packed if we're going to do this. She'll need help. And I want to get back in time to shower. I have no idea what I should wear to Stu's party. I wish I knew why Maya isn't responding to me. I texted her to say I had to go to New York. I apologized for leaving her a note about a sex dream that mentioned her husband. I said I miss her. No reply. I can't stand it.

DAY 58

Maya.

　All night.

　Maya.

　I couldn't stop thinking about her.

　And him.

　That was him, wasn't it?

　It's all so surreal.

　I hope she's okay. I wonder if Stu's with her? Does he know? Does he care?

　It's hard to make sense of what happened. I keep replaying the night from beginning to end. The strange smell of the club when I walked in, which was a kind of cologne and beer stew. There must have been 50 people there that I didn't recognize. You think you're entrenched in someone's life until you go to a surprise party for their husband's 50th birthday and discover there are dozens of people there who you've never met or heard about who also feel entrenched in their lives. I don't remember looking over at the band, but I do recall they were playing Joe Jackson covers. Everyone in the room was cheerfully bopping as they milled about. I scanned the room for familiar faces—where in the world were Bobby and Erick? I spotted Fiona and Michael in a circle of parents that I sort of knew and walked over to them.

"How are you guys?" I asked. The fathers replied by saying, "Good, good," as if one good wouldn't be good enough. These fathers were two-goods good. The mothers responded by updating me on their kids. I've noticed this is a thing that mothers sometimes do. You ask a mother how she is, and she gives you an update on her kid.

When Maya and Stu arrived, the band started playing "He's So Fine" and got a huge laugh. That's when I first really looked at them. The lead singer looked familiar, but I couldn't quite place him.

Maya was wearing a black dress that hugged her still slender-at-50 body and black boots that had a 104-inch heels. Stu, perennially boyish at 50, wore a blue pinstriped shirt and khakis. Maya and Stu are not a perfect couple, but something happens when they enter a room together. It's like we're all a little better for them being together.

I know that Maya wanted Stu to be confused, to walk in and have his eyes graze over his old friends, one by one, and start putting the pieces together, but that's not what happened. Someone shouted out: Happy birthday Stubert! And then we were all shouting, "Stuuuubert! Stuuubert! Stuuubert!"

I turned my head back to the stage when the lead singer—I was wracking my brain, where did I know him from?—launched into a kind of Violent Femmes-meets-the Talking Heads version of "Happy Birthday." I moved closer to the stage. Our eyes caught. His gaze grabbed mine. That's the best way to describe it. I still wasn't absolutely certain it was him though.

I turned around to find Maya.

There was an amp screech and I turned back to look at the stage again. Oh my God! This time when our eyes met, I winked at him. I don't think I've ever winked at anyone before.

Not like that at least. He winked back and I considered rushing the stage.

He started talking about Stu—their drummer and college buddy.

Stu was a Jekyll and Hyde, he said. "Cum laude by day, drum loudly by night. Stubert, buddy, come up here and hit the drums."

We all turned to watch Stu walk to the stage. To see him embrace his old bandmates, to be moved by the emotion it all. We searched the room with our eyes. Our necks twisted to the left, to the right, and to the left again. We stood on our toes. We furrowed our brows. We waited for Stu.

Stu didn't jump onto the stage. He didn't lift his arm and wave from the back of the club. He didn't shout out, "Thank you all for being here!" There was no Stu.

The sound of silence in a crowd echoes. Not in the pin drop kind of way, but in the clickity clack of high heels walking alone.

Maya stepped up onto the stage. A clump of hair fell onto her face and she didn't seem to notice or care. Her body was shaking, not quite convulsing, but almost. She was teetering. The lead singer—yes, it was him. What was he doing there?— put his hand on Maya's shoulder, which seemed to steady her. He whispered something into her ear and she gently shook her head and took the mic from him. At first it was just sad—listening to her explain, listening to her apologize.

"Thank you all for coming. Stu was definitely surprised. Not in the way I had hoped. I'm really sorry. I know some of you traveled to get here and I appreciate all the effort you went through. I thought he'd be happy. I thought he'd be so happy.

I just wanted him to be happy. Stu left. I don't know why he would leave with so many people here that he loves."

She stopped talking, and I guessed she was figuring out what to say next. I couldn't read her expression. It wasn't a look I had seen on her face before. She was still holding the microphone, but it was no longer directed at her lips, and her words, amplified but not entirely, started coming out indecipherably gibberishy—a bundle of disconnected syllables incoherently strung together. Then she collapsed.

He helped her up. She could walk. She was okay. He was keeping her steady, but she was walking. I think. Am I remembering this correctly?

I tried to rush the stage, to push my way through, but I was stopped by some ass-wipe who commanded, "Don't!"

"Move!" I yelled. "She needs me."

By the time I had maneuvered around him, the band and Maya were gone.

And the rest of us? What did we do then? I suppose we claimed our coats and bags and piled out onto the street and dispersed without knowing what to say and saying what we didn't know.

And now, after a night of twists and turns and drinks of water and trips to the bathroom to pee and turning lights on and wandering the house and turning lights off and lying in bed, looking at the blank screen of my phone and checking my email, it's 5:55 in the morning and all I can think to do is write these Morning Pages.

DAY 59

Mom and I hit the road early yesterday morning. I had stopped to get gas when Stu called.

"Maya asked me to call you," he said. "She's okay."

I think I said something like, "That's great news! Thank you for letting me know, Stu. Are you okay?"

It was hard to hear him and I thought he said, "No."

I wasn't sure if he could hear me. "What? What did you say? Stu, what did you say?"

This small voice. "Maya's not actually okay."

"What? What? What!"

"She's at Mass General. We don't know what's going on yet. She may have had a stroke. Or it's possible she may have a brain tumor, or it could have just been a reaction to stress. They're running tests on her and haven't ruled anything in or out yet. She seems a lot better though."

"What are you saying, Stu? I don't understand."

"Maya wanted me to let you know. They're running tests. We'll let you know when we learn anything."

"I'm on my way to New York. I'll drop my mother off and turn back around. I can be at the hospital by tonight or stay at your place with the kids."

Stu kept talking. "Had you noticed she's been different lately? Moody. I don't know, something's been off. I figured it was hormones. I know I'm probably not supposed to say that."

"It's okay. I noticed too."

It was little things, like being late, or messing up a seating arrangement at a dinner party. I told him that she came over recently and fell asleep on my couch. Stu said he felt awful about ditching his party, like an inconsiderate selfish ass. He told me I shouldn't come to the hospital and that the kids are fine. Maya admitted that she was having what she called little episodes but plowed through them. Figured they were nothing. I said I wanted to be with her. He said it was too soon. That I should stay with my mother as long as I needed to. That he'd keep me updated.

"Send her my love."

"I will."

"Happy birthday, Stu."

"Thank you, Elise."

"She'll be okay."

"I know."

Mom slept for most of the drive. Even with the radio on and the phone ringing.

Aunt Rosemary called while we were driving past Worcester.

"Elise, what time will you be getting back to the city? I miss my sister."

"We're on our way."

Elliot called right after I got on Route 84.

"I heard something happened last night with Maya."

"I don't have details. She may have had a stroke." I couldn't repeat the rest.

I didn't mention I was on my way to New York. I didn't tell him I told Marsden he could stay in Dedham by himself while I was gone. I owed Marsden one for hanging out with Mom, and he promised to work on his applications.

Sammy Ronstein called on the Merritt Parkway right after Larchmont.

"Elise, I need to see something. What can you send me? Nancilla Aronie wants to know how it's going."

Mom slept until the George Washington Bridge flittered in the rearview mirror.

"This has been a wonderful trip, Elise. Thank you."

When I walked into the building, Alan said, "Welcome back, Elise. Welcome home, Mrs. Hellman."

I brought Mom upstairs. I needed to get some air, so I told her I was heading out for a short walk.

I should have expected that he'd be there. He seems to always be there. But he looked different. I suspect I looked different too.

"Small world," I said.

"Small world indeed."

"I spoke to Stu and he said Maya's at Mass General."

"Yeah, I know."

"So, you went to college with Stu?"

"We had a band. But I guess you know that. We were pretty good."

"Small world."

"Small world."

He reached his hand out. I put mine in his and he pulled me into him. And held me. That happened.

DAY 60

Yesterday, Mrs. Harris from the long-term care insurance agency stopped by to assess Mom.

Mom said she wasn't feeling well and refused to get out of bed, which was a gift from her to me, but I didn't realize it at the time. At 9:00 sharp, Alan called up to announce that Mrs. Harris had arrived. Mrs. Harris. That's how she introduced herself, even after I greeted her at the door by saying, "Hi, it's so nice to meet you, I'm Elise."

"It's nice to meet you too, Elise, I'm Mrs. Harris."

I offered Mrs. Harris coffee. "No, thank you." Tea. "No, thank you." Water. "No, thank you." Mrs. Harris needed nothing. I am the one in need. I need Mrs. Harris to approve our request to have Mom's long-term care insurance pay for her to move into an assisted living home.

Mom was wearing her stained sky-blue nightgown. Her hair was unwashed and unbrushed. Mrs. Harris was wearing a royal blue suit, and I hoped Mom would be gracious. I was wrong.

"I'm not feeling terribly well, so I'm not getting up to greet you," Mom said.

"That's not a problem at all, Mrs. Hellman," said Mrs. Harris. "I'm sorry you're not feeling well today. I promise I won't take up too much of your time. I just want to ask you a few questions. Would you mind if I sit down next to you?"

"You can sit over there." Mom pointed to a chair on the other side of the room. I picked it up and brought it over closer to Mom.

"Not there. I said over there." Mom was pointing to where the chair used to be.

Mrs. Harris sat in the chair next to Mom. I went to the corner of the room and tried to push myself into the wall.

"How are you feeling today, Mrs. Hellman?" Mrs. Harris asked.

"Why should I tell you?" Mom replied.

"Can you tell me what year it is, Mrs. Hellman?"

"I think it's around 2005. No, wait, maybe it's 2010? I really can't remember."

"Do you know what day of the week it is?"

"Elise, what day is today?"

"Mrs. Hellman, I need you to answer these questions."

"Okay, what was the question?"

"What day is today?"

"It's Saturday. I was watching a movie. Is this going to take long?"

"Do you know what state we're in?"

"New York."

"I'm going to say three words and I want you to repeat them back to me as many times as you can. The words are: *cup, house, ball.*"

"What are the words?"

"*Cup, house, ball.*"

"I don't want to do this."

"Mrs. Hellman, please repeat the words *cup, house, ball.*"

"*Cup, house, ball. Cup, house, ball. Cup, house, ball. Cup, house, ball. Cup, house, ball.* Can I be done?"

"Mrs. Hellman, can you count backward from one hundred by fives?"

"I'm not good at math."

"Okay, then spell the word 'world' backward."

"D...L...O...R...L...D."

"Can you remember the three words that I asked you to repeat before?"

"Yes, of course."

"Will you tell them to me?"

"No, I don't want to."

"Mrs. Hellman, I'm going to give you a piece of paper and I'd like you to write a full sentence on it. You can write whatever you want, but your sentence must include a noun and a verb."

Mom propped herself up and placed the piece of paper on her bed table. She took the pen and hunched over the paper. When she was done writing, she picked up the piece of paper and waved it at Mrs. Harris.

"Thank you, Mrs. Hellman. I appreciate your time. Elise, would you like to join me in the other room for a minute to chat?"

We went into the other room and Mrs. Harris told me that she would recommend coverage for Mom and handed me the results of the assessment for me to look over. The sentence Mom wrote was a mere two words. One noun. Bull. And I suppose one verb. Shit.

Bull shit.

DAY 61

THE DOCTORS STILL haven't figured out what's going on with Maya and they're keeping her in the hospital and if that wasn't shitty enough news yesterday, there was this—Marsden had a party. He got caught. He's always getting caught. He gets caught when he isn't even doing anything wrong. I don't know why he's so bad at being a teenager.

He ditched school. He called in. Said he was on a college visit. The school said to have one of his parents call to confirm. Of course, neither parent called. A few friends stopped by in the afternoon to get high. A few more stopped by later for a beer or two. They knew not to smoke and drive. They knew not to drink and drive. They've been taught well. Being responsible kids, they spent the night. Marsden and two of the boys decided to skip school. "Our heads were pounding," Marsden explained, as if being hungover merited an excused absence.

I learned about all of this because Mrs. Yule called me. I told her I was in New York taking care of my mother who has dementia. It was the first time I'd used that word. Dementia. My mother has dementia. It's such a monumental word. I can't believe I wasted it on Mrs. Yule.

"I'm sorry," she said.

"Thank you," I replied. It felt like we reached a rapprochement.

But it didn't last. Her tone returned to scolding and accusatory. One of the kids who didn't cut told the school that the three absent senior boys had been partying at Marsden's. I don't understand why Marsden's generation has such a hard time covering for themselves. They're always squealing, these overly-pampered kids whose parents have assured them that if they tell the truth, they won't get in trouble.

Mrs. Yule said they will need to take disciplinary action. It might mean suspension. I argued that this happened outside of school. Mrs. Yule said they are cracking down on student smoking and drinking. I didn't see many options, so I decided to tell Mrs. Yule that Marsden has been having panic attacks lately. That the divorce has been very difficult for him. That I'm worried.

High schools don't want to hear that kids are having panic attacks. I laid it on. I don't care that what I am doing is ethically suspect. I know it's wrong on so many levels, but Marsden cannot have a suspension added to his lackluster transcript. Mrs. Yule listened as I talked. There was a pause. "Are you still there," I asked. My voice cracked, but not too obviously. She said she didn't know about this situation, that she would take that into consideration. She told me not to worry and recommended that Marsden should stay with his father until I returned home.

I didn't want to call Elliot. I searched for flights to Buenos Aires instead. Buenos Aires is a place where people fleeing their lives fly to. I could be amongst them. Playwright flees with unfinished play and unfinished business with ex-husband before she finishes raising her son.

It always comes back to finishing.

I didn't book a flight.

I drove back to Dedham instead.

Aunt Rosemary agreed to stay with Mom. "I wouldn't abandon my sister in her time of need." Sometimes I feel like even though Aunt Rosemary wears bifocals, she sees the world through a set of *my-focals*. The world's issues are her issues. Its pain is her pain. Murders, muggings, drug addiction, typhoons, and cancer, they are all hers. She once told me, "Elise, I don't just have empathy for other people, I have empathitis." But she has been totally there for Mom, and mostly without her usual dose of high drama, and I am grateful for her, grateful that I can go home and be with Marsden.

"Thank you so much, Aunt Rosemary. I can't tell you how much I appreciate this."

"Trudy is my right arm. My left arm. My soul. My heart. Go home and do what you need to do. I'll call Julie if there's a problem. Take care of your messy life, we'll suffice."

"Thank you, but you should call me, not Julie. I'm sure Julie is busy with patients."

"Of course she is, but my daughter is a saint."

"Yes, she is. And so are you."

(LAURIE and GRANVILLE are chatting as they walk into Laurie's house. They hear something as they enter and stop talking. LARRY and GRACE can't be seen-or maybe just their bare legs are visible-but the sounds of vigorous lovemaking are quite clear.)

                    LAURIE
What's that? Do you hear that?

                    (Laurie walks further inside
                    and screeches.)

Oh my GOD! Oh my God. Oh my God. Oh My God. Oh my God. Oh my FUCKING God!

                    GRANVILLE
Ohhhhhhh wow!

                     GRACE
(Moaning) Shit! Laurie?

                     LARRY
Laurie? You're home already?

                     GRACE
Larry. Stop. Laurie, what are you doing here?

                    LAURIE
What? It's my house. That's what I'm doing here.

                    GRANVILLE
Laurie.

                         (Grace stands up and covers
                         herself with a smattering
                         of her clothes.)

                    LAURIE
Mom! Ewww. Dad!

                     GRACE
Darling, we weren't expecting you until tomorrow.

                    LAURIE
What is going on in here?

                     GRACE
Your father and I were simply—

                    LAURIE
No. Don't say it. What are all these boxes
doing here? Mom, I can see your—oh my—Granny.
Turn around.

                    (Laurie and Granville turn
                    their backs to Grace.)

Please, will the two of you get dressed.

                    GRACE
The boxes belong to your father.

                    LARRY
I needed to get a couple of things from
the house.

                    GRACE
Larry, get up.

                    LAURIE
This is a couple of things? Pops, get up. I
can't believe you brought all this stuff over.
I can't believe you and Mom were...Oh God.

                    GRACE
It was your father's idea.

                    LAURIE
Well, it sure didn't sound like you thought
it was a bad idea.

                    LARRY
I...I...I can't seem to....

                    GRACE
Give us a second, we're not young, you know.
Larry, get up.

                    (Grace turns her back to the
                    audience and puts on her
                    clothes-she can either be

> behind boxes or not while
> doing this.)

LARRY

I can't.

LAURIE

Pops. Are you kidding me? Are you kidding me!

GRACE

Get up and get dressed Larry. Stop making a scene. This isn't a good time for your antics.

LARRY

Grace, I'm serious. I can't get up.

GRANVILLE

Let me help you, Mr. Herman.

LAURIE

Thank you, Granny.

> (Granville steps behind a
> box and looks at Larry.)

GRANVILLE

You look like you're in terrific shape. I'm surprised you can't get up.

LARRY

I'm not so bad for a man my age, if I do say so. So, you're the man they call Granny? Does that bother you?

GRANVILLE

Not really. The only time it was a problem was when I was about twelve and one of the prettier girls started to—

LAURIE

Granny, this isn't the time for stories.
Will you just help him up. Please.

> (Granny reaches down to
> help Larry.)

LARRY

I don't think I should try to get up.

LAURIE

Pops, are you okay?

LARRY

I think she did something to me.

GRACE

Of course I did something to you. I fucked
you in a way you probably haven't been fucked
in a long time. No offense to your nubile
young wives.

LAURIE

Jesus. Mom! Must you? Really? I can't believe
you did this.

GRACE

There you go-blaming me again.

LAURIE

I'm not blaming you. But Dad's stuck on the
floor naked. What am I supposed to say?

GRACE

Larry. Get up! I said get up. Please. Now.

LARRY

Grace, I don't feel right.

GRACE

I don't believe you. Get up Larry.

LARRY

Maybe it was the quiche. Laurie, your mother made quiche.

LAURIE

Pops, maybe you've had a stroke. Oh my God!

GRANVILLE

Laurie. You should try to calm down.

LAURIE

Don't tell me what I should do. Don't ever tell me again what I *should* do. I am done being the only person around who does what they *should* do. I am tired of being *shoul*ded on and I am done, finished, *should*ing on myself. *Should* my mother and my father have been having sex on my floor? Was that what they *should* have been doing? Mom, tell me-is D for Doing the Deed? Maybe E is for Erection. Clearly, it's not for Erectile dysfunction. And F, let's make F for Fucking your ex-husband who you hate. You. Hate. Him. Pops, are you okay?

GRACE

Let's all sit down and talk.

LARRY

I can't sit down. I can't get up.

LAURIE

I don't want to sit down. I never want to sit down again.

GRANVILLE

Laurie, you're being irrational.

LAURIE

For once I get to be the irrational one. I'm tired of making all the pieces fit together like a well-formed equation.

LARRY

Laurie, Princess—

LAURIE

Do not call me "Princess!"

GRACE

Laurie, you're going to have an aneurism. Larry, do something. I feel faint.

LARRY

Well don't faint on me.

GRACE

Get up you bastard! You're faking this. You're looking for some sort of sick sympathy. I knew it. I knew you couldn't be trusted, Larry. I am sick. No, you are sick. What you're doing is wretched. Your father is a sick man, Laurie. A very sick man. He's fine. He can get up. I don't know why he's doing this, but he's faking. He's trying to make me look bad. Like I can't make a quiche without poisoning him. He's always accusing me of trying to kill him. He spent his life trying to make you hate me. This is what he does.

LAURIE

I'm gonna call an ambulance.

GRACE

You'll see. He's fine.

LAURIE

Mom, what's wrong with you? Why are you being like this?

LARRY

This is what she does. This is why I had to leave.

GRACE

Larry, you will rot in hell before you even get there. For one minute, I let my guard down...

(Grace finishes getting dressed, picks up Larry's pants from the floor, and grabs his car keys from his pants pocket.)

LARRY

What are you doing, Grace?

(Grace dangles the keys in front of Larry.)

GRACE

Get up, Larry.

LAURIE

Mom, give me Dad's car keys.

GRACE

Get up Larry or I'm taking your car.

LAURIE

Mom, stop it. Please.

GRACE

You want me to stop. I'll stop.

(Grace storms out of the house. Laurie tries to grab ahold of Grace's arm, but Grace slithers free. We hear the sound of a car engine starting and then-crash.)

LARRY

Oh my God, my car! Oh my God. GRACE!

> (Laurie and Granville run
> out of the house. Larry
> stands up slowly and hobbles
> out after them.)

BLACKOUT [Crash should
be the final
sound

DAY 62

I RETURNED HOME to a talkative son. It's as if his words and syllables had been released from their long hibernation, at least for a short time.

"I know I screwed up. I promised you I'd be responsible, and I wasn't. I'm really sorry. I'm not just saying that. I am embarrassed and ashamed, and you deserve more. I know you're dealing with a lot right now and I don't want to add to your burden."

He was talking. He was being thoughtful and considerate. I knew my sweet boy was still in there somewhere. Maybe Marsden needed the threat of suspension to get the words flowing again.

I didn't want to let him off the hook too easily though. I tend to parent from a wishy-washy-open-minded-acceptancy-it's-okay-honey place, but yesterday I invoked an authoritarian tone.

"You promised me you could stay here for a few days by yourself. Explain to me what happened."

He said he skipped school to work on his applications.

"Really, Marsden, you skipped school to work on your applications?"

"Really, I did, Mom. Maybe I smoked some weed too, but only 'cause it helps me write, and I know you like it when I write."

"Don't try justifying getting high as a way to please me."

"Did you know that Shakespeare got high?"

"I've heard that. He probably experimented a bit. I doubt he could have been as productive as he was if he smoked regularly. Are you comparing yourself to Shakespeare now?"

"No, I'm comparing you to Shakespeare. You should try. It might help you finish your play."

He's smart, my son. When he talks, he knows the right words to say. He looked so sweet. His limby lankiness and sleepy eyes that somehow twinkle even when he's high. I asked him for a hug. I overstepped. We're not at hugs yet.

Then Elliot came over. He insisted on having a family meeting, as if we were still a family.

The three of us were standing in the kitchen and Elliot was aggressively lobbing questions at us.

"Why didn't you tell me you went to New York?"

"How come Marsden stayed here by himself?"

"Marsden, why didn't you come over and stay with me and Midge?"

"Elise, how did you think this was going to end?"

"Did it ever occur to you that something really bad could have happened?"

"Tomorrow is Thanksgiving, Marsden. Is this the kind of thanks we get?"

It was one question too many. Something in me snapped— that sounds cliché—but it's what happened.

"That's enough, Elliot! Stop with the questions and get out of my house!"

I have never yelled at Elliot in front of Marsden. I rarely yell at Elliot in front of Elliot. My biggest fights with Elliot have been without Elliot. I have yelled and hit and thrown things at him, but not when he's around. It's not that I didn't want to give him the pleasure of my pain, it's not that I didn't want him to know how heartbroken and angry I was. I didn't yell at Elliot in front of Elliot, and especially in front of Marsden, because if I did, I would become my mother. I felt like I was seeing him clearly for the first time since our divorce. I was no longer looking at him through the lens of my misery and desire for him. I wanted him out of my house.

I did the math. Three days left to finish *Deja New*, and one of them is Thanksgiving. I have failed. I was never going to finish. From the day I accepted the commission, I embarked on the excruciating process of coming to terms with the fact that my place in this world is not as a playwright.

From day one, this has been an exercise in letting go, of understanding that the forces around me are greater than the forces within me. The purpose of these Morning Pages was not to help me finish writing *Deja New*, it was to plot out the points of why I cannot and will not finish. My Morning Pages are my map to failure. My husband cheated on me, then cheated with me, and my writer's block defeated me. This morning ritual of writing three pages has not served up the focus to finish, but rather has become a journal of a playwright doomed to failure—not because of big and magnificent events, but because of daily distractions. All the moments when I'm focused elsewhere. The moments when I'm dealing with Mom, or worrying about Marsden. The moments when I'm not writing. There are so many moments. All the moments in a day of fighting the distractions of life instead of writing.

Moments + moments + moments + moments + moments = time escaping, time not finishing.

My heart might have missed a beat or put in a few extras. I'm not sure which way it went, but it was doing something it surely shouldn't have been doing and I started sweating. Soon I was dripping wet and smelled like under-boob stink.

I'll have to pay back the commission. Sammy Ronstein will hate me. I will be gossiped about.

Did you hear that Elise Hellman couldn't finish writing her play and had to return her commission with interest? How much interest? Her future as a playwright. She had to forfeit it all.

I'll be written about in cautionary "What Not to Do" articles that will be widely available online.

The former playwright, Elise Hellman, put family first, friends first, the mutterings and mumblings inside her undisciplined head-first, and she never wrote again.

"Mom, are you okay?" Marsden asked.

"I want you out of my fucking house! Elliot, get out of my house!" It was tree-toppling, full-throated screaming.

"Calm down, Elise."

No, Elliot—I will not calm down! Why would I calm down?

"So, this is what's going to happen," I announced. "Marsden and I are going to go on a college tour."

"That sounds like a good idea," Elliot said.

"But before we go on a college tour, we're driving down to New York and we're going to pick up Grandma Trudy."

I paused because I wanted to watch their faces. The flickering of the eyes, the frowns, the deepening lines of confusion cutting through Elliot's forehead.

"And we're going to combine Marsden's college tour with an assisted living homes tour for Grandma Trudy."

"What?" Marsden asked.

"I don't think that's a good idea," Elliot said.

"The two of you both need to start thinking more seriously about the future."

"But?"

"Elise?"

"I'd like you to leave now," I said. No ambiguity.

"Who?" asked Marsden.

"Both of you. Marsden, pack for a week. Make sure you have a few pairs of clean khakis and nice button-down shirts and a few sweaters. Then go spend tonight at Dad's. I hope you have a good Thanksgiving dinner with Dad and Midge tomorrow. I'll pick you up after dinner is done and we'll drive to the city."

"You're not going to join us for Thanksgiving this year?" Elliot asked.

"No, Elliot, I won't be joining you."

That's how it played out. I spent the rest of the day making appointments to tour colleges and leaving messages at assisted living homes.

I may not have finished my play, but this trip will be my tour de force.

DAY 63

TODAY I WILL give thanks for:

★ Marsden, for being my son

★ Maya's friendship, unmatched

★ Aunt Rosemary, for always being there in her own way

★ Alan, for having to always be there

★ Mom, for encouraging me to express my uncensored self

★ Dad and Lucy, for forgetting to call on Thanksgiving again, as I know they will

★ Handsome men in elevators who used to play in bands

★ Sammy Ronstein, for having faith in me when he shouldn't have

★ Nancilla Aronie, for being a brilliant director

★ Thanksgiving dinner, alone

DAY 64

We were driving to the city. I was deep in thought, thinking about Maya. They found a lesion on her brain. I cannot believe I am writing those words. How is that possible? How can that be? More tests and then a biopsy to determine if it's benign or—I'm not going to write that ugly word. I talked to her yesterday, finally. When I heard her voice, it felt like the clouds parting. I apologized for being so needy and acting like an ass. And of course, Maya being Maya said, "You're weren't, Elise. You're fine. I was being withholding. I knew something was wrong, but I didn't want to worry anyone and so I didn't tell you. You didn't need more stress in your life. I didn't even tell Stu. I shouldn't have waited but I had a feeling that once I looked into what was going on with me, it would be a game changer, and I really didn't want the game to change."

Somewhat surprisingly, instead of not knowing what to say or stumbling for the right words, I knew exactly what I wanted to tell her. I wanted her to know how much I love and respect her. How our walks get me through the day. How our talks fuel me. How I will be with her throughout whatever happens. How she's the strongest and smartest person I know. How I'll distract her with good gossip and walk the rescue dogs. And how I'm planning to lose my divorce virginity. And I got her to laugh. And then I heard Stu in the background, and he was laughing too.

We spent the rest of the drive listening to music. It didn't matter that Marsden had stopped talking. I just wanted to be in the car with him. I thought about staying on Route 95 and driving us to Florida instead of New York. As we crossed from Connecticut to New York, I watched the exits peel off, knowing that too soon our exit would be up next. I celebrated each exit we passed that wasn't ours—the exits that fed off to smaller highways and roads that went through towns where people who weren't us lived and worked and sent their kids to school. Where people fought and cheated on each other. Where people celebrated birthdays and anniversaries, got bored and drunk, went to basketball games, sometimes littered, and let their toenails grow too long. Where people laughed until they cried and choked on their food, overdosed, and hugged. Every exit we passed made me happy that we weren't those people, because if we were those people, it would mean the end of the car ride.

We hit traffic in the Bronx, but it didn't hold onto us long enough. I drove past the sign announcing that our exit was coming up in two miles. I had two miles to decide. Should I skip it and keep driving?

We found a parking space quickly—too quickly—just a block from Mom's building. Alan wasn't working. He must have taken Thanksgiving weekend off. I rang the doorbell, but Mom didn't hear it, so I used my key to let us in.

"Bitch!" Mom was yelling at someone.

"Mom?" I called out. "Is everything okay? I'm back. Marsden is here too." I wanted to make sure she remembered he was coming.

"Hi Grandma!" Marsden called out in his deep baritone of a voice that I will never get used to.

The volume on the TV must have been set to a thousand. Mom was holding the clicker like a lance and stabbing it toward the TV.

"Mom!" I said loudly.

"Elise, you scared me. I didn't hear you come in. I'm watching *Mommy Dearest*." I yanked the clicker out of her hand and turned off the TV.

"I'm here with Marsden."

"Marsden is in the city?" She sounded joyful.

"He is. Remember, our little road trip starts tomorrow."

"My grandson is here?" She practically jumped out of bed. "Marsden, my phantom grandson. The child who never calls his grandmother. What am I, already dead to you?"

"Sorry Grandma Trudy," Marsden said. "I've been busy."

"That's bullshit. Your mother keeps you away from me. Come here and give me a hug."

Marsden bent over and enveloped his grandmother in an uncompromising hug. He went all in.

DAY 65

BELIEVERS MIGHT PIN what happened on "the universe." Cynics say irony is dead. Since I'm neither believer nor cynic, I posit the possibility that the universe is ironic.

We were on our way out of Mom's apartment. Mom asked Marsden to help her with her suitcase: "You're a strapping young man, help your old Gram out."

Then she scolded him for lifting it the wrong way.

"How can he be lifting it wrong? It's got a handle. He's carrying it by the handle, which was put there for this very purpose."

"It's a very old suitcase. He needs to pick it up and carry it."

Marsden picked up her suitcase and cradled it in his arms.

"Not like that," she said.

"Let me show you."

"Mom, it's fine."

"Elise, mind your own business," she snapped.

I turned away from them. Pivoted toward the bookshelf and that's when I saw it. There was a fissure on one of the lower shelves, a crack in the continuity, and there it was. Mom's missing copy of *Madame Bovary*.

When we got to the car, I asked Marsden if he wanted to drive.

"You want me to drive? For real?"

"Yes," I told him.

"Why? Are you sick?"

"I'm fine."

"Then why do you want me to drive?"

"You have your permit. You need your practice hours."

"But we're in New York."

"That's a good observation."

"For real, Mom, you want me to drive in the city?"

"You only have to drive a few blocks before we get on the highway. It'll be good practice."

"I would drive but I can't find my license," Mom said.

"Marsden needs the practice," I said. "He should drive."

Mom settled into the passenger side of the front seat with her portable oxygen tank, Marsden got behind the wheel and pushed the seat back to accommodate the sprawl of legs on his six-foot-two frame, and I squeezed in behind him in the back seat. I'm not entirely sure why I thought he should drive, but I think it had something to do with encouraging him to take control of his future while I was losing control of mine. Maybe life doesn't really work in literary metaphors—but writers are always seeking metaphors and this one seems apt.

I needed to think about how I would tell Sammy Ronstein that that I wasn't able to finish. That I would never finish. He's been emailing and calling. I am scared of his fury. I need to fortify myself. After Marsden successfully steered us onto the Merritt, after I could see Mom's eyes close, after the hum of the portable oxygen tank was the only sound in the car, I pulled Mom's copy of *Madame Bovary* out of my coat pocket and started to read.

DAY 66

I NO LONGER need to be doing these Morning Pages. They've failed me, and yet they sustain me. Over the past two months, they've become my morning kiss and tell, and I'm not ready to let them go. Not after the events of yesterday.

Our hotel room came with a complimentary buffet breakfast, and we were sitting at a table with plates full of scrambled eggs, hash browns, bacon, sausage, pancakes, granola, croissants, and fruit salad. Mom had her gaze set on Marsden. I took a sip of coffee. My first for the morning. I was preparing to mentally prepare myself for the day ahead—pre-prepping for the preparation—when Mom said, "Marsden, the girls must be crazy for you."

He was too busy being tired and consuming his plate of food without chewing to respond, so I gently swatted him on the arm.

MARSDEN: Why'd you hit me?

ME: I didn't hit you. Grandma Trudy was talking to you.

MARSDEN: Oh.

MOM: Marsden, the girls must be crazy for you.

MARSDEN: Not really.

MOM: Do you have a girlfriend?

MARSDEN: Nup.

MOM: Do you prefer cock?

ME: What? Mom!

MOM: I want him to know that I accept him no matter who he wants to love. After all, I've had relationships with both men and women.

ME: What? You have?

MARSDEN: Mom, does that bother you?

ME: No, of course not, but I would have liked to know.

MOM: I didn't think you could handle it.

ME: I can handle it. I'm just surprised. I wish you hadn't kept this from me.

MOM: Why? You yell at me when I try to talk to you about my lovers and tell me I'm being inappropriate. Marsden, do you think it's inappropriate to discuss your lovers with your child?

ME: He wouldn't know. I never do.

MOM: That's because you don't have lovers.

ME: How do you know?

MARSDEN: Mom, for the record, I don't care if you want to date women.

MOM: I believe every woman should be fucked by a woman at least once in her life.

ME: We're in a hotel restaurant!

MOM: Elise, you're never going to be a successful playwright if you're so timid. What are you possibly able to write about with all those restrictions you put on yourself? That's your problem. Your writing is constipated. You're constipated.

ME: Fuck you, Mom.

MARSDEN: Don't say that to Grandma Trudy.

ME: You're right. I apologize. I am sorry.

MOM: Marsden, am I shocking you?

MARSDEN: Kind of, yeah. But that's okay. It's cool to hear about your sex life. You're definitely the coolest grandma I know. Most grandmothers don't talk about their sex life.

MOM: Your mother would prefer that I talk about something else, like knitting or the weather.

MARSDEN: I'd rather you say cock again.

ME: How about if we don't talk at all.

Marsden was turning into a normal conversational being, and all I wanted was for us to all to stop talking. Instead, I changed the topic.

I started rattling on about my research into the school we were to be visiting.

ME: Springfield College was founded in 1885, which honestly was not a terribly interesting year, as far as years go. Though, you might be surprised to find out that the magazine *Good Housekeeping* was published for the first time in 1885. I found a copy of their launch issue online and it had an article about how a model housewife can maintain a model home and a piece about the philosophy of dessert. Who knew dessert needed a philosophy?

MARSDEN: Mom, nobody cares what happened in 1885.

ME: I care. And you should too. The first appendectomy was performed in 1885.

MOM: Your Aunt Rosemary had an appendectomy about that time.

ME: I also found out basketball and bodybuilding were invented at Springfield College.

MARSDEN: That's an excellent fun fact, but not as fun as Grandma Trudy's stories.

I wasn't trying to be bothersome or boring, I wanted to change the topic and give Marsden a little context about the school he was about to visit, which played a big role in our nation's sports history. Admittedly, it was during the actual tour of the school that I became bothersome.

We parked in a lot close to the admission's office, but Mom was walking so slowly I feared we'd miss everything, so I yanked on the rubber tubes to her portable oxygen tank a few times to try to get her to walk faster.

MOM: Elise, stop treating me like I'm on a leash. I'm not a dog.

ME: Marsden, you go ahead, and we'll catch up with you. I don't want you to miss anything.

MARSDEN: No, Mom, you go ahead. You're the one who's most interested in finding out everything you can about this school. You need to calm down.

ME: I am calm.

After the informational session, Mom waited for us in the admission's office while Marsden and I took a student-led campus tour. We were with a group of eight other prospective students and their parents. Our student guide was a junior named Keisha and she walked backward while pointing out the different buildings on campus. Skillful as she was, I couldn't stop myself.

ME: Be careful, Keisha, there's a crack in the pavement.

MARSDEN: Mom, she's fine.

ME: Keisha, do you see the step behind you?

MARSDEN: Mom!

The campus had mostly emptied out for the holiday weekend, but the few students we saw looked happy and I pointed them out to Marsden.

MARSDEN: Yes, Mom, there are students here. It's a college campus.

I asked Keisha questions. Marsden had the look of someone who wanted to let out a huge sigh but didn't dare. After I
said, "Keisha, I know you said that we wouldn't be able to see
a dorm room on the tour, but I was wondering if maybe you'd
be willing to show us your room," Marsden whispered to me, "I
don't want to see a dorm room. Let's go get Grandma Trudy."

When we arrived at Sunrise Village, we were greeted by a
woman who looked to be around my age, give or take ten years.
I really can't tell how old anyone is anymore, but she had an *I
don't want anyone to know I'm hitting fifty* look to her. I think it
was her plump fuchsia lips that screamed, *Hey, I'm still in the
game.* Her name was Marjorie, or maybe Miriam, and while she
didn't walk backward during our tour of Sunrise Village, she
did greet everyone by their name who we walked by. We were
introduced to at least two Sarahs, an Alice, a Florence, a Paul,
and a Norton. She took us through "the lodge" and into one of
the stand-alone apartments that bordered the "campus quad."
In addition to apartments, the lodge had a library filled with
cozy couches, a theater for movies, guest speakers, and concerts, and out of the way nooks filled with partially completed
500- and 1000-piece puzzles. Miriam informed us that there
were no immediate openings, but Mom wanted to put down
a deposit. She pulled a checkbook out of her purse and wrote
out a check for $5,000.

ME: Do you have five thousand dollars in your
checking account?

MOM: How would I know?

ME: You just gave them a check for five thousand dollars.
Maybe you shouldn't be handing out checks.

MOM: It's my money.

ME: You don't even know if you have the money.

MOM: Then it's my bankruptcy. Either way it has nothing to do with you, Elise.

MARSDEN: Mom, it's okay. Don't worry about it.

ME: What?

MARSDEN: You're always jumping all over Grandma Trudy. Give her a break.

Mom and Marsden were becoming a team. By dinner—at a Greek restaurant 20 miles from our hotel—they were ganging up on me. We were seated at a table with a fake candle flickering up at us.

ME: Does anyone want a bite of my moussaka?

MOM: Marsden, what did you get?

MARSDEN: Souvlaki.

ME: How is it, honey?

MARSDEN: Good. Do you want to try some, Grandma Trudy?

ME: Would either of you like to try the moussaka? Mom? Marsden?

MARSDEN:

MOM: Marsden, your souvlaki is delicious.

ME: So, I have some big news to tell both of you. I am no longer a playwright.

MARSDEN: Have more if you want, Grandma Trudy.

MOM: Thank you, dear, but I'm fine. Here, let me give you some of my salad.

ME: Can either of you hear me?

MOM: Marsden, take a few more of the olives.

ME: I didn't finish my play. I am going to have to return my commission and go back to subbing.

MOM: Elise, what are you saying?

ME: I didn't finish.

MOM: That's bullshit.

MARSDEN: Yeah, Mom, what the fuck? Finish your play. You've been working on it forever. How could you not finish it? What's wrong with you?

ME: I couldn't figure out how to end it.

MARSDEN: If I told you I couldn't finish my math homework because I couldn't get the answers to the equations right, you would have a huge a hissy fit. Sorry, Mom, couldn't get the ending right to 12x46.

ME: That's different.

MARSDEN: Is it?

MOM: Elise, go finish your play.

ME: I'd prefer to finish my moussaka, thank you very much.

MOM: Forget your mouss-shitka. Leave Marsden and me alone here to eat in peace and go back to the hotel and don't leave until you've finished your play.

ME: I obviously can't do that, Mom. Remember we're here to tour colleges and assisted living homes.

MARSDEN: We don't need you for that, Mom. We can write you out of the scene. It'll be better with two actors anyway.

MOM: And we'll have a lot more fun without you dragging us down. Marsden, don't you agree?

MARSDEN: It'll be way less stressful.

MOM: I've decided that I'm not talking to you again until you finish your play.

MARSDEN: Good idea. Me too.

I handed the car keys to Marsden and took a taxi back to the hotel. I wrote an email to Sammy Ronstein apologizing for missing my deadline—there was a family emergency, blah, blah, blah—and read through the last draft I had written.

DAY 67

MOM AND MARSDEN left before 8:00. Mom was wearing a striking, indigo, button-down shirt and a pair of slimming black slacks. She put on mascara, which framed her milky hazel eyes, and the rubber tubing of her oxygen tank broadcast what appeared to be an extra layer of lipstick. Marsden looked unspeakably handsome in a pinstriped Oxford and khakis. He was holding the portable tank and they hurried out of the hotel together, connected by a cord.

And I thought to myself—*how dare she call me constipated!*

After about an hour later, my indignation turned into questioning.

Am I constipated?

And the answer. Yes, I am. I've been holding it in. It was time to shit it out.

I didn't stop for lunch. I stayed away from Act 1 and punched up Act 2, finessing a surprise plot twist. I walked around the hotel room reading aloud. I tidied it up—the play, not the room. I let it breathe and I let it simmer.

I didn't eat until we met up at a Chinese restaurant for dinner.

MARSDEN: You wouldn't believe it, Mom. We were sitting in the admission's office and it was full of students and parents and everyone was trying to look smart when the Dean of Admissions walked in and Grandma Trudy yelled out, like really loudly, "Excuse me, sir! Sir!"

ME: Oh no!

MARSDEN: The guy turned to look at her. And she was like, "Roy! Roy! Is that you?"

MOM: He looked just like him.

ME: Who?

MOM: Roy Levinson. I fell in love with him when I was fifteen. Roy was twenty, and a real man, not at all like the boys at school. My father was furious when he found out. He thought Roy would soil me. That's the word your great grandfather used—*soil*. I wanted to play in the dirt. Roy would take me to the movies, and we'd fool around. We called it *petting* back then. There were such great movies and real movie stars, not like the ones today. Marlon Brando. Vivien Leigh. Hedy Lamar. Lana Turner. I remember Roy fingering me in the dark theater and I'd close my eyes and pretend he was Brando.

ME: Mom, please stop talking like this in front of Marsden!

MARSDEN: I'm cool with it. Grandma Trudy already told me this story. But you're not going to believe this, the admissions dude said that Roy Levinson was his dad.

MOM: And I told him that I was a close personal friend of his father's.

MARSDEN: So, he invited us into his office and canceled his appointments for the next hour and we hung out in there. First, he asked me a bunch of questions about what I thought I might be interested in studying and then Grandma Trudy told him everything.

ME: Uh-oh.

MARSDEN: But she kept it clean. You would have been proud. And then the guy called his father and Grandma Trudy talked to him.

MOM: Roy told me his biggest regret in life was letting me slip away.

ME: This world gets smaller every minute.

MARSDEN: He lives nearby, in an assisted living home. We're going to visit him tomorrow.

MOM: I needed something to wear, something sexy to remind him of what I used to be, so Marsden and I went shopping.

ME: You went shopping with your grandmother?

MARSDEN: I picked out a hot outfit for her.

MOM: We're going to charm the pants off of him.

ME: Literally, no doubt.

Mom says something saucy and winks at Marsden. He smiles when she talks. I had forgotten that smile. He looks different. He looks happy. And Mom seems less confused. She seems present. Also happy. I had a moment of transcendent happiness while eating lo mein and watching the two of them engage with each other.

We got back to our hotel room. Marsden checked in with his phone. I fixed a few lines of dialogue. Mom went into the bathroom. I heard water running. A long soothing silence.

And then:

"Elise!"

"What Mom?"

"Can you come in here."

"Why?"

"I need you."

"The door to the bathroom is locked. Unlock it please."

"I can't."

"Why can't you?"

"I think I'm stuck."

"Stuck where?"

"I'm taking a bath. I can't get out of the bathtub."

(LAURIE and GRANVILLE are sitting at a table at a pastry shop - shelves of delectable pastries can be projected on a large screen behind them. If possible, a delicious aroma of fresh baked goods should be emitted into the audience.)

LAURIE

You know, hindsight isn't actually 20/20. I still didn't see any of it coming.

GRANVILLE

It was a shock. I mean, who would see that coming?

LAURIE

In a weird way, I'm glad it happened.

GRANVILLE
It's great to see you, Laurie. I don't really
understand why you've been avoiding me.

LAURIE
I needed time away from everyone. Quitting
my job and going to Argentina was the best
thing I've ever done. Once I knew Mom was
fine, I knew I needed to escape from their
dysfunction. She could have killed herself.

GRANVILLE
I'm glad she didn't.

LAURIE
You know her plan was to total his car.
To destroy his prized Jaguar and maybe to
destroy herself too. Thankfully she's a lousy
driver and couldn't even crash straight.

GRANVILLE
She was pissed!

LAURIE
She gets that way. And he's lied to her so
many times over the years that she didn't
believe him when he said he couldn't get up.
She figured he was playing some sick game.

GRANVILLE
Well, she was right.

LAURIE
I guess so. I don't really know what to
believe. But you know, Granny, I don't care
anymore. Whether he was looking for some
sort of warped sympathy or really couldn't
get up at that moment, it doesn't matter to
me. I've moved on. Finally.

(A waitress who looks exactly
like NICOLETTE walks over
to their table.)

WAITRESS
What can I get for you today?

LAURIE
(Looking up at the waitress) Oh my Gosh,
Nicolette?

WAITRESS
Laurie? I thought that might be you. You look
different somehow. Older.

LAURIE
I am. It's my birthday today.

WAITRESS
Oh, I didn't mean it like that. You look
young and gorgeous, but something about you
seems, I don't know, older. I'm not sure what
I'm trying to say.

(She puts her hand out
to Granny.)

Hi, I'm Nicolette. I used to be Laurie's
stepmother.

GRANVILLE
I can see the resemblance.

WAITRESS
Oh, we're not genetically related.

GRANVILLE
I mean between you and Grace. Laurie always
told me that her father has a type.

WAITRESS
I didn't realize that until I met your mom.
Boy, that was a shock.

LAURIE

Nicolette, I want you to know that he once told me that he really loved you. And I believe him. He's complicated.

WAITRESS

That's nice to hear. Honestly it is. I know how proud he is of you. When he mentioned you, the room lit up.

LAURIE

I would never guess that.

WAITRESS

I haven't talked to him in months. How is he?

LAURIE

You know, I haven't talked to him in months either, so I'm not really sure. I think he and my mother are back together. The last time I saw them, they were together. Did you ever get your boxes back?

WAITRESS

He delivered them all back to the house. You know, your father was very generous with me.

LAURIE

That's a first, but I'm glad to hear it. I suppose I should reach out to him.

WAITRESS

When I was with your father, part of me believed that he was still in love with your mother. It was all the bad-mouthing, almost obsessively. He didn't stop talking about her, even if it was all complaints.

LAURIE

(Genuinely curious) How are you doing?

WAITRESS
I've been working here for the last few months. Even though I have the house and a nice settlement, I wanted to be making some money on my own. It's great here. I love the people I work with and I'm taking classes to get licensed as an interior designer.

LAURIE
That sounds great. I'm happy for you.

WAITRESS
So, what can I get for the two of you?

LAURIE
Birthday cake! We're here to celebrate my forty-first!

WAITRESS
Well you've come to the right place. Our pastry chef is known for his one-of-a-kind cakes. Today he's baked his vainglorious vanilla with hibiscus meringue and buttercream-puff frosting. We also have his signature red velvet-rope cake. And a standing ovation celebration cake.

LAURIE
Those sound fabulous! We'll have two slices of the standing ovation.

GRANVILLE
How very decisive of you.

LAURIE
I've learned to make decisions. It's liberating.

GRANVILLE
Leaving your job after all these years was
certainly brave.

LAURIE
I've rented my house for a year. I'm going to
travel. By the time I return, I hope to have
seen a bit of every continent.

GRANVILLE
Running away from your parents?

LAURIE
No. Just taking a break. I'm trying to grow
up and let them grow old. My hindsight vision
may suck, Granny, but I feel like I can see
a different future from the one I had envi-
sioned for myself before.

GRANVILLE
So, what do you say, shall we revisit our
pact when we turn sixty?

LAURIE
And then again at eighty?

GRANVILLE
Promise me, if we make it to a hundred, and
we're both still single, that you'll marry me.

LAURIE
Hmmmm. We can talk about it then.

> (Nicolette comes out holding
> two slices of cake. One has
> a candle in it.)

WAITRESS
Here you go, Laurie. Here's your standing
ovation.

BLACKOUT

END OF PLAY

DAY 1

Again.

Today I start again. A new play. A new notebook. New morning pages. So much is new.

I realized I had left my notebook at the hotel the morning after we got back from our college and assisted living homes tour. When I called, the man who answered the phone at the hotel—he sounded more like a 12-year-old boy than a man—promised he'd send someone to look for my notebook and FedEx it back to me. A month later, it arrived by snail mail. By then, I suppose I had gotten out of the habit of doing Morning Pages.

Yesterday, though, I took myself shopping and picked up this beautiful notebook that will hopefully get me through the writing of a new play. And today I start again.

I already wrote that. But that's okay. It doesn't matter.

So much has happened since I last did these Morning Pages.

Marsden is officially a high school graduate!

And life feels settled at the moment. Well, not entirely. Maya is still undergoing treatment, but her prognosis is good, and she and Stu have worked things out. We haven't walked since they found the tumor, but I pick up the rescue dogs and we talk on the phone while I walk with them.

Nancilla Aronie saw things in *Deja New* that I had no idea were there. "I think the play is about repressive expectations on daughters that shape and then choke us," she told me after she read it. Of course, Sammy Ronstein wasn't able to forgive me for missing my deadline or for believing that I wrote the play I wanted to write, rather than the one he wanted me to write, even though the final play did actually incorporate some of his ideas. He just refused to see it that way. He started turning his back to me when he saw me enter a room. He only reluctantly talked to me, and then usually with a fake smile and some sort of criticism, which always began with him saying my name, as if to remind me who I was and, more importantly, who I wasn't. But not even Sammy Ronstein could be mad about the reviews. "We've been poking and prodding at the American family for generations, but Hellman still managed to find a new twist." "Devious and delightful." The *New York Times* called it "a captivatingly provocative comedy of serious intent." I'm not sure what that actually means other than it led to a sold-out run. I'm done this time with Sammy Ronstein for good, but Nancilla wants to work with me again and I am writing this play with her in mind to direct.

Marsden finally finished writing his college essay, but only after all the application deadlines had passed. When Mrs. Yule found out, she told him, "I hope you have a good back-up plan."

I couldn't really be angry with him for missing his deadline after I missed mine. I'm just glad we both finished. I'm not even sure what finishing means anymore.

Is anything ever really finished?

Marsden's been volunteering as an usher three nights a week at the American Repertory Theater, where the musical version of *Finding Neverland* just premiered on its way to Broadway, which means that three nights a week he gets to watch a play about a struggling playwright, the pressures of growing up, and the power of the imagination. He also got a job scooping ice cream and is looking around for classes to take during his gap year, or who knows, maybe it'll be a gap decade. On the morning he graduated from high school, I made him crepes stuffed with blueberries, strawberries, bananas, and chocolate. He swallowed them down and said he had something for me. He handed me an envelope and asked me not to open it until after he graduated. I sat with Elliot and Midge, and we watched a robed procession of students walk onto a stage as undergrads and walk off as high school graduates. After the caps were tossed in the air, the student cheers, and the parental tears, I escaped into the ladies' room and locked myself in a stall so I could be alone when I opened the envelope. In it was Marsden's college essay, a beautiful essay that no college admissions officer has had an opportunity to read, and I could not stop reading.

A lot has happened, but maybe the biggest thing that's happened since the last time I wrote any Morning Pages is that Mom has found someone who loves her for who she is. Roy Levinson left his assisted living home and moved in with her two months ago. "We both like watching old movies and then fucking," she told me. We have someone who comes in during the day to help them out, and it seems to be working out. I've been going to New York frequently. To check on Mom. To take meetings. To ride the elevator with the handsome man with the luscious lips who lives on the 16th floor. We like to go up to the penthouse, then down to the lobby three times for floorplay before rushing into his apartment and ripping off each other's clothes. And I now know his name.

I guess that's it for easing my way back in.

Morning Pages, Day 1 is completed.

And today I will start writing my next play, *The Divorce Virgins*.

༄

Instructions. *The essay demonstrates your ability to write clearly and concisely on a selected topic and helps you distinguish yourself in your own voice. What do you want the readers of your application to know about you apart from courses, grades, and test scores? Choose the option that best helps you answer that question and write an essay of no more than 650 words, using the prompt to inspire and structure your response. Remember: 650 words is your limit, not your goal. Use the full range if you need it, but don't feel obligated to do so. (The application won't accept a response shorter than 250 words.)*

This fall, I wrote a play. Writing it helped me think about issues from the perspectives of different characters. The title of my play is *The Divorce Ferret*. It was inspired by the ferret that my parents gave me a week before they broke the news that they were getting divorced.

Here are a few lines from *The Divorce Ferret*:

BOY: What are you doing?

DAD: Building a five-star playhouse for the ferret.

BOY: Since you moved out, all Mom talks about is the ferret.

DAD: She likes to read up on things. I suspect by now she's got a Ph.D. in ferretology. She knows you've wanted a ferret for a long time.

BOY: I wanted a ferret when I was eight.

DAD: And now you have one. Do you think the ferret would like a turret?

My parents have high hopes and expectations for me. I've often felt like I haven't met their expectations and I think it's because I am an introvert. I tend to be a thinker, not a talker. Adults are easily impressed by precocious and loquacious children. My mother sometimes complains that I'm monosyllabic, and precocious and loquacious are two words that I usually don't use. But when I wrote *The Divorce Ferret*, something happened. All sorts of words started falling out of me. It felt like my play was writing itself. I've heard my mother, who is a playwright, talk about this happening. I never understood what she meant or never really believed something like that was possible until it happened to me. The characters in my play were telling me what to say. I wasn't in charge. They were. It was crazy.

I am working on a new play now, and I think I want to study playwriting in college. I'd like to learn about the great playwrights, historical and contemporary. I want to study William Shakespeare and Anton Chekov, Samuel Beckett and August Wilson, Wendy Wasserstein and my mom, Elise Hellman, who is one of the greatest playwrights I know. And maybe, if I work hard and keep writing, I will one day become a great playwright too.

This is another scene from my play:

BOY: I want you to have this.

GIRL: It's so cute. Is this your ferret? Why would you give me your ferret?

BOY: I heard your parents were getting divorced. When my parents got divorced, they gave me this ferret. I call him Divorce Ferret. My parents thought I'd be so happy about getting a ferret that I wouldn't be sad about them getting divorced.

GIRL: Did it work?

BOY: Not really.

GIRL: So why are you giving it to me?

BOY: Because maybe it'll work for you. And if it doesn't, maybe you can give it to somebody else. Maybe it'll work for them.

GIRL: I think it's already working.

My parents never knew what happened to Divorce Ferret. They assumed he got out and ran away, but the truth was I gave him away because I believed Divorce Ferret had powers that could help people. Maybe someday my plays will have that kind of power too.

ACKNOWLEDGMENTS

THIS BOOK WAS essentially workshopped, as a play might be workshopped. It was tested and tried in sections with two wonderful writers' groups. I am beyond grateful for the encouragement, laughter, insights, and suggestions I received from the talented women in both these groups. My Martha's Vineyard writers' group has been there from the beginning of this project and this book wouldn't exist without them. Nancy Slonim Aronie, Nicole Galland, Melissa Hackney, Lara O'Brien, Jamie Kageleiry, Laura Roosevelt, Catherine Walthers—you are so much more to me than just a writers' group. My New York-based writers' group of Judith Hannan, Lisa Liman, and Robin Rivera was formed later in the process and their fresh eyes and spot-on critiques got me to the finish line.

I was first exposed to Morning Pages and *The Artist Way* in yet another writers' group. Julia Cameron, who I've never met, has helped millions of people break through creative blocks, and I am grateful to her for the work she does. (I do hope she likes this book.)

I owe a bountiful round of thanks to Geraldine Brooks, Glenn Korman, and my agent Rosemary Stimola, for their invaluable feedback during different stages of this process. My sister Halley Feiffer, a playwright, answered my questions about playwriting, and showered me with her unfettered enthusiasm.

How lucky I am to be able to call Gretchen Young a friend and an editor. I am honored and thrilled that *Morning Pages* gets to be part of Regalo Press's magnificent inaugural list. Working with Regalo editor Adriana Senior was a dream. I am so appreciative of her keen eye and spot-on editorial suggestions.

I'd also like to thank Jeremy Kareken, whose playwriting class I took. Gail Hochman kindly gave me advice. Marty McDonough got me to Dedham and Sheila Corkhill provided information about Wellesley.

During the writing of the book, we had two private readings of *Deja New* so I could hear and get feedback on the play within the book. I am very grateful to the actors who took part in those readings: Brooke Adams, Amy Barrow, Scott Barrow, Nicole Galland, Jonathan Lipnick, and Tony Schalhoub.

My mother, Judy Feiffer, first exhibited signs of dementia in 2011. Over the following five years her memory may have declined, but her spirit never did. I was lucky to have had this extraordinary, complicated, and ever supportive woman as a mother. She used to say to me, "I've given you the material. You should use it." And so I have.

I have friends and family who haven't yet read a word of this book, but it's hard to imagine it could have been written without their love and support. Topping that list is Chris Alley and Maddy Alley.